Praise for Amita Murray's *Unladylike Lessons in Love*
A Julia Quinn Selects title!

"Sizzling romance with a splash of intrigue."

—Julia Quinn

"A superbly crafted historical novel, *and* a romance that doubles up as a mystery, with a delicious Indian twist—what's not to love? Amita Murray's brilliant take on a traditional Regency romance is smoking hot—and haeartbreakingly realistic about the racial and class divide that dominated eighteenth-century English society. I can't wait to read the next book."

—Harini Nagendra, author of *The Bangalore Detectives Club*

"Lila Marleigh is a smart, unconventional and independent English-Indian beauty who controls what's allowed into her iced champagne punch, her gaming establishment, and her life . . . till Ivor Tristram turns up and, yes, it's a romance and mystery and Lila is charming, but it's the painful secret at the heart of her family that leaves me wanting even more. Are the Marleighs going to be the next Bridgertons? I can only hope!"

—Ovidia Yu, author of the Crown Colony Series
and *Aunty Lee's Delights*

"This romantic adventure bolts from the first page while following professional hostess Lila Marleigh as she untangles a crime and finds lust—or is it love? You'll have to finish this in one sitting—call in sick!"

—Sumi Hahn, author of *The Mermaid from Jeju*

UNLADYLIKE
LESSONS
IN
LOVE

ALSO BY AMITA MURRAY

The Macabre Cozy Mysteries Series

Arya Winters and the Tiramisu of Death
Arya Winters and the Cupcakes of Doom

Standalones

The Trouble with Rose

AMITA MURRAY

UNLADYLIKE
LESSONS
IN
LOVE

A Marleigh Sisters Novel

AVON
An Imprint of HarperCollins*Publishers*

UNLADYLIKE LESSONS IN LOVE. Copyright © 2023 by Amita Murray. All rights reserved. Printed in the United States of America. No part of this book may be used or reproduced in any manner whatsoever without written permission except in the case of brief quotations embodied in critical articles and reviews. For information, address HarperCollins Publishers, 195 Broadway, New York, NY 10007.

HarperCollins books may be purchased for educational, business, or sales promotional use. For information, please email the Special Markets Department at SPsales@harpercollins.com.

Published in the United Kingdom in 2023 by HarperCollins Publishers Ltd.

FIRST U.S. EDITION

Designed by Renata DiBiase

Library of Congress Cataloging-in-Publication Data
has been applied for.

ISBN 978-0-06-329648-0

23 24 25 26 27 LBC 5 4 3 2 1

To my tiny peeps

Thanks for teaching me all about love

It turns out I can belong somewhere after all, and it's with you

1

The banquet room shone. The staff had done an outstanding job, even though Lila Marleigh was hardly a stern mistress. The chandeliers sparkled, the sunset curtains gleamed, and the peacock-blue mirrors, hand-painted in Rajasthan, reflected Lila's customers faithfully—more faithfully than some of them wanted at this hour of the night.

Lila's salon was a fashionable destination for men and women who wanted to spend an evening gambling and listening to music in an elegant town house in the heart of Mayfair in the city of London, but who didn't go to the more notorious gambling hells. At two in the morning, the salon was packed and that, along with the hundreds of candles that studded the room, was making it hard to breathe. Lila fanned herself with her pretty cockade fan, painted with a trellis of roses, desperate tonight for the salon to end so she could make her way up to bed, collapse on the cool sheets, and not wake up again until noon at the earliest.

She stifled a sigh. Her customers looked as if they could keep going for hours. The piquet table and faro were the busiest, but her customers came to her salon because they liked that it had a hint of something different, a magical something that only she could bring, and so the Indian rummy and Shatranj tables had takers too. No, no one looked in a hurry to call it a night.

As she sat at one of the piquet tables, Walsham entered the banquet room. He looked so severe—even more than usual—that Lila's heart sank. He walked over to her, his back rigid, dodging the card tables and the huddles of standing people. When he reached her, he bent and said in a hushed voice, "A *person* at the door, Miss Marleigh." He may as well have said *a cockroach, Miss Marleigh.*

Lila blinked but nothing else showed on her face. Her mind was racing. Who on earth had turned up at her house at two in the morning that would make Walsham look so constipated? He normally showed customers straight into the salon. He didn't keep them waiting at the door.

Smile firmly in place, she leaned forward and tapped the Dowager Countess of Ellingham's hand with her fan. "You must allow me to refill your glass, Lady Ellingham."

The Dowager Countess might not have allowed this kind of familiarity from anyone else, but most things could be forgiven an eccentric, and Lila Marleigh had spent nearly five years learning to be one. The dowager harrumphed, keeping her eyes on her cards.

"I will find you some punch, my own special brew."

This was one of her eccentricities. Lila blended her own iced champagne punch (some of her guests called it The Lila) and she liked to play with what she put in it. Tonight, it was apple cider with a hint of ginger, a touch of sugar, and the secret ingredient, the tiniest pinch of cardamom from the Indies. The dowager inclined her head.

Lila sprang to her feet as if she weren't completely exhausted and her butler Walsham wasn't making her anxious. Her dark curls were coiled high on the top of her head and then left to fall down her back. She pushed away unruly strands that were clinging damply to her forehead. Her net silver overdress sparkled, and she shook out the folds of the midnight-blue silk dress that hugged her figure and, followed by the stiffening Walsham, turned to make her way out of the heaving room.

But this was easier said than done. The room was packed, and everyone wanted a piece of Lila Marleigh—some wanted as many pieces as they could get.

Donald Barrymore, Viscount of Herringford, was the first to stop her, with a hand squeezing her upper arm, which she batted playfully away with her fan. His face was purple. The waistband of his trousers was bursting and his cravat more wilted than the hothouse lilies that one of her admirers had sent her, fresh from his estate, just this morning. Herringford had that tottering look that said he should have stopped drinking about three drinks ago—Lila could calculate these things down to the mouthful. She sighed inwardly.

"Lord Herringford, what a hot summer we're having," she said in her usual vibrant voice. She checked herself. The cheery tone was grating on her nerves tonight.

The man didn't notice the complete lack of originality in the remark. "I heard you're backing Kenneth Laudsley to win the race to Brighton, m'dear," he said, leaning closer, licking his lips at the deep V of her neckline. "You know his racers don't hold a candle to the ones I'm putting up for m'nephew?" He squinted at her cleavage as if he was thinking about diving into it.

Her smile widened. She placed her fan under his chin and lifted his face so he was forced to make eye contact. "You're quite right, Lord Herringford. At this rate, I'll be forced to run the race myself."

She was turning away. She meant it as a joke—after all, it would be the scandal of the summer if a woman raced a curricle to Brighton—but, to her surprise, it created an excited hum.

"I'd lay a monkey to see that," said Henry Alston. She turned to look at him. He was pink-faced too, but in a young and overeager way. He was slim, only nineteen, and his chestnut locks were flying in all directions. He blushed. In his own way, he was just as painfully eager as Lord Herringford, but it was hard to be anything but kind to him, he was just a boy.

Lila's eyes darted toward Walsham. He looked as though he was willing to be patient until the end of time. She bit her lip but gave her guests her sparkling smile.

At this late hour the women were laughing louder, and the men were swaying dangerously close. It took several minutes to disentangle from the group. It was a good thing, Lila thought, as Herringford pawed at the air behind her, that she had given up trying to save her reputation a long time ago.

As she started to wind her way to the door again, she noticed a man she hadn't seen in her salons before, standing nearby, speaking to no one, an amber glass of brandy held carelessly in one hand. He was over medium height and his broad shoulders and chest made him look imposing. Her practiced eye noticed the strength of his thighs and the understated but elegant clothes. He was wearing pantaloons and Hessians, but she imagined he would be more comfortable in riding clothes. The hair was dark, the face broad, the eyebrows shapely. But these were not what caught her attention. She couldn't look away from the piercing crystal-blue eyes that were looking at her, not lasciviously like Herringford, nor with a deep blush like Henry Alston, but with strong dislike.

As she stared at him, he didn't turn away, but instead took a deliberate sip of his drink. She was startled, wondering who he was and why he was looking at her with such loathing. She made herself turn away.

When she finally made it out of the ballroom, she shut the door behind her and sagged. A sliver of longing pierced through her, though for what she didn't know exactly.

She opened her eyes and shook herself. This wouldn't do. Whatever the longing was for, it could never be hers. She squared her shoulders as Walsham led the way to the front door.

"I told the person that the back door would be more suitable. But she is refusing to leave until she has seen you, Miss Marleigh."

"Since when do you let people refuse you anything, Walsham?" Lila murmured.

But then she stepped out into the humid night air and saw the reason for Walsham's disapproval and his reticence. The girl standing outside was dressed in rags, big with child and fuming, and she looked as though nothing—no woman, no man, no mountain—would dislodge her from Lila Marleigh's front door.

2

"Why he can't let me in for two minutes—*two min-utes I said and not a minute more!*—why he has to stand in the way of an honest lass . . ."

Walsham cleared his throat. Whether this was at the girl's shrill tone or her description of herself as honest, Lila didn't know. The girl was sputtering she was so mad. She glared as Walsham sniffed.

"Does he have a cold?" Her eyes were blazing. "Can't a girl have a word with you, Miss Lila? Are you so high in the instep now?"

"Here now—" Walsham said, but Lila held up her hand. She peered at the girl's face.

For she was no older than a girl. Seventeen maybe, at most, at least eight years younger than Lila. Tiny, even shorter than Lila herself. She had a heart-shaped face, a cloud of frizzy dark hair, sharp kitten eyes, and a ferocious mouth that looked ready to bite anyone who got too close.

Time stopped for Lila. Darkness threatened to engulf her, darkness that she normally kept at bay.

"Maisie?" She could hardly believe it, but then as soon as she said the name, she knew she was right.

The girl lifted her chin. "I'm surprised you recognize me."

Lila grasped the girl's cold fingers. "Maisie, of course I recognize you. Do you think I've left the house even once in the last ten years and *not* looked for your face?"

"Didn't look hard enough, I reckon."

Walsham stirred again at the insolent tone, but Lila ignored him. "How far along are you?" she asked, looking down at the girl's belly.

There was a constriction in her chest, almost like a rock was wedged there. Maisie! Maisie Quinn! Lila wasn't lying. She did look for Maisie's face everywhere, desperate to find her. Though maybe less and less over the years, she thought guiltily. Did she try hard enough? Yet here she was, still no more than a girl. And very pregnant.

"What?" the girl said.

"How many courses have you missed?" Lila asked patiently.

"Oh, the lord love you," the girl said, "how is a lass to keep count of something like that? Seven, maybe?" She fidgeted with the folds of her thick skirt, looking uncertain for the first time. "Wouldn't come to you if I had anywhere else to go." The face was uncertain, but the voice just as stubborn. "I need help."

"You must come in," Lila said firmly.

Walsham cleared his throat. "The back door, miss."

Lila lifted a hand again but didn't look at him. "I have a full house right now," she said apologetically to Maisie.

"I can't come back tomorrow. I have the rat pit," the girl answered, "and that's a busy night for me. I can't miss a night. Not now, I can't. A girl's got to eat."

Lila didn't bother trying to decipher the cryptic words. "You can't leave. Not now that I've finally found you. But Walsham is right, the back door may be better." She was uneasily aware not only of Walsham standing rigidly behind her, but also the many guests in the ballroom. As it was, her credit with the *ton* was precarious. If she lost its goodwill, she would lose her only source of livelihood. The salon might sparkle, but it took everything Lila had to hold things together.

"I'll help you," she said firmly

The girl was working away at her skirt again. And her chin looked even more stubborn. "You said that—back then. And it didn't come to naught. I trusted you."

The guilt came flooding back. Ten years ago, when Lila was fifteen, and Maisie no more than seven, Maisie's mother, a maid in the Marleigh house, had been accused of stealing a box of jewelry. Lila had known that Annie Quinn couldn't have done it, she knew the woman too well. And she had promised Maisie she would help. She tried to help, but it came to nothing, and Maisie's mother Annie—who Lila sometimes thought was her only friend in the large, cold house—was hanged for her crime. Maisie ran away soon after. Now here she was, and Lila couldn't imagine why Maisie should trust her now.

"Will your man not help you?" Lila asked, looking down at the belly. Though she didn't need to ask. Of course, he wouldn't help. That was why the girl was here.

But instead of outrage or even shame, the girl's eyes filled with tears that she was quick to bat away. "He can't," she said abruptly.

"Can't or won't?" asked Lila cynically.

The fierce look was back. "He . . . he's in trouble. He can't. It's why I need your help. He's been accused of something he didn't do."

"A crime?"

Maisie's chin quivered. "Of attacking a hoity-toity miss."

Lila's fist tightened on her dress. That didn't sound good. "Did he do it? Did he attack this girl?"

Maisie quivered with rage. "He didn't do it! He wouldn't hurt a fly! But a girl who looks like me and a man who looks like him—what chance have we got?"

Maisie's mother Annie had come all the way from the Caribbean with a family that wanted her to look after their children on the journey, but who then abandoned her to the mercies of London. The Marleigh family had hired her, and she worked in the house for seven long years, but then they had thrown her to the dogs in the worst possible way.

Lila could see that the girl was skinny as a stick, despite the distended belly. If she gave birth now, the baby would die and so could she. "Come in now, Maisie."

The girl was dithering.

"I won't bite, you know," Lila said gently.

Some of the ferocity left the girl's face. "It's just you're a grand lady. I knew you were, but I hadn't seen you or believed it, not till I saw it with my own eyes."

Lila held out her hand to usher the girl toward the back door. Just then the door to the ballroom opened behind her. It was down the hall, and Lila lifted her chin and decided to battle it out with whoever came out—but thankfully no one did. It was just someone looking for more drinks. Johnny, the first footman, hurtled forward to replenish the glass. Lila looked back at the girl, at Maisie Quinn, and was surprised to see a look of horror on the girl's face.

"What is it, Maisie?"

Maisie didn't answer. She was staring at the doorway into the ballroom. Lila turned in confusion to see what the girl was looking at. It was just a glimpse of the large room. Clusters of people inside, dressed in jewel colors, yards of Belgian lace, rivers of spangles. Her friend Mrs. Annabel Wakefield was laughing at something someone said. She could see Lord Herringford, nearly falling over now, but with yet another glass in his hands. The stranger who had been looking at her as if he despised her, he was there too, speaking to someone, to Henry Alston. Some others she knew. She turned back to the girl. Maybe Maisie Quinn hadn't expected such a thing, all the people and the glitz.

"Him!" The girl looked terrified. "Don't know why I thought *you'd* ever help me."

Before Lila could stop her, the girl, distended belly or not, lifted her skirts and took off down the street.

Lila stifled an oath. Before she could stop *herself*, Lila lifted her silk skirts and took off after her. But the girl had a head start and apparently shoes that weren't as delicate as Lila's satin slippers, because by the time Lila was halfway down Brook Street, the girl had disappeared.

Lila stood there panting. "Well! The stupid chit. What will I do now?"

She turned around and nearly got the shock of her life because Walsham was standing right behind her, dignified as ever, chest thrust out like a true London pigeon, and she hadn't even heard him walking, much less running, after her. "Miss Marleigh," he said in a long-suffering voice, "perhaps we can return to the house now? It is *starting to rain*."

He said this in the same way most people would announce the arrival of the Black Death.

"I won't melt, Walsham. Could we send someone to look for the girl?"

"It is highly unlikely anyone would be able to find *the per-*

son now," Walsham said. "But perhaps if you come back to the house, miss, *the person* will return tomorrow."

"Someone scared her." Her brow creased. "She could die. She's poor and hungry—did you see how thin she was?—and her rags." Lila shivered, the exhaustion hitting her all at once. Where had Maisie been all these years, and what had happened to her in that time?

"Miss Lila," Walsham said, his voice gentler, "you can't solve the world's problems."

"No, I can't," Lila said. "I won't try to, I promise, Walsham."

Walsham melted enough to give her a kind smile. "If you'll come out of the rain, I'll fetch you a coffee. You'll feel much restored—"

"Not *all* the world's problems," Lila ruthlessly interrupted. "All I have to do is go to the rat pit tomorrow night to find Maisie. That's all."

3

L ila ignored the horror on her butler's face as she entered
the house again.

Right this second, all she wanted was to leave it all and
run away, but she hadn't become one of London's most successful hostesses by being a craven fool. She ignored Walsham and
entered the startlingly bright ballroom. She stood for a moment
staring at it all as if she had never seen it before.

When she came out seven years ago, she had the opportunity
to find a husband, get married, and live a safe and steady life. She
chose not to. Society was never going to accept her, not really.
Her fortune was small; worse than that, she was the bastard of
an earl and his Indian mistress, transported all the way across
the ocean to England at the age of seven, along with two of her
sisters, when their mother and father had both drowned. Sent
to live with the Earl's wife and his sickly son—whose existence
none of them had known about until after the Earl died. To
say that the woman embraced the three girls like the daughters
she had never had would be grossly untrue. The woman had
loathed them on sight.

After four years living under Sarah Marleigh's roof in London, Lila was the first of the sisters to be sent off to school in Yorkshire. In those four years, instead of herding together like sheep, the girls had turned on each other, encouraged by the sickly Jonathan, their half brother, and their stepmother Sarah Marleigh, who thought herself the unluckiest woman in the entire world and played the girls off each other by alternately gaining their sympathy and then turning on them when they weren't expecting it.

Now the sisters were estranged, though, Lila thought with satisfaction, each had defied society and gone her own way. Her younger sister Anya was a singer and sitar player in the Queen's court, and Mira, the youngest of the three, was a writer of society gossip. Lila, the oldest, hosted card parties, accompanied by the best music and sumptuous dinners and wines. The gambling at Lila's salon was nothing compared to the stakes in gambling hells, but the house allowed men to bring their mistresses and their wives (though ideally not at the same time), and allowed women to gamble, too. Her house had a reputation for honest play and she had built it from scratch.

Still, respectable it was not. The way society mamas shooed their young charges away from it, it might have been labeled with skull and crossbones.

She was so sick of it all that it was like a physical hurt some days. Not the business side of things, which she was good at. But the ogling men, the tedious conversation, the constant need to be playing her part. Her cheeks hurt from smiling.

She looked around the ballroom. The remains of the midnight supper had been cleared away by her faithful staff. As usual, judging by her happy customers' faces, the staff had outdone themselves. Not only did her house serve slivers of salmon and scalloped oysters and apple tartlets, but she had made sure they could fry a samosa and serve colorful milky sweetmeats. The ingredients weren't always easy to find, but she had her reputation to maintain—she was renowned for adding a hint of *je ne sais quoi* to everything she offered.

All her guests seemed to be speaking at once, sounding like a swarm of bees. "You must tell me what you put in your champagne punch, Miss Marleigh," someone was saying. "Miss Marleigh, I heard you're planning to have theatricals at your salons?" someone else asked. And of course, people were asking if she would run the Brighton race. Annabel Wakefield, one of her few female friends, who always had a kind word to say to her, walked by and asked if she needed anything. She quickly shook her head and Annabel wandered off, talking to some man who was ogling her. Annabel was forty if she was a day, but she was soothing and pretty and men tended to like her.

Next it was Henry Alston. He went beetroot red as he handed her a glass of champagne. Sweet boy. She *was* parched. She took a gulp. She couldn't help placing her hand on the boy's arm. "What would I do without you, Mr. Alston?"

She regretted the impulse as she saw the ardent look in his eyes. She watched him walk away when a friend called to him. She couldn't bring herself to rebuff him, but his attentions were hard to bear, and the older men laughed at him.

The room was hot. She was dizzy from the heat. And she felt dizzier when the stranger suddenly appeared at her elbow, the man she had seen before, with the piercing eyes. He was staring at her, with that same dislike. "Ivor Tristram, at your service, ma'am. Could I have a word?"

He was looking at her as though he was weighing her up, not so much as horseflesh, but as you might appraise an opponent. She shot him a penetrating look before unfolding her fan. "I'd love to," she said, taking his arm—rigid as a log of wood—and letting him lead her to the door out of the room.

She drew him into an antechamber off the hall. The ballroom was decorated in Indian blue and sunset silk, but this room was lighter, airier, decorated in morning colors, simply furnished and rarely used except when someone needed to discuss business. She sank down on one of the chairs, grateful for the break in playing hostess, and drained after the abrupt meeting with Maisie Quinn. How on earth would she ever find her again?

She tried to focus on the man. He was powerful, as if he boxed for exercise, but also understated. Not that he needed flamboyant clothes. Those eyes would be enough to catch anyone's attention. What did he say his name was? He stood there, his eyes trying to drill a hole in her face. "Would you prefer somewhere less secluded?" he asked.

She couldn't help laughing. "I can't remember when someone was last worried about my reputation."

He was studying her face with those eyes of his. "You don't care about your reputation?" He leaned back against a table and crossed his arms. It was an easy pose and it suited him. She was probably staring at him, but she was so tired she didn't know what she was doing. His eyes were glittering beads, their expression inscrutable.

"No, I don't."

"I don't believe you," the man said.

She raised her brows. "Think about it, Mr. Tristram." Ah, yes, that was his name. "Women mind their reputation if they want to marry. I don't want to marry."

"Not even if someone rich and titled offered for you?"

She didn't answer, wondering where this was going.

He didn't enlighten her. "Do you like your work?"

Now that was a difficult one to answer. "Sometimes." With anyone else, she would have laughed and said she loved it. But it was hard to lie to this man's direct eyes. "When you're good with people, working with them is a sensible way to earn a living. But I often think there is nothing more exhausting than people."

He was studying her face as though he was trying to unpack her words, or as if he didn't believe anything she was saying. He picked up a cast-iron ship from the mantel and touched the sharp ridges. He seemed to be trying to assess what to say to her. "You know, Miss Marleigh, I can't help thinking that with you it's hard to know what is true and what not."

"What on earth do you mean?"

"The Brighton race, amateur theatricals, there are always rumors about you."

"I made a joke about the Brighton race . . . As for the theatricals, so what?"

"It would attract a lot of attention. I suppose that's what you're after."

"I am not especially looking for attention."

"Men are attracted to you like moths," he said, those eyes watching her again.

She bristled. "I know how to do my job."

"To attract hapless men into your web?"

A laugh escaped her. "I'm not a spider, Mr. Tristram. I would have said my job—as a hostess—is to be amiable." She was surprised at the things he was saying. Where was it all coming from?

"You do it rather well." Her brows knitted. But before she could speak, he spoke again. "I will keep it brief. You know my father, Benjamin Tristram."

"Your father?" She was surprised. Benjamin Tristram was a lush, a man who paraded a string of mistresses in front of his wife. A weak-chinned man who had to be escorted to his carriage in the middle of the night by a footman. It was hard to reconcile that man with this. She noticed again the strong set of his shoulders, the severely cut coat, the hard face. Something twisted in her heart. She remembered now. Rumor had it that Benjamin Tristram squandered his fortune and lost land in gambling and debt, but his son took the reins and saved the family from ruin. "It can't be easy being his son," she blurted out.

He looked at her in surprise. "I can live with it," he said shortly. There was a slight frown on his brow now, and his eyes seemed to have shut her out, even more than before. No, this man didn't easily let people in. She doubted he ever let anyone in.

Then his eyes narrowed. "As I said," he said, his lip curling—at her or at himself, she didn't know, "you know your way around men."

She looked at him in surprise. "Why on earth do you hate me?" she asked, forgetting her hostess persona. The dislike felt like a physical blow. It reminded her of her stepmother. Of being sat down in front of Sarah Marleigh and being told what a little worm she was for never being enough of a Marleigh, for being the daughter of a "native woman" and never learning how to hide it.

She was brought back to earth by the man's voice now.

"I will get to the point. My mother is ill. She does not have long left. If you let my father go, I will compensate you for the income you will lose."

His words didn't make sense. She was staring at his face in an exhausted daze. But then they struck her like a punch in the guts and, all of a sudden, the exhaustion vanished. She came to her feet, her face blazing. Words flooded her brain. *How dare you! I am not your father's mistress! Get out of my house!*

But she couldn't form them. She wanted to punch the man. But even that paralyzed her. A crippling sense of weakness hit her. This, she thought. This hadn't changed. When she was at her maddest, she froze. And she dealt with it now the way she always dealt with it.

The blazing heat left her face, leaving her drained. She lifted her chin. "You can't afford to compensate me, Mr. Tristram." Her voice was weary, but it was also resonant. For some reason, the man's words, his assumption that she was Benjamin Tristram's mistress, hurt her more than Lord Herringford's leers. The casual assumption. *You know your way around men.*

"I can make it worth your while," he said.

"Can you now?"

"You're a beautiful woman, Miss Marleigh. You can have anyone. He's an old man."

That thing that was in her chest twisted again. A beautiful woman. The assumption that she was sleeping with his father. For money. Using an old lush for what she could squeeze out of him. Her insides curled with distaste. At him or at the picture he carved of her, she wasn't sure. She couldn't—she wouldn't—deny it. She wouldn't stoop so low. Her eyes were hooded. "I can have anyone?"

"Yes."

She looked at him for a long time. "How about you, then, Mr. Tristram? If I were your mistress, I would bear the loss of your father."

Disgust crossed his face, and he didn't even try to hide it. It pierced her like a shard, even though she had just done her best to rile him.

"Stay away from my father, Miss Marleigh. Or you will have me to answer to."

He was gone before she could respond.

4

"**H**ow dare he! How *dare* he! If I'm ever near him again, if I'm ever within a hundred yards of him, I'll punch him and break his nose!"

Lila raged about her room. Her bedchamber was designed to be soothing, in colors of silver and chalk blue. She could hide inside her four-poster in the early hours of the morning when her salons were done, hide away from the world and shut it out.

None of this magic was working today.

"Now, now, miss," her maid Hannah Bowers said, "is he another one of your admirers?" Hannah was tall and wore her brown hair in a pretty bun. Her figure was neat and she had a soothing manner. She had soft brown eyes, like a doe. And unlike Lila, she was rarely in a flap. "I swear you had about fifty at last count."

This inexplicably filled Lila with even more rage. "I do *not* have fifty admirers!"

Hannah was folding Lila's midnight-blue dress away, ready to be steamed. She put it to one side and started gathering the hairpins that Lila had torn from her head and scattered all over the floor in her rage. "Men *like* you, miss, and what's wrong with that?"

"Aah!" Lila cried and, throwing herself on her bed, burst into tears.

Hannah kept on gathering the hairpins and making soothing noises. She bent and straightened, bent and straightened, her noises muffled. She laid the neat bouquet of hairpins on the dresser. Then she walked to the wardrobe and chose clothes for the next day. She was murmuring to herself, reciting what she was doing. "The blue velveteen in this weather, I reckon," she was saying. "The sateen isn't needed, is it, miss? Maybe you'll have a beau call on you tomorrow and I could do your hair ever so pretty?" When this produced a fresh bout of crying, she said, "It's not like you try to attract them, miss. It's your nature and your large eyes. They laugh, you know. Your eyes, I mean."

"I hate it, I hate every minute of it!" Lila cried through her hands.

"As to that, I'm sure you don't. You hate your work sometimes and at other times you don't. Just like the rest of us."

Lila wiped her nose and looked guiltily at her maid. "I suppose you hate this side of things."

Hannah was smoothing down riding clothes for Lila, her hands efficient and experienced, teasing away a crease, picking at a piece of lint, scowling at a hint of dirt. "Oh no, miss. I like this bit. I know how to calm you down. I reckon most people don't. But I do. It's the cleaning I hate. It never ends. Just when you finish one thing, there's another pile ready and waiting to be cleaned." Hannah glanced at Lila. "Now don't you be feeling guilty, Miss Lila. I'm saying just because you hate some of it don't mean it's all a load of horseshit."

Lila squeezed her eyes shut and sighed. "A man was completely disgusted today when I offered to be his mistress."

"Now, miss," Hannah said reprovingly, turning away from

the clothes and tidying the things on the dresser, "why would you do that? You can have any man for the asking. Why do you need to beg?" She moved the silver brushes one way, the empty box of hairpins another. She picked up the wilting flowers that she had woven through the coils in Lila's hair earlier in the evening and stuffed them in her pocket so she could take them downstairs.

"I didn't beg! I didn't really *want* to be his mistress!"

"Well then, you shouldn't have asked to be. You can see how he might have got the wrong impression. In any case, you don't care about anyone's opinion. I admire that about you. Who cares if the man looked disgusted? I would choose you as a mistress if I were a wealthy man." She picked up the bouquet of hairpins, ready to be replaced in the box.

"Thank you, Hannah," Lila said meekly. "You're quite right. I'm being idiotic. Who cares what that man thinks? I have better things to think about. Tell me what I should wear to the rat pit tomorrow, because I have to say I have no idea."

Hannah shrieked and dropped the hairpins all over the floor again. She had borne with equanimity Lila begging men to let her be their mistress, but now her face filled with horror. "You can't go to the rat pit!"

"I can and I must," Lila said. "This scrap of a girl came around last night. I owe her. And anyway, I can't not help her. She . . ." Lila yawned. "Look, I'll tell you tomorrow. Or do I mean today? Try and get some sleep. I will too. Just get something together, will you? I have no idea if I should go as a man or a harlot. What think you?"

5

Lila tossed and turned all night. Dreams haunted her sleep, dreams that she had kept at bay for years. Maisie's face. *I'll help you, Maisie. I promise, I'll help. I'll never let you down.* Except it wasn't Maisie's seventeen-year-old face. It was Maisie as a child. Big amber eyes, heart-shaped face, trusting, completely trusting of Lila. *I know you will, Miss Lila.* Maisie's trusting eyes. Maisie put her little hand in Lila's. *I know you will, Miss Lila.* There had been no doubt in Maisie's mind that Lila would help, that she would make it her priority to help. None. Not in those days. In those days, she had more faith in the world.

At one point in the night, Lila woke covered in sweat, and gulped down a tumbler of water. She was exhausted, her body aching with tiredness, but she dared not sleep again, dared not be confronted by Maisie's face. And she wasn't.

When she fell asleep again, into a restless slumber, it wasn't Maisie's face she saw, it was Annie's, it was Maisie's mother's. It was Maisie's mother Annie Quinn, hanging from the gallows.

She gasped and struggled in her sleep. She battled with her damp bedsheets. But no matter what she did, Lila couldn't wake up. Couldn't unsee Annie's face. She tried for a long time to claw herself awake, and then finally woke up with a jerk and lay there panting and stifling sobs.

Lila had seen the hanging. Her sisters hadn't. She had never told Anya or Mira that she saw Annie hanged. In fact, she had never told anyone. She often wished that she hadn't seen it, and hated herself for wishing it, for not wanting to be Annie's last witness. She had begged one of the footmen to take her. She didn't know why. Had she wanted to bear witness to Annie's death, be there for her, or had she believed somehow, at the last minute, that she could do something rash and save Annie? She made a dash for it at the end, when that rope was put around Annie's throat. She screamed her name over and over and tried to run to Annie. No one heard her screams in the melee, Annie never even knew she was there, that anyone who loved her was there, and the footman—Andrew—had held on to Lila until she stopped struggling. In the years after the hanging, she had woken up many a time, struggling to get away from Andrew's death grip, years after she had felt it.

Lila found the night unbearable and was up early, after no more than three hours in bed.

Through her breakfast, through dressing for the morning, Lila couldn't get last night out of her mind. Annie. Annie Quinn. Annie, who was hanged for a crime she didn't commit.

She hadn't committed it, had she?

Lila rubbed her face and tried to clear away the cobwebs. Did she have it wrong, after all? It wasn't in Annie's character, but desperation could make people do strange things. Yet, had Annie been desperate? Or what if she'd only wanted a thing or two from the jewelry box, and meant to put the rest back? What if she only wanted a little more spending money, or money for her daughter Maisie? And who could blame her?

Lila tried to pierce the veil of time, but the harder she looked, the denser became the fog. Maisie had the same heart-shaped face as her mother. But Annie's eyes had been a darker brown, smaller and gentler. Maisie's were almost amber, and they flashed dangerously when she was mad at the world. She was often mad at the world. Lila remembered this from when Maisie was little, and nothing she had seen of the ferocious young woman last night made her rethink it.

Lila had only been eight when Annie arrived in the Marleigh house. At the time, Annie was already pregnant, and no house of any quality would have hired her. A brothel or the workhouse would have been her only options. But surprisingly, Sarah Marleigh hired her as the girls' nurse. Lila suspected it was because she had no intention of hiring a regular servant, someone who would need a decent salary. She took Annie in because she hardly had to pay her anything. Annie was grateful to have a roof over her head. She barely had five days off after Maisie arrived in the world, and then it was up to the servants, the horses and the dogs to raise the little baby. Maisie spent many hours crawling around the girls' nursery.

Lady Marleigh always threatened to cast off the child, but Annie promised that Maisie wouldn't interfere in her duties and she lived up to her promise. Lila had gone off to school three years after Annie arrived, but Annie was the one person she could trust in the house. Maybe not a substitute for her mother, whom Lila had known only for a few short years. Not making up for all she lost when she moved to England at the age of seven—the heat, the mangoes, the bustle of Delhi city, the parties of East India Company members that took place in the wide open veranda of her father and mother's large, airy house, even the geckos that roamed the walls inside the house, the fans, the swirling smells of cardamom, cumin and rain-beaten earth, the feel of the mosquito nets on her fingers, the sea of stars and the chirruping of crickets that she never saw or heard in London ever again—but at least there was one person who seemed to love her, who brushed her hair and stayed up at night with her when she had a cold.

When Lila moved all the way to London on a ship that never stopped heaving, she wasn't allowed to bring much with her. But she had hidden some treasures away in her trunk and Annie helped her look after them. A tiny portrait of her father and mother, her father with his serious face and gentle eyes, standing with his hand on her mother's shoulder, and her mother, sitting on a chair, dressed in a sari of a vibrant magenta, the color of dawn in the monsoons. There was not much in their expressions but, for some reason, Lila thought she could see the thick knot of love that bound them together, a knot neither had been able to resist, even though it could not have been easy. Her mother had told her a long time ago that when the portrait was painted, Lila had been growing in her belly. A shiver of pleasure and pain crawled up her spine when she looked at that picture.

Also hidden away was an empty bottle of attar of roses that still smelled like Mama and some dried and pressed marigold flowers from a garland the girls had made together when they were little. All of these Annie had taken care of as if they were made of gold and silver and weren't scraps of a lost childhood.

When Sarah Marleigh's missing box of jewelry was found in Annie's room, Lila was sure nothing would come of it. No one who had lived with Annie for seven years could imagine that she could do such a thing. She had a neat little figure, her frizzy hair was combed back, and she hardly ever used any adornments except the daisy chains that the girls or Maisie wove for her. To think she would steal jewelry—it was unthinkable. Annie herself was vehement that she never touched the box. In fact, as the girls' nurse, Annie didn't enter Lady Marleigh's room. She had no reason to.

There was a period of two hours in which the box could have been stolen. But no one could vouch for Annie for the entire two hours. She was in and out of the kitchen, in and out of the girls' rooms to look after their laundry. She spent some of it with Lila. But no one could vouch for every single minute. Annie was frantic. Maybe she had already guessed how it would all end. Lila hadn't.

Lady Marleigh had turned cold eyes at Lila, asked her if Annie was with her for those two hours. Lila could have said yes at once. But she dithered. Because Annie wasn't with her all that afternoon. The word *yes*, it was on the tip of her tongue, but then she saw the cruel smile playing on Sarah Marleigh's lips, a smile Lila knew intimately. That made her dither. She was sure even if she said that Annie was with her the entire time, Sarah wouldn't believe her. She finally murmured, "Yes, Annie was with me the whole time."

Sarah's lip curled and Lila knew what she was going to say before she said it. "No matter how many years you live here, there is no getting the native out of you, is there, Lila? You will always be your mother's daughter, unable to tell the truth. I suppose that is how she trapped my husband?"

And of course, Lila should have stuck to her guns, but whenever Sarah looked at her with so much derision, Lila froze. The rage, the pain froze inside her and she couldn't speak.

And Annie couldn't account for how the box ended up in her room.

Over the years, Lila was ravaged with guilt, a guilt not only about what she had done—or in fact, not done—but also for who she was. She burned with shame for letting Annie down, for letting poor Maisie down, Maisie who had disappeared one night and was never seen again. It wasn't just that Lila had faltered. It wasn't just her stepmother's face or that awful knowing smile. It wasn't just that she *couldn't* have said where Annie was all of that afternoon because she didn't know. Lila knew that at that time she was so in love with Robert Wellesley, a young man about her age, the brother of a school friend, that she didn't take the threat to Annie's life seriously. Her days and nights were clouded with one thing, and she didn't have a thought to spare for anything else.

She didn't imagine that Annie wouldn't be believed, much less that she would hang. Selfish, she was so selfish. And Robert Wellesley! The sniveling, spotty, peevish son of a baron who dangled Lila for years and then told her there was no way he could marry someone like her, someone with no fortune and no birth. A face and a willing body, they didn't count for much once he was a baron, he said kindly. *You do understand, Lila, I'm sure you wouldn't want me to marry beneath myself.*

For him! For him, she couldn't lie convincingly for her only friend.

Yet even now she couldn't say *how* the box ended up in Annie's room.

Sarah Marleigh could have done something that sneaky, but she had no reason to. If she had wanted rid of Annie, she simply had to turn her out of the house. Could one of the other staff have done it? But why? It was hardly a happy, harmonious household. People were suspicious of each other. Sarah encouraged it. A servant could have framed Annie.

Lila wished she could speak to her sisters Mira and Anya about it. But she couldn't. Because they never spoke. And it wasn't just because Annie's face and the clamoring crowd—hungry for blood at Annie's hanging, which had nearly suffocated Lila—haunted Lila's nights. The toxic pools of guilt that lay between the sisters couldn't be bridged. Guilt for how they treated each other in the Marleigh house.

Yet it wasn't just that either. It was other things, things that would never heal. That would be an open sore forever. The past lay between them. What they had done. What had happened because they had not had courage. Because even at the time they were moved to London, even then they had played Sarah Marleigh's game. A game that Lila still didn't completely understand. After all, why had a woman who had no maternal instincts transported the girls all the way to London in the first place? She had barely bothered to look after or care for Jonathan. Even with Jonathan, she had only shown an interest in him when she wanted him to do something for her, especially to torment the girls. Beyond that, she had little affection for him. So, why the girls? Just to torture them? But surely it wasn't worth torturing her late husband's bastards if it meant also torturing herself, making herself uncomfortable. She had sent the girls off to school as soon as she could, but seminaries had to be paid for. So, why? It was a question she feared would never be answered now because it was too late. Sarah was dead. Had been for two years. Was it destined to remain yet another source of darkness?

That darkness would always lie between the sisters. Darkness that threatened to consume her if she looked too closely at it.

6

Hannah chided her when she found her in her bedchamber looking through her clothes not four hours after she had gone to bed. She checked to see if Lila was still bent on going to the rat pit, and then seeing that Lila was adamant, she accepted it. She eyed Lila's full bosom somewhat ironically when Lila asked if she could go as a man. "Harlot?" Lila asked, to which Hannah frowned and shook her head. "I'll work something out, miss. Don't fuss. And I wish you'd get more sleep. I know you say you don't want to marry, but bags under the eyes help no man nor no woman. What is bothering you, miss? It isn't like you to look so wan."

"Nothing. It's nothing, Hannah," Lila muttered.

Hannah glanced at her once or twice but said no more. She promised Lila she would find something for her to wear and urged her to get some sleep. Lila glanced through her correspondence. There were notes and flowers from her admirers. A note from Henry Alston. *Thank you for yet another unforgettable evening.* She sighed. Oh dear, how to get the boy out of love with her? A huge bouquet from Herringford. *My only regret is that we never get time to be private.* Dear lord. Even the thought of being private with Herringford made her queasy. A note of thanks from Annabel Wakefield. *You know the state of my marriage. Your salons are a haven for me.* Poor Annabel. But she couldn't help feeling the tiniest bit proud. Whatever people thought of her and her "gambling den," it *was* a haven for men and women who found their own homes anything but havens. Annabel was only one of many. There were other notes, like the ones she received after all her social evenings. Lila gave up the fight to try to read all of them. She paced her room.

The truth was it wasn't just Maisie Quinn's visit that was haunting Lila this morning. Every time she thought of the glittering eyes of *that man*, she could barely breathe. She would stop her pacing, clench her fists, and stare murderously into the distance. How dare he! How *could* he! He didn't even know her. To make such an assumption about her. Based on what exactly? Some hours he spent in one of her salons?

She remembered the way he was watching her. Scrutinizing every millimeter of her face. The color rushed to her face at all he might have seen. Her arch words at Lord Herringford when he was nearly licking her cleavage. The playful and sympathetic smiles at Henry Alston. The stupid boast about the horse race! She burned; she didn't even know with what. It couldn't be with shame, because what on earth did she have to be ashamed of? Nothing! She could murder the man. She saw herself as he saw her. His father's mistress. The disgust in his face when she challenged him to take her as his mistress. The disgust.

She would get back at him. Somehow, she would get back at him. She never wanted to see him again. But she would find a way to get back at him. The insufferable self-confidence, the complete self-belief. She was sure he was one of those horrible people who never questioned anything they thought or did.

Who were always right and anyone who didn't agree was wrong. The eyes that seemed to read her mind, and yet couldn't read her at all, were fooled by the hostess persona that everyone else was taken in by too. And anyway, why was it that a woman was expected to put her real self on show when she was working? Did a man go to Parliament and burp and fart his way through a speech? Did a man wear his drawers to an appointment? No!

"Not so discerning at all, then, Mr. Tristram," she growled.

And here she was again. Thinking about some stupid, insufferable man, when there was only one thing to think about. Maisie. Maisie and how to help the girl. Or even to find her.

As she was pacing, the doorbell rang.

"Finally!" Lila hurtled all the way down the stairs and to the hallway.

The front door opened and one of the footmen ushered in a vision.

It was her friend Kenneth Laudsley. He came in, sauntered in, one should say, looking resplendent. His coat was a muted purple velvet, his waistcoat gold floral silk. His pantaloons fitted him so well they may as well have been painted on, and the eyes, the disdainful eyes and the walking stick he twirled were a work of art. The artful clothing and demeanor hid the muscled thighs and the hands that were steady as a pin when managing a sporting vehicle, but then, he made sure of that. Indolent, he wanted to come across as nothing so much as indolent. People who tried too hard, he said, were the very worst kind of people.

He stood there, staring at Lila. "Darling, you look positively inflamed. Whatever is the matter? And can you not give a chap a chance to wake up at a decent hour before sending urgent missives? You know what time I got to bed?"

"I don't care!" she said, dragging him into the living room.

"Here, mind the coat!" he said, sounding more like the Kenneth she had known since they were both twenty and met at Vauxhall and she was crying about Robert Wellesley and he about someone or the other whose name she couldn't remember now. Come to think of it, the idea of her salons was born on that very evening. She was desperate not to marry conveniently just to escape Sarah Marleigh, and of course she had sworn off men at the time. So an opportunity to think about earning a living, she took what was perhaps a casual chat very seriously indeed. Kenneth wanted nothing to do with it, it sounded like too much work, but he helped her figure out what she could do and how she could go about it. Not to mention that he knew everyone, all the right people, and knew exactly who to send her way. It was Kenneth who had said that she was good with people, she had energy, and she had a boundless determination. Not to mention that she always beat him at cards. *A gambling salon, Lila, it would suit you down to the ground.*

"Never mind the coat," she said impatiently. "I need you to take me to the rat pit tonight. I would go by myself, but I have a feeling it wouldn't be the thing. And I don't even know where it is. Though I'm nearly sure it must be in Covent Garden. I mean, I suppose I could find it myself. It can't be that hard. How big is the place anyway? It'll be heaving. Though if I go myself, I suppose I might attract too much attention?"

He was looking askance at her. He had the most beautiful cherub curls, made of spun sunshine. In fact, they reminded her of nothing so much as the sheaves of wheat that grew in the fields outside Delhi. Though silkier perhaps. He had a chin dimple. His eyes were apprehensive. "Darling, you're alarming me."

"I know women don't go to the rat pit. At least not women with a reputation. But I don't have one!"

"It's mostly harlots, it's true. Though that isn't the main thing that is worrying me. It's the energy in your body. You seem like you want to *do* things. It's wearying. Just looking at you makes a man wilt."

But Lila knew that. It was fashionable to lie half the day on a chaise and not want to do things. She knew it wasn't attractive that she always had an urgent purpose—usually five different urgent purposes. No wonder *that man* was disgusted at the idea of her as his mistress. Not that she wanted to be his mistress. "Yes," she said meekly. "I see what you mean. My teachers at the seminary found it horribly unfeminine. They were sure I would end up joining the Bluestocking Society, or worse, remaining a spinster all my life, with all the reading and energy. But there's no point worrying about something you can't change. I told them much the same. You couldn't find out for me where it is, could you? The rat pit, I mean."

He placed himself, puddle fashion, on a chaise longue, and looked to be blending into the upholstery, trickle by trickle. He already looked half-asleep. "I suppose you'll go whether I escort you or not?"

"Yes."

"Then you take matters out of my hands. Which, as a matter of fact, I greatly prefer. It's exhausting trying to make decisions. I'd much rather you put a leash on me and told me where to sit."

"You'll take me?"

He widened his eyes, by way of trying to keep them open. "I expect so. Though it's only boring people who plan ahead. Why do you want to go, can one ask?"

Pacing about the room, she gave him a quick explanation, but he lost interest in it halfway and focused on the coffee Mrs. Williams, the housekeeper, brought in for him. He said no to the delicate and flaky *boudoirs*, shuddering and saying that if he lost his figure his valet would quit on the spot. He looked with sleepy eyes at Lila. "You know, I am hearing the most riveting rumors that you're planning on driving the curricle in my stead, for the Brighton race. You know every man between here and the Brighton tollgate will gawk at you, look you up and down, and take you for a fast one? You'd lose your reputation entirely. If you had one, that is." He raised his quizzing glass at her because she had come to an urgent standstill in the middle of the room.

Her eyes glittered. "They will, will they? And how is that different from what they already think? I have a good mind to do it, you know. It'll teach people a lesson, that's for sure. Oh, and apropos nothing, do you know someone called Tristram? Ivor Tristram?"

Kenneth's leg was dangling off the chaise. A streak of sunshine was hitting him square in the face from the window and he was shielding himself from it as if it was a musket attack. "I don't know why anyone would ever *choose* to draw their curtains back. I suppose you can't stop your servants from doing it? They probably think it's their job? Ivor Tristram. He spars at Jackson's."

"Any good?" she asked. Though she had no idea why she should care if he was any good at boxing or not. "In fact," she said, even though Kenneth had not said anything, "I'm convinced he's not very good. His arms looked . . . weak."

"Nothing of the sort. He has a punishing left. He plays fair. Very sporting. But it's hard to get around him. Nimble on his feet. Looks good without his shirt on. Not everyone does."

A vision of Ivor Tristram without his shirt on flashed across Lila's mind.

"A good rider. Nifty pair of hands. But one of those boring men who work hard minding their estate or whatever it is these men do. I've heard he invests in coffee or some such thing and has an additional source of income from that. I mean, don't get me wrong. He's not in my set and I don't know him very well. But I see him riding in the park now and again, of an afternoon."

Lila, who had been abstractedly looking out of the window with a frown, turned and looked at Kenneth again. "Oh, just the thing. I was thinking of going riding today. Would you like to come, or shall I see you later on for the rat pit?"

Kenneth peeled himself off the chaise. "I have business to attend to, even if you don't. I will see you promptly at seven tonight. Until then, m'dear, try to stay out of trouble. And take a nap or something. It's reviving to the system. It's the main reason I would love living on the continent. That and all the mindless rutting!" These would have made for splendid parting words, but he paused and said, "I nearly forgot. You do have an over-energetic way of distracting a man. Vauxhall Gardens in three nights. Will you come? One can't help thinking a dashing woman on one's arm would be just the thing." He kissed her goodbye on the tips of his fingers.

7

Lila dressed with unusual care for the park that afternoon.

In India, as a little girl, she was given horse-riding lessons by a master. But instead of riding sidesaddle, she was taught to ride astride, wearing breeches just like the boys did. It was only once she came to London and then went to the seminary that she learned to ride "the correct, less hoydenish way," as her stepmother described it. But then a few years ago, she decided—with the help and encouragement of Kenneth Laudsley—that flouting society's conventions only halfway didn't work. People didn't respect you, and in fact they ignored you. You may as well go all out.

Lila didn't think she hankered after anyone's attention, but she enjoyed doing what she liked and not what everyone else wanted her to do, and when all was said and done, her eccentricities were good for business. When she wanted a proper ride, she chose to put on her breeches—though draped with pomegranate velveteen to look more like a dress—and ride astride.

Her groom Roger Manson rode behind her, but other than that nod to respectability, there she was in her eccentric glory, riding astride, a plume in her hat that curved and fell, to blend gracefully with her curls. Even though the *ton* had gotten used to her over the years, dowagers still stared at her through quizzing glasses. The younger men gave her admiring glances and the older ones stripped her naked, no doubt. Not all of them did that. But as Lila often thought, one or two unpleasant people made *everything* unpleasant, so that you could hardly remember the ones who weren't judging you or ogling at you.

Of course, they could have been staring at the silk eye mask Roger chose to wear. Another one of *her* eccentricities, a groom that wore an eye mask in broad daylight.

She raised her chin high, adjusted her posture though it was already enviably perfect, and looked around her. She was attracting a lot of attention and the solitary, secretive part of her was squirming, but she sat even straighter and was pleased when Henry Alston rescued her from her internal writhing. He looked as bright-eyed as always. "It's lovely to see you here, Miss Marleigh," he said, riding up to her.

She noticed one or two young women—one with poetic red curls and bright green eyes—who were looking, and at the same time trying not to look, first at Henry and then with less kind eyes at Lila. She looked clinically at Henry. It was difficult to see him as anything but a child, but she supposed that if she were under twenty years of age she might find the bashful face and the soft hazel eyes appealing. He needed to fill out and, more importantly, grow in confidence, but he had potential. When he got over her, he'd make some girl his own age—some respectable girl with a proper name and family—very happy.

She chatted with him as they rode together. When he got over his shyness, he talked about books and politics, subjects that men didn't normally touch on with a woman. And she relaxed.

But then, seemingly emboldened with the easy conversation, he said suddenly, "Miss Marleigh, I have wanted a word with you these past few weeks." He blushed. "But it isn't the kind of thing I would—or could!—bring up when you are busy at work in your salons. I wonder—"

Oh, dear God. She ruthlessly interjected. "It's such a pleasure to see you in my salons! Don't get me wrong, I enjoy them. But I'm always thankful to have a few friendly faces I can turn to as the night wears on."

This distracted him for a second from what he was about to say, but she regretted her words when he gave her a shy but glowing smile. "I'm pleased to hear you say it. I can't tell you how much. Do you think we could find—?"

"Oh, is that a blackbird? Aren't they very unusual? I've always wanted to see one. Haven't you?" She was babbling now, pointing at . . . a pigeon.

"Miss Marleigh!"

Lila turned her head to look at who was calling her. It was Lord Herringford. Not someone she ever looked forward to seeing, but right this second, just what she needed to stop Henry Alston's declarations.

"Lord Herringford," she said, inclining her head.

Henry looked irritated, but he was too well bred to do anything but greet Herringford in a friendly way.

Herringford stared at her up and down, declared that he had never seen anyone ride so beautifully. "I suppose it don't chafe?" he inquired, looking down at her thighs.

She sighed inwardly and was going to say that she had seen an acquaintance and must be off when she spied a dark blue riding coat with bronze buttons, perfectly fitting buff riding trousers and natty riding boots. It was Ivor Tristram. Of course, now she would see him everywhere. There would be no getting away from the man. Wherever she went, there she would find him, looking disdainfully at her. Not that he was looking at her.

He was riding with two other men, but then he caught her eye. Lila laughed loudly and batted a hand at Herringford, though she was pretty sure he hadn't said anything. She slowed her pace and so did Henry and Herringford, to match hers. But no matter how much she slowed down, she would have passed Tristram by quick enough, except Henry Alston waved to him. She looked up through her eyelashes to see what Tristram would do. But instead of ignoring them, he rode up to her group.

"Miss Marleigh, Lord Herringford," he said. His eyes gave nothing away. He gave her one of his direct looks, but there was nothing in it. Hardly even recognition, given they had spoken just last night. Maybe he was used to fighting off his father's mistresses and they all blended into one. She felt that unexpected pang again that she had felt last night, wondering what it would be like to be Benjamin Tristram's son. Would he feel disgust or shame? At his father, or even—as an extension—at himself? But then she dismissed it. He was too self-confident to care.

"Mr. Tristram," she said in that loud resonant salon voice of hers, her eyes sparkling. "Aren't I lucky to bump into so many of my friends this afternoon? It makes it worthwhile to put up with the humidity. I was wilting before I came across Mr. Alston and Lord Herringford." She had the sinking feeling she'd never be able to speak to Tristram in anything other than this cheery voice.

Her admirers protested. "You could never wilt!" Henry declared.

"As I always say," Herringford said, "a bit of perspiration only makes a woman more desirable, not less."

She cringed. But her smile got wider. She laughed. "You always know just what to say, Lord Herringford. I swear my clothes are clinging to me in all the wrong places!" She felt disgusted at herself and even Henry looked a little surprised, but he was still smiling at her with glowing eyes. Herringford was falling into her chest again. She wanted to slap him. She gripped her horse's reins harder.

"There is nothing you could wear that would not become you, m'dear," Herringford said.

"Lord Herringford, I plan to go to the rat pit tonight. And my maid wants to make me look like a milkmaid. You wouldn't notice me in those clothes." She eyed Tristram sideways.

Henry looked surprised again. "I never knew you'd like to go to the rat pit."

"You find yourself in a bloodthirsty mood, Miss Marleigh?" Tristram asked.

"Yes, you know," she said, "I really do."

"You don't find it a vile sport?"

She did. She had a feeling she was going to faint the first time a rat was decapitated. It sounded horrific and the poor, poor rats. But she batted a hand. "We have a rat infestation problem in this city, don't we? This is one way of taking care of it. And rat-catchers need to live too. Or their guilds wouldn't survive."

"And it's a great way to catch everyone's eye," Tristram said, sounding genial. "If that's what you wanted."

"Oh, yes," Lila said. "I love catching everyone's eye. I *thrive* on it." The smile was brighter than ever. She looked straight ahead so none of the men would catch the dangerous glitter in her eyes. "Do come, if you can, Mr. Tristram," she said, glancing at him from under her eyelashes. "I have to say now that I've met you, I can't get enough of your company."

He said nothing, but merely smiled. She was wondering how

to extricate herself from this odd group. She was already irritable at the better-than-everyone Mr. Tristram. But then Herringford said, "Heard about the kerfuffle at your place, Tristram. Don't suppose you caught the fellow?"

She looked at Tristram. His face didn't change. She wondered what kerfuffle.

"No," he said briefly. "We didn't catch him. But I will. I have evidence against the man. It's only a matter of time."

She was mildly interested now. "Oh, what is this? A mystery? A romance?"

Tristram's mouth twisted as if he didn't believe in such a thing. "Hardly. A man—a lascar—savagely attacked my cousin Tiffany. He got away before we could hand him over to the Runners. But Tiffany managed to tear his dagger off him. And I still have it."

Lila frowned. Her heart was beating painfully hard. A lascar. A sailor from India. Attacked Tristram's cousin. It couldn't be. Surely it couldn't be Maisie's man. Isn't that what Maisie had said though? That her man had attacked some *hoity-toity miss?* What—or who—had Maisie seen in Lila's salon last night that made her run away?

"Damn those natives. You can't move them all the way to a civilized country and then expect them to behave civil," Herringford said.

Lila's hands gripped her reins harder, but she didn't say anything. Both Henry and Herringford seemed deeply oblivious that Herringford had said anything that could offend her. A lascar—a sailor from the colonies, employed on British ships at horrifically low wages and then let loose in the city to fend for himself. *A girl who looks like me and a man who looks like him—what chance have we got?* Maisie's words.

She looked up to find Tristram looking at her. The heat

rose to her face. So, he understood how Herringford's words might sound to her. Damn the man! She didn't need his knowing eyes. And who knew what was behind that look—pity or disgust? She didn't want either. The man was no different from Herringford. He had found a sailor from the colonies in the room with his cousin and immediately made him the villain.

She thought uneasily of the dagger. A lascar could be carrying a distinctive dagger, an Indian one, something recognizable. Did that mean that the man—this lascar, if he *was* Maisie's man—was in fact in the room with Tristram's cousin when she was attacked? And if he was, had he attacked her?

They rode for a while, chatting of this and that, Lila keeping her face amiable as her mind raced. Henry's family barouche caught his attention and he excused himself, saying that he hoped he would get the chance to spend more time with her soon. Perhaps in Vauxhall Gardens in a few nights' time, when there was supposed to be a hot-air balloon launched from there? She murmured that she might be going there with Kenneth Laudsley. He looked pleased that he might see her there and tipped her his hat before he cantered off.

Herringford, who was red and panting, finally said that he would die of the heat if he didn't get out of it. This left Lila alone with Ivor Tristram.

She thought he would make an excuse and be off, he had no reason to linger and would not want to be seen with a woman he thought was his father's mistress, but he didn't leave, and they rode quietly together. They stopped their horses in a shady spot under some sweet chestnuts. He turned his magnificent gray half toward her. She soothed Polly, her mare, a little larger than average for a female rider, and who loved a good gallop in the mornings. They were surrounded by fashionable riders in the park, but Lila couldn't help thinking that there was something about the dappled sunshine under the trees that made it seem like they were the only two people there, perhaps the only two people in the world.

For some reason, she was acutely aware of the way he looked at her, as if he could see every feather of movement in her face, hear every inflexion, even those she didn't want him to hear. She was aware of his hands that held his horse easily. The thighs, the way his coat fitted him perfectly. It was as though the awareness wasn't just in her eyes; it filled her entire body.

If she were in her salon, there would be twenty things she could think of to say to the man. Affable, meaningless things. Right now, she couldn't think of even one.

"Did he rape her?" she blurted out. She bit her lip. Where did that come from? "The lascar, I mean," she said feebly.

He must be shocked at her words, but he was simply looking at her with those piercing eyes. "No. No doubt he would have if he hadn't been stopped."

"What makes you so sure it was him who attacked your cousin?"

"The room was dark. When light was brought in—when people heard my cousin screaming—there were only two people in the room. Tiffany and this lascar."

That sounded damning. Yet Maisie was sure her man couldn't have attacked anyone. And it was a big risk to take. If the man already had a woman—Maisie—why take such a huge risk, why attack someone? Surely, he knew he could hang for it. A brown man attacking a white woman, she was surprised it wasn't already a bigger scandal. Lila was frowning hard. The man's voice broke into her thoughts.

"Which one will it be, Miss Marleigh, the innocent Henry Alston or the less than innocent Lord Herringford?"

She turned her face to him and gritted her teeth. She made herself smile, not a wide, obvious smile, but one that made her eyes flash. "You are forgetting your father. And yourself? You can't expect me to choose between just two men."

"You aren't really thinking of going to the rat pit?"

She looked at him in surprise. He was looking at her from under those shapely dark brows. "What do you care?" The question jumped out of her. And the sharp tone.

His eyes became a little sharper. She tried to get the smile back on. The man was too irritating for words.

He didn't say anything at first, then said, "Even mistresses must have some reputation to maintain. Surely you can't expect me not to care?"

She blinked. The color rushed to her face. "How dare you? If you think that I would be *your* . . ." She stopped abruptly.

He was smiling slightly. "Funny," he murmured, "here I was thinking you really wanted me to choose you as a mistress."

She growled before she could stop herself. She leaned forward. "Maybe the question isn't so much whether or not *you* would choose *me* as a mistress, Mr. Tristram. But whether or not *I* would choose *you* as a lover."

Some passing children had ruffled Tristram's horse slightly, but though he was soothing his horse with a steady hand, he was looking directly into her eyes. Her words hung in the air. And she was annoyed to see that she was completely aware of him. A drop of sweat trickled down her back and she felt dampness between her legs. He glanced, as if against his will, at her lips. "I was hasty last night, and I was rude."

She was surprised. She searched his eyes.

"It can't be easy for you to let go of guaranteed income. I will happily compensate you."

She drew back as though she'd been slapped. Just for a second, just then, she had felt that maybe he did see her, did understand her. That underneath the self-assurance there was understanding, even a hint of kindness. But there he was, pretending to be kind by offering to compensate her for what she would lose if she stopped being his father's mistress. Oh, there was desire in his eyes. Maybe just a flicker, but it was there. She could see it. But then there was that disdain too.

Her eyes flashed at him. "And perhaps I won't let your father go so easily, Mr. Tristram."

His eyes glittered. "Yes, you know, you'd be stupid to, really. I am a wealthy man."

He took his leave and, spurring his horse, rode off, his back straight, his legs shapely on his horse.

Lila growled some more before turning in the direction of home.

8

Ivor was disgusted at himself. He was turning out to be no better than his father. And that was one thing he hadn't seen coming. He knew his other faults. He could be obstinate and overbearing, making up his mind too quickly about things. He kept himself from getting close to people. He ordered things for himself, as he liked them; he wasn't used to asking for or needing the opinion of others. He was good at running his estates, because he consulted people but then took his own decisions, instead of endlessly dithering. He knew these things about himself. They were qualities and faults he more or less accepted. But this, this was a new one.

He had seen her, seen her in her salon and then today on her horse. The bright smiles, the flashing eyes, the arch words that were designed to attract attention. Exactly how you might imagine the mistress of a gambling salon would be.

She was beautiful, there was no doubt about that. It wasn't just the dark curls that looked as though they were hardly dressed at all. The face clear of rouge and patches. The skin, pale and creamy, yet not the same as his, a whisper of something that set her apart. The dresses that fitted her perfectly, that weren't understated, but weren't flashy either. The hint of difference in everything she did. Simple things, like the mirrors cut into the cushions in her parlor, the tiny bells that hung from her earrings, the way she used her hands when she spoke, as if she wasn't aware she was doing it, like a dancer. The excellent seat on her horse, second to none. A strong, maybe even athletic woman who stirred a strong desire in him. But it wasn't just those things.

He placed his whip and gloves on the hall table of his house in Bloomsbury and walked to his study. It wasn't just those things. Lila Marleigh's face hovered before him. It was the awareness in her eyes, the confidence, the sonorous voice. Her clothes, perfectly chosen, but worn in her own particular way, not coupled with the same jewelry as everyone else might choose. It was hard to forget those things once you'd seen them.

And there was something else, something less definable. Something hard to put his finger on. That he couldn't see. Only sense; like she was keeping a part of herself tucked away where people couldn't see it.

That there was something else there, more than the hostess that everyone else saw. Something underneath that almost no one got to see. Or touch. And he couldn't help it. The hidden, private part of him wanted to reach out to that side of her, to link fingers, to see and be seen, to hold on for dear life.

Good God.

He stood at his desk, a pile of correspondence in his hands that he wasn't looking at. She was exactly what she looked like: a bright-eyed hostess who knew how to find and keep her customers. She was dangling Henry Alston and Herringford, and who knew how many other men, off the tips of her fingers. He had seen it with his own eyes. It didn't matter how much Herringford encroached or how young Alston was. She was keeping them both hanging after her.

And yet, *yet* knowing all that, when he was with her, he found himself watching the quick flash of expressions on her face, the impatient way she brushed her hair back from her forehead, the way she shrugged away thoughts she didn't like. The keen intelligence and the deep privacy that was hidden behind such a public persona that it didn't look like privacy at all. You could blink and miss it entirely.

She was his father's mistress.

The disgust twisted in his belly. He was frozen, the correspondence still in his hands, though he scarcely knew it was there, staring out of the window to the rose garden. Was he disgusted at her? Not really. She was no different from any woman of her profession. An accomplished hostess, who knew her music and food like she did her piquet tables. She knew her conversation and she understood her customers' needs and their pockets. And she seemed educated. In fact, he had done his research before he met her. She was educated at a select seminary. She could have chosen to be a governess if she needed to earn a living, a school mistress. But she chose to host card parties. That told you a lot.

Being someone's mistress could supplement her income nicely, and she didn't look like she was choosy about her men. He went to her salon expecting exactly her. No, not exactly her. She was intelligent and perceptive; he hadn't expected that. And there was a warmth to her that he hadn't expected at all. She was nothing like his father's other mistresses, in fact. There was no hartshorn or smelling feathers—these were a given with his father's other women. No artificially dyed stiff curls. No patches or rose balm. No flaunting of the jewels bestowed on her by her men.

No, he was disgusted at himself. Well, perhaps a little bit at her for attracting him so easily.

Ivor grew up with a series of his father's mistresses. He watched as his father paraded them. There was nothing so obvious as taking his wife and his mistress to the same ball, nothing like that. And none of the mistresses showed up in their home. But he didn't hide the women from society, he took them to the theater, he took them to the park, he took them shopping, he didn't hide that he spent nights in their homes, so that everyone knew about them and pitied Ivor's mother, Heather. It was from these pitying looks and whispers that Ivor had first gotten a sense as a boy that things weren't right. His parents rarely spoke to each other; often one was to be found in town, the other in the country at their estate in Sussex, and they didn't share a bedroom. They had little in common. His father, though emotionally weak, was an energetic and restless man. His mother kept to her bed when she could. One or two social engagements per week, even at the height of the season, were too much for her. And she tended to wheedle and complain, not ask for what she wanted directly. And his father was always impatient.

He saw what his mother went through, how she would escape to her bedroom for weeks sometimes, be as unavailable to her son as his father was. And the guilt, the guilt that Ivor felt. The guilt at being his father's son. The guilt, he sometimes thought, at being a man. Of sharing his blood with Benjamin.

And yet here he was. He couldn't get Lila Marleigh's words out of his head. She had thrown them at him. Would *she* choose him as her lover?

He flicked his head. It would pass. It was a mild infatuation, hardly even that. Hardly more than—curiosity, say. She was a beautiful woman, and she knew how to attract men. He would get over it. He would make *sure* he got over it.

He riffled restlessly through his correspondence. He couldn't bring himself to sit at his desk, so he took the letters outside and sat at the iron grille table. He imagined his gardener, valet, and butler would all have something to say about him sitting at a garden table and working in his shirtsleeves. Bees were buzzing around him and the sunshine touching soft fingers at his neck. The mixed colors of the rose garden—gold, sunset, pomegranate, a deep burgundy, clotted cream—and the confusion of perfumes swirled. He answered a few letters.

At the back of his mind was his mother's response. Three days ago, he had written to her. He told her he would speak to Lila Marleigh and was confident he could peel the woman away from his father. *You are sure she is entangled with my father, aren't you?* He found himself cursing at those words now. His mother had years of experience. She knew. She had her sources. Why did he bother asking that question? And then he met Lila Marleigh last night and she didn't deny it. Yet there was something distasteful about it. Something that made him writhe in revulsion.

And just this morning, the answer had come back. *I have confronted your father with the woman. He doesn't deny it. He tells me it is none of my damned business and he'll thank me to stay away from his mistresses. Ivor, I only have you to turn to. The woman is young enough to be his daughter. Does he have no sympathy for me? The doctor confirms I could be gone in months. Some consideration at the end, that is all I ask.*

It was proving harder than he had anticipated to discuss terms with Lila Marleigh. After two meetings, he should have an idea of how much she wanted. He wanted to get on with it.

He didn't want to see her again. But she wasn't letting him get to an amount. Of course, it was a dammed good way to negotiate.

As he was sitting there, writing to his agent Trevor Symonds, the doorbell rang. A minute later, Tiffany, his cousin, came skipping in. She was dressed in primrose muslin, her glossy hair, the color of fresh straw, lay over one shoulder, and her light blue eyes were bright. He was happy to see she hadn't suffered too much from the shock of the other night when that man had attacked her.

Tiffany's father, Ivor's uncle Arthur, was a very wealthy man, having supplemented the income from his estates by some sound investments in tea, soap, and sugar. But since he was from an old and respected family, people didn't mind his involvement in trade. Tiffany was an eligible catch, an heiress, the only child of her parents, and pretty to boot.

She dropped herself into one of the garden chairs, then shrieked, stood up and swiveled to look behind her. "Have I ruined it, have I, Ivor?"

He was still glancing at his correspondence. "I expect you have twenty that could take its place in a wink," he said casually.

"You know, you haven't even looked at me," she complained. "Most men think I'm something special to look at, you know."

"Of course, you are," he said, still looking at the accounts from his agent.

"Tell me what color my eyes are," she demanded.

"Blue."

"Oh, all of us have blue eyes," she said petulantly. She popped inside and brought out a rug that she draped on the garden chair, making sure not an inch of offending metal was poking through and touching her dress, and then perched herself on the edge of the chair. "Other men do admire me, you know, Ivor."

"I don't doubt it."

"I suppose you have some wealthy widow or some opera singer you're involved with?" she said, as if that would explain why he didn't notice her.

"Can't say I do at the moment."

Mrs. Manfield, his housekeeper, brought the tea tray outside.

"Mrs. Manfield, would you say I'm pretty?"

Mrs. Manfield's gray eyes twinkled as Ivor exchanged a quick smile with her. Her silver crimpled curls were neatly pulled back into a bun and the black dress she wore didn't have a single crease in it. Her buckled shoes shone like a mirror. "I would say exceedingly so, Miss Tiffany."

"Well, Ivor doesn't think so. Though he's not easy to please, is he? I mean, he's twenty-eight, which is practically ancient, and still unmarried. And he scorns the idea of mistresses."

Mrs. Manfield didn't seem alarmed at young Miss Tiffany discussing her cousin's mistresses or lack thereof. She smiled and said no two men were the same, nor two women. "Some come to love late," she added placidly, "but when they do come, they fall hard."

"Oh, yes," Tiffany said. "I imagine Ivor would be as obstinate and pigheaded in love as in everything else."

Tiffany elaborated on her theme for as long as Mrs. Manfield was bustling around the tea tray. When the housekeeper left, Tiffany turned to Ivor again. "Twenty-eight isn't that old," she said to his surprise. "Even thirty-five isn't. Not really." She was twisting her dress in her hand, a frown playing on her brow.

Ivor put his pen down and gave her his full attention. "Now who are you dangling after, Tiff? Someone completely unsuitable?"

"He's a bit older, that's all." She lifted her chin. "An earl to boot."

"Fifteen years older than you. But an earl, I suppose. That

should make up for the age difference," he said, somewhat iron-ically.

She flicked her head. "As if I care what you think."

"Exactly. I wouldn't have thought you did. Which is making me wonder why you're here," he said amiably. He pulled his chair back from the table and leaned his elbows on his knees.

"Because Papa won't like the match, and I want you to convince him that it's what I want, and it'll be good for me."

"If the man's an earl, I can't imagine that there would be a problem." He interlaced his fingers.

She was still fidgeting. She picked up a biscuit and started squishing it into powder between her fingers. "I'm just saying. You men always have *notions*. If Mama was alive, she would talk sense into Papa." She came to her feet. She brushed her hands of biscuit dust. "Anyway, I thought I'd give you a little warning, that's all. I mean, so what if the man has lost money . . ." She stopped abruptly.

Ivor was watching her steadily. "Gambling?"

"Some."

"Debts."

"There may be. But so what? Just because there are debts doesn't mean a man only wants you for your money. I must be off." She turned to leave.

"Tiff?"

She turned.

"Substantial debt?"

"I don't know. And I don't care! If a woman is penniless and if a wealthy man loves her, the *ton* allows it. Why not the other way around? He loves me. He wants to spend time with me. There isn't another appointment, another letter, another tour of somewhere or another he is always off on. I would rather be with a man who wanted to spend time with me than one who was always itching to be somewhere else!" Her voice was defiant now and her color raised.

His eyes softened. "Tiff, not everyone is like your father."

"I know my own mind. I'm young but that doesn't mean I don't know what I want. I like that he pays attention to me. He *listens*, Ivor. And he looks at me when he listens."

"I can see how that could be compelling."

"*You* don't even look at me when I talk. It's not just Papa. Do you ever look at any woman when she's speaking to you?"

He sat completely still. A face flashed across his eyes, a face framed by dark curls and a direct, challenging gaze. "Sometimes," he said finally. He looked down at his hands, then lifted his head to look at her. "This man you like, what do you like about him, besides that he pays attention to you?"

Tiffany, whose name came from the Greek name Theophania, flounced down in the chair again, raising a froth of hair and dress at her sudden movement, and tossed her head. "I know Papa will disapprove."

Ivor studied her. It wouldn't be the first time Tiffany chose to do something just because Arthur forbade her to do it. How often had she befriended someone—most notably, a disreputable and aging actress a few months ago, who had managed to get quite a bit of money and jewelry off Tiffany in the end—just to annoy Arthur? Or rather, as Ivor suspected, to get Arthur's attention firmly on her. Ivor had often thought it would be better if Arthur spent time with her and didn't tell her so clearly and forcefully what she could or couldn't do. He thought Tiffany would be more accommodating if Arthur showed her some affection and patience. But subtlety wasn't Arthur's middle name.

"Don't lots of men pay attention to you, Tiffany?" he asked gently.

She was playing with her dress again. She didn't respond. In a way, she didn't have to. As recently as two years ago, Tiffany had been twice the size she was now, her face covered in unbecoming spots, her dresses cut to hide her size. She had grown out of it, the weight and the spots, but he couldn't help thinking that she still saw herself as the awkward girl fresh out of the schoolroom, and thrust into her first social season where she had had to compete with fairy-like ethereal girls, with flawless complexions and just as flawless a confidence in their own worth.

"You're very pretty, you know, Tiffany," he tried.

She looked annoyed now. "Don't patronize me, Ivor."

The truth was, though, even after she had lost the weight and the spots, somehow or the other, she had had a few men dangling after her, but then they tended to disappear. Despite her prettiness and her wealth, no one had made her an offer, and she had been out three years.

"Why didn't things work out with Herbert Long?" he asked now. He wondered why he had not thought of asking before. Maybe he did ignore her, just like she said.

She raised her brows. "He was young and stupid, that's why." She frowned heavily. "He said I needed him too much. That I was always hanging off him. That a man needed space to breathe." She pursed her mouth.

Ivor was annoyed on her behalf. "And the others? Weren't there one or two other men before Herbert?"

She stood up again. "I suppose you will throw my failures at me like Papa does? Well, no more. Jonathan does want me. He doesn't think I get too attached and that I don't let him breathe. He doesn't mind that I want his company. It isn't a crime to want to be—to want to be seen and loved."

And at that, she turned again. Ivor had the grace to feel

ashamed. Is that how she felt? That her love and her need weren't wanted. God, men were stupid. He was glad, suddenly and acutely, that she wasn't his daughter. And then, just as quickly, he was ashamed of the thought. Before she made it to the door into his study again, he stopped her. "Tiff, the other night." He stopped, feeling uncomfortable. Damn it, it wasn't his job to play big brother. But her father rarely thought about her, other than to throw money at her. She had no siblings and her mother died when she was three.

She raised her eyebrows at the question. "Oh, don't worry. No lasting damage done, you know."

"Did the man hurt you?"

"You mean, in any significant way? No. Some bruises on my arms, a scratch or two."

"I know it was dark, but I don't suppose you can remember anything about what happened?"

She pouted. "Do I have to, Ivor?"

This was Tiffany all over. She wanted pets but not the heartache that came when they died. She wanted to ride her ponies but only as long as she never fell off or got out of breath. She had no use for the unpleasant side of life. A true Tristram. He could see she was eager to be off. "It's important, Tiff. Give me two minutes of your time."

"I really don't know. I can't remember it perfectly. I suppose I don't want to. I can hardly even remember why I went into the study."

Still, she walked all the way back and sat down yet again, carefully, on her rug-covered chair. She was silent for so long, Ivor expected her to get up again and say she couldn't remember. But then she suddenly looked surprised. "You know, I've just remembered why I went to the study. I saw a maid. You haven't employed any new ones, have you?"

"Not that I know of."

"She was petite. She looked—determined. She was from the colonies, or, you know, not *from* the colonies, but perhaps one of her parents was. From Africa or the Caribbean."

"I haven't employed anyone new."

"I didn't think so. She was dressed in black, like the other servants. But she looked—oh, I don't know—you know how when you're staying somewhere new you aren't familiar with all the rooms, so you walk less certainly? It was something like that. But as I said, she had such a determined look on her face, I was curious. I followed her, but then I lost sight of her. I thought she turned in to the study, so I did too. But it was dark. That's when I was attacked."

"What did he do?"

She clutched her hands together. "He grabbed me by the throat and backed me up against the wall. I had no time to react. I couldn't breathe." She took a shuddering breath. She started again. "I haven't thought of this before. But I think he said something. Like, *you wanted me, did you?* Something like that. I'm not sure. I was thrashing about. To tell you the truth, I didn't even have time to think—to think what he wanted or what he might do. I froze. But then I managed to knee him, hard enough so his grip loosened. I pushed him away. I thought I heard footsteps. I thought maybe he ran out of the room. I groped my way about but there he was again. I grabbed at something and managed to wrench it off him, and it later turned out to be his dagger. I was screaming by this point, though I wasn't aware of it. And suddenly there was light and people in the room." She shrugged. "You know the rest." She sat a little straighter. "You know I feel better already," she said lightly, though she still looked pale. She tried to smile. "There, Ivor, aren't you proud of me? Not such a ninny, after all."

"I never said you were a ninny," he said gently, feeling rattled by what she had described, and feeling a rage inside him at the man, the lascar, who had run off and been out of the window before Ivor was firmly in the room. Ivor had caught sight of his bearded face though, a lean face, a compact body, a tunic worn over a pair of cotton trousers. He thought he would recognize the man if he saw him again. "I never said it, Tiff," he repeated.

"Oh, you think it. You think just because I like pretty things and I—I want to be loved that that makes me weak. But the thing is, a woman just wants to be loved, Ivor. All women do." She looked defiantly at him. "And what's wrong with that?"

He thought of another face. With those dark, almost black eyes. A face that was determinedly animated. Completely aware of what it had to do in order to live a comfortable life. "All women, Tiff? I don't think so. Some women want other things." He came to his feet and offered her his hand.

She stood up and took it. Looking a little surprised. "Are you going soft in your old age?"

He laughed. "You know, I'm worried about the same thing. In any case, I'll find that lascar, Tiff. I promise you."

She gave an exaggerated shudder. "You look so serious when you say that you're making me tremble. And if I didn't know better, I'd say you almost care about me." She gave him a quick kiss on the cheek and headed to the door into the study again.

He was ruefully shaking his head. "Of course, I care about you."

She turned around. She inclined her head like a pigeon. "Yes, maybe you do. But caring for someone and letting someone see *you*—it isn't the same thing at all, darling cousin."

9

Lila was deep in thought as she dressed for the rat pit. Hannah had recommended that she be as inconspicuous as possible. It was a plain linen dress, sky blue with a pattern of little roses all over it. Hannah had found some scuffed boots and dressed Lila's hair casually with tendrils escaping everywhere, but Lila drew the line at Hannah yellowing her teeth or blacking some out to look like gaps. Hannah shrugged and said if she wanted to look poor, she couldn't have all her teeth. But Lila pursed her mouth and said maybe she was a maid in a doctor's house and had learned all about tooth hygiene.

"And don't talk," Hannah said sagely. "Open your mouth, talk in that aristocratic way you have, and the game's over."

"Maybe the doctor educated me. Maybe his wife was nice and taught me to read and write. She treated me just like a daughter. She was the kindest thing. She made me—seed cake and—and custard!" Lila sighed. "I miss them. They died—in a horrific collision with something or the other. A runaway stagecoach, that was it."

Hannah, who was used to her ways, shook her head. She was kneeling at her feet, trying to make the hem of her skirt scruffier and more threadbare. "You should be a writer. Like your sister, Miss Mira. The stories you tell."

Lila did up her cuffs. "I don't have any talents, not like my sisters." Mira was a writer. She wrote society gossip and was astonishingly good at it. She wasn't cruel but had a dry wit that people loved to read. Anya was a sitar player in Queen Charlotte's court and her voice and her sitar playing were so in demand that she was often offered work outside the court too. Two genuinely talented women. "I'm not good at anything."

"You're good at your work. You're good at knowing what your guests want and need. And you give it to them. You think that's not a talent? Understanding people?"

Lila frowned.

"It's that you never stop and think what *you* want and need that's the problem, miss, if you don't mind me saying." Hannah had a needle in her mouth, as she used both hands on Lila's skirt, but her words were clear enough.

"Oh, fiddlesticks. I want a comfortable life. I don't want to worry about bills all the time. I don't want to be bored looking after someone else's ungrateful brats. I don't want a husband I don't love because he can buy me security. I want to be my own mistress. I know what I want."

Hannah came to standing and unconsciously smoothed Lila's hair, then realized what she was doing, and tried to make it less tidy again. "Those are good things to want, miss, I'm sure. There now, that should do. If you don't want me to brown your teeth, then I reckon you're done."

"Thank you, I'll keep my teeth as they are. *And* I can see you don't believe that those are the only things I want."

Hannah walked across the room and stood at the door. "Oh, no, miss. You do want those things, I reckon. It's just they don't warm your bed at night. And *you're* not one of those women who might be happy with a cold bed. Not for long."

With this parting shot, she left the room.

Fifteen minutes later, Lila waited downstairs for her Kenneth. And he wasn't late. Whatever his faults, he was never late. He entered the parlor where she waited, stopped dead and looked at her in horror. "Dear God. Have you swapped lives with your twin who grew up in poverty, most likely in the workhouse, and who cleans houses for a living? I can almost smell the slops on you. Is it cabbage?"

"Don't be such a snob," Lila said crisply. Though her heart sank. She had forgotten to tell Kenneth how she was planning to dress, and he looked just as much of a dandy as ever. He wore a natty coral coat over a delicious indigo silk waistcoat and nicely fitted trousers. There was no way anyone would believe she was with him.

"Change, darling. Right now," Kenneth said. "You're making me feel unwell. It's as though someone was horribly sick and you are the result."

"I won't change. Hannah is right, I'll be less conspicuous like this."

"And you will take your maid's advice over mine, will you? I suppose she has some success in moving in society circles? I told you years ago, Lila. What you need is to *be* conspicuous, not hide your light under a thin veneer of respectability that no one will grant you anyhow, no matter how well behaved you are. People don't employ bastards, they don't marry 'em, and they don't invite 'em to things," he said ruthlessly. "Not the right people."

She didn't flinch. She was used to Kenneth's brutal ways, and he was right in any case. Over and over his words had proved correct. She had friends at the seminary, but even there she didn't fit. She wasn't invited to summer at her friends' houses; no Christmas parties for her. There was hesitation at introducing her to parents. Even the girls who were close friends with her would have been horrified if their brothers looked at her as a prospective wife. Lila was the one to have a good time with, and then you went back to real life. The women in her life, not to mention the men, all saw her like that.

This was a lowering thought. Her mood was already dark, and they hadn't even left the house.

"I'm going like this," she said stubbornly. "You don't have to know me. If you're there, in the—room, or whatever it is, a tavern?—then I'll feel safe."

"No."

She growled. "Kenneth, I'm not changing."

"Darling, listen to me. Men who are like me, they do go to the rat pit. And some go with women. But women don't go to the rat pit and see a terrier murder a hundred rats—unless they're obedient wives, or women of a certain kind. If you go dressed like that, you'll look like a woman of a certain kind. The kind," he said, just in case his meaning wasn't clear, "who're paid by the hour, you do see what I'm saying?"

There was a standoff. In the end, she won. But he told her he would pretend not to know her. "People'll think you're a common prostitute I picked up! Do you think I have no reputation to mind?"

"No one in their right mind would think you'd pick up a common female prostitute," Lila said.

"You are so droll, darling, full of tricks," Kenneth said, his words dripping with sarcasm, clearly deciding *not* to remark on her slight emphasis on the word *female*. She smiled widely.

10

Many parts of the city became quieter as night crept nearer, but Covent Garden came alive after dark. It was almost nine and there was the last lingering spell of daylight in the sky, but the lights of Covent Garden were twinkling and there was a buzz in the air of people just about to start their evening. In Covent Garden, at night, anything was possible.

On the rare occasions when she was there, Lila had the magical feeling that she could be anyone she wanted to be. She could be giddy and careless; here she didn't have to be continually fighting to make things work, hold things together, or paying bills, making sure she could survive on her own, feeding and clothing her staff while reconciling herself to being more or less a social outcast.

There was a hum in the air, of people alighting from barouches, girls giggling, setting their masks straighter, men and women saying everything in a glance. A hum of anticipation.

The hum became a din as Kenneth opened the door of the public house they were going to. Lila thought she was prepared, but she gasped to see what looked like thousands and thousands of men jammed into the room. A cloud of cigar smoke hung about the place. And there were women too. Some heavily made-up with powder and rouge, eye-smacking furbelows and petticoats and silk scarves; women sitting in laps, drinking out of tankards, laughing as loudly as they could, eyeing the other men in the room to line up their next customer. But then there were other women too. Women who were just there for the entertainment. Women who came with their young men, their brothers and fiancés and husbands.

"I wouldn't have dreamed that there were so many blood-thirsty people in London," Lila yelled over the clamor. Even though Kenneth was more or less ignoring her. Though she could see that he knew where she was and was keeping half an eye on her. "I've never seen so many prostitutes in my life!"

Kenneth frowned. "Try not to be such a greenhead," he yelled back, to make himself heard. "If you're going to act like a prude, you'll cast a bit of a damper on the evening."

"I would think a bloodthirsty terrier and a load of helpless rats would be enough to do that," Lila retorted.

"It is a little gory for my liking too." Kenneth grimaced.

Lila wondered how she would ever spot Maisie in this crowd. It seemed impossible now she was here. And if she couldn't, or if Maisie didn't show up, there was no way Lila would be able to find her or help her.

Kenneth handed her a tankard of ale. Lila made a face, but then before she had the chance to take a sip, there was an announcement that the most wicked show of the century was about to begin and would everyone make their way downstairs. The announcement was made by a red-faced, round-bellied, middle-aged man, with enormous whiskers that were so long he wound them about his face and tied them together at the back with a ribbon. He was called Diehard Dickie. Everyone stood up to head downstairs.

In a corner of the room there was a trapdoor leading down to the cellar. There were four iron ladders strung there, and down they all had to go, stockings and corsets or not, four at a time, all the way down to the basement. Lila and Kenneth were not too far from the trapdoor, but by the time they wound their way to it, Lila realized with some surprise that her tankard was empty. "How did that happen?" she said, staring into its depths.

"Stop swaying about like a man on stilts and go down the trapdoor, Lila!" Kenneth hissed. "And stop tugging at my sleeve! I don't know you."

Down the steps she went, giggling because her feet kept getting caught in her skirt. She was wearing the narrow skirt that was fashionable these days, not the hoops of twenty years ago, but even her skirt wasn't made for a ladder. And she was swaying. How strong was the ale in that tankard?

Down in the basement, there was a round circus arena with a low wall all the way around it, and tied on the outside of this wall was a sturdy rope. Around the rope, the spectators gathered. Lila had the mad sensation of being swept along by the crowd. Somewhat to her surprise, she found herself giggling again.

As the others made their way down, she felt a press of hot bodies behind her; young, old, able-bodied and infirm, poor and well-off. She was being pushed and jostled, but to her surprise, she didn't mind. It was strangely intoxicating, to be part of this mad crowd. Just for a few seconds, she forgot to look for Maisie.

"All righty then, folks!" Diehard Dickie shouted. "Jacky has done us proud. We have 'ere some three hundred or so of the juiciest brown rats you can find in London. Now then—I'm going to warn you once, and once only. If you don't stay behind the rope, and if you fall into the pit, then you stay in! Steer clear of the rope and try not to push the gent in front of you into the arena, no matter what the provocation. Especially you with the large melons, Bosomy Betty!" A woman with an enormous cleavage laughed, made a rude gesture with her fingers, and told him what he could do with his tiny prick. Lila couldn't help laughing. Even Kenneth, who wasn't standing far from her, was grinning. He had forgotten to be bored by everything. "Now, now, Betty, don't be like that," Diehard Dickie said. "We both know where my prick is sleeping tonight. And it ain't in my bed. And maybe if you're lucky, you'll find out just why I'm called Diehard Dickie!"

There was a roar of approval. He went on to explain the betting system. There were seven dog owners competing tonight, and the winner would be the one whose bull terrier killed the largest number of rats. People had already placed their bets.

Rules explained, the contest began. The first contestant, an angry bull terrier with the most maniacal look in its eyes that Lila had ever seen, was let loose in the pit. Lila shrieked as it bared its teeth, saliva flying everywhere, and took a running leap at a rat. It bit down on the poor fat creature. And that was all Lila could bring herself to observe. She turned away, stumbling, and fought her way out of the fray. The cheering was so loud and echoing so wildly about the basement, her head was ringing.

Lila stood there, at the back of the crowd, swaying. She was pretty sure she had drunk another tankard of ale that Kenneth—or maybe someone else—had thrust into her hands. She stifled a giggle. She looked about her, trying to get her bearings. All along the edges of the cellar, there were little cubbyholes, for keeping large barrels of liquor when this was a real cellar. She walked about for a bit, jostling people, peering over heads, craning her head, trying to spot Maisie. Was the chit even here? How could anyone find anyone in this crowd? Not only were there a lot of women in thick dark skirts and linen shirts, but there were all races and colors, and it was hard to separate them. It was a mass of writhing bodies. For that matter, how would she even find Kenneth again?

Lila climbed a set of steps that were at one end of the room to see if she could spot Maisie in the throng. She stood there for ten minutes, and the baying of the crowd, the snarling of the dogs, the shrieks of the rats were making her hot and giddy. She was starting to wonder if this whole thing was a bad idea when Maisie ran past the bottom of the steps.

11

Lila gasped, pelted down the steps and ran after her. A man was running in front of Lila and got to Maisie first. Both Maisie and the man disappeared into the crowd. Lila growled in frustration. Where the devil did they go?

By the time Lila spied the two of them again, it was in the dark of one of the cubbyholes, the man's trousers were a puddle around his ankles and Maisie was kneeling in front of him, her mouth full of his engorged penis. He was clutching at her hair and making her go faster.

"Stop, you bastard!" Lila cried out, before she could stop herself. No one heard her, and it was just as well, because though the man was holding on to the back of Maisie's head, he was not forcing her to be there. She was doing the work willingly enough, even throwing him a saucy glance or two upward. Before Lila knew it, it was all over. The man spent himself in Maisie's mouth, gave her a few coins which she quickly put down her bodice. He gave her a grateful pat on the head and was off. Maisie spat in the corner, picked up someone's stray tankard of ale that was standing outside the cubbyhole and washed out her mouth.

She came out of the cubbyhole and banged straight into Lila, who was standing there glowering at her.

"You! Are you following me or what? I told you I don't need your help, Miss Lila." Her eyes were blazing, and she was stalking off.

Good God, could the chit not stand still for a minute? Lila grabbed her elbow and turned her around. "Don't you dare run away again! And stop spitting at me. It was you, as far as I remember, who came to *my* house."

The anger left Maisie's face and she grinned. "If I was a grand white lady, Miss Lila, I'd be a redhead and no mistake. I have the temper of a banshee. Sunil says the same. Though *your* temper don't seem much better than mine."

To her dismay, Lila hiccuped. Then inconsequentially, she said to Maisie, "You're drunk."

Maisie grinned again. "You're rat-arsed yourself, thanking you very much, swaying like a willow in the wind. But in my line of work, it helps. What's your excuse, Miss Lila?"

Lila giggled. She couldn't help thinking she was fifteen again, and Maisie no more than a scrap of a child, urging her to climb trees and find illicit fruit. Lila had done it too. In fact, she had been Maisie's willing coconspirator. She realized with a pang that she missed Maisie. Had missed her for a long time. Maisie and her mother Annie were a gaping hole in her heart, along with all the other gaping holes that were drilled there.

Somehow or other there was another tankard in her hands. How did that get there? She half guzzled it down. But then she looked sternly at the girl. "Does your Sunil know that you are sucking another man's prick?"

Maisie's face was livid again. "He sees me as lily-white—black or not though my face might be. So, I'll be thanking you not to say anything. I have to live. He has to live. And it's not like he can get work, not if they're looking for a lascar all about the city who attacks young women of society." She hiccuped. "You're right. I'm pissed."

That at least meant that Lila was right. Sunil and Ivor Tristram's lascar were one and the same. She had been hoping they weren't. The lascar was in trouble, there was no getting away from it. She gripped Maisie's arm. "Tell me what happened."

Maisie pulled her arm away. "I have to work. You see these men laying bets on the dogs? They're going to come out of there hungry to put their seed somewhere. And I can tell them just where, if you get my drift, Miss Lila."

"You're not going to shock me, you know, so you may as well quit trying. Where is this Sunil of yours hiding anyway?"

Maisie burped. "Excusing my pardon, ma'am. Your Majesty, please thank you." She gave Lila a curtsy. Then held out her hand for Lila to kiss it.

"I know where that has recently been," Lila said, eyeing it distastefully, "so if you don't mind, I will just wave at you." My God, how could anyone get the chit to focus?

"That man's spunk is making its way down my gullet as we speak." Maisie was rubbing her tongue on her palm. "Anyway, Miss Lila, *you* can't help me. And you're disturbing me at my work."

"Oh, for heaven's sake. I'll pay you whatever measly sum those horrible old men are paying you and you don't have to lick my dick for it!" She pulled at Maisie, until Maisie almost toppled over and sat heavily on a step. Lila gingerly followed. Maybe she should have had less to drink. The floor was heaving.

There was a cheer now. The two women looked up. But it was not for the rats or the terriers. A fight had broken out between two men and the spectators were laying bets on which of them would win the round. There was a man with an accordion who was ignoring the crowd, the rats, the terriers, and the fighting men, and playing away. Some of the crowd, tired of the carnage, were dancing to the man's tunes. It was pure bedlam.

Maisie sat drinking some ale someone had left in their tankard and Lila finished the rest of hers. The lights were winking and twinkling now, and Lila was dazed at the pandemonium.

"You saw that man—Ivor Tristram—in my house. Is that what frightened you?"

Maisie scoffed. "Frightened, my arse, Miss Lila. It's just I don't see how I can get any help from you if you and him are friends. See?"

"Friends?" Lila said with as much venom as she could put into her voice. "The man is insufferable."

"Why was he in your house then?"

Lila briefly told Maisie how she earned a living. "Ivor Tristram was one of the guests. *Not* my friend. The man is an especially aggravating specimen of masculinity. You don't need to worry about him."

After some more persuasion, Maisie flicked her head impatiently and began to tell her story. Maisie and Sunil had been at Ivor Tristram's house one evening. Maisie opened her mouth to go on but Lila ruthlessly interrupted. "Why were you there?"

Maisie blinked but didn't respond.

"If you don't lay all the facts on the table, I can't help you."

"I told you I don't need your help, Miss Lila!"

"And how do you plan to have this baby and keep on earning and looking after your fella who can't leave the house without being caught by the Runners?"

Maisie looked mutinous. She struggled with herself for some

moments but then seemed to give up the fight. "I went to keep an appointment with someone. It may not seem obvious to you, so high and mighty as you are, but I hate the whoring. It's the worst thing that's ever happened to me. I went to talk to a man about a thing. I can't tell you more. *You* wouldn't understand."

Lila wasn't satisfied but urged Maisie to go on.

"I was heading to the garden outside the study to keep this meeting. But when I arrived, there was no one there. Next thing I knew there were screams coming from the study. Before I could do anything—run inside, see what was going on—Sunil leaped out of the window. He was frantic. He grabbed me and we made off. He told me later, when he heard the screams, he thought it was me and rushed into the study. It was dark as a horse's arse, and someone brushed past him. Just as he was steadying himself, someone else collided into him, and managed to get his dagger off him. And then there was light in the room and people were pointing at him, and this young woman in a gown made of taffeta or whatever it is you lot wear, was screaming. She was pointing at him too and screaming her head off, saying how he attacked her. *Rape, rape!* she was going." Maisie shrugged. "We didn't exactly know what happened, but the papers next day said a bearded Indian lascar attacked this young miss in that house and that the Runners were after him. It said he was dangerous, and people shouldn't go anywhere near him. There was a drawing of him and everything." Maisie looked troubled now. "He's holed up with me now, in a room in the East End, and though we've shaved off his beard, he still can't go anywhere because the Runners are stopping *all* Indian men and all lascars. And it was your Mr. Ivor Tristram who put the notice in the papers."

Lila eyed her. "*Could* he—could your Sunil—have attacked the girl?"

Maisie turned a fuming face at Lila. "He didn't! He didn't touch a hair on her head! Why would he?" She stood up and brushed herself off. "Now you're making me lose a night's work, miss, so if you please, I have to be off. I've told you all I know. And I knew you wouldn't believe me. You society people all stick together when push comes to shove. Ma always said so too. And she was right."

Lila came to standing. "Tell me where I can find you."

Maisie impatiently clicked her tongue, but then said to meet her tomorrow at the park at noon.

It flashed through Lila's mind that people would gawk if she kept an appointment with Maisie in the park. She was annoyed at herself for thinking like that. So what if Maisie was not of her own class? She bit the edge of her thumb. Some of her feelings must have shown on her face, because Maisie was giving her a smug look. "Don't you worry, Miss Lila, I'll make it so it don't look strange."

With that, Lila had to be satisfied. She handed Maisie some coins. "Here, I hope this makes up for the work you had to miss because of me."

Maisie laughed. "If you think a couple of poor sods would have given me half as much to suck their balls, Miss Lila, you're greener than a monkey's bottom!"

When Maisie disappeared into the crowd again, Lila looked around for Kenneth, but kept her eyes averted from the arena. She was fuzzy, almost like her brain had been dipped in syrup. Bodies were swaying around her, the lights swooping in and out. The accordion was louder now and there was a lot of clapping and cheering. For a second, she had the wonderful feeling that no one in the world knew exactly where she was this instant. She laughed out loud.

Suddenly, she was pulled into the fray and, before she had a moment to catch her breath, she was dancing and whirling.

She was too shocked to do anything at first, but then instead of pushing out of the mad mass of people, she found herself laughing, shrieking, joining in. The lights were whirling and swirling about her, the heat was rising in spirals, she passed from man to man, as did all the other women, holding their skirts up, laughing. She forgot that she was here for a purpose, or that she didn't know anyone, or that she should hide her teeth. She was laughing so hard she had a stitch in her side. But she couldn't stop. She felt as if she was made of pure movement and nothing more. Most importantly no thoughts, no endless questions.

She realized with something of a shock that this feeling, this feeling of doing something just for fun, she had forgotten it existed.

The next time, legs kicking, arms at her waist, that she changed partners to yet another smiling young man, she realized with a shock that it wasn't a stranger. It was Ivor Tristram.

Her smile faltered. "What are *you* doing here?" she yelled over the music and noise.

"Didn't you ask me if you would see me here tonight?" he yelled back, leaning closer and speaking into her ear.

She was surprised she recognized him. He was dressed in a loose white linen shirt tucked into brown trousers. A plain waistcoat hung loosely on his frame. A couple of shirt buttons were casually undone, and she could see his neck and the beginning of his chest hair over the top of the shirt. His hair was undressed, even wild and unkempt. He looked like a farmer. He looked—in short—delicious.

She scowled at him. The dancers were still jigging around

them and changing partners, but Lila and Tristram were dancing only with each other now. "Why are you dressed as a farmer?"

"You told me it was the right way to dress for the rat pit."

He was in a strange mood. He was smiling but his eyes glittered. As they moved, as their hands touched and parted, she found she couldn't stop looking into them. Those eyes that were like snowflakes patterned over ocean waves. She had no conscious idea of what her feet were doing. She didn't know if she was smiling or not, her legs kicking, her body moving to the left, then swaying to the right, if the music was still playing and if the other dancers were still in the room. All she knew was she was dancing, and then when the dancing stopped—or maybe only she stopped—she was kissing Ivor Tristram.

At first only their lips met. And they parted. But then they found each other again. Her hands clutched his waistcoat, then the hair at the back of his head. His hands were clasped at her waist, but then, as the kiss deepened, his arms wound so tightly around her that he was almost lifting her off her feet. No, she was wrong, the music was still going, mingling oddly with the thumping of her heart. And now a pulse was starting between her legs, an ache filling her that she normally only allowed herself to feel when she was alone, in the early hours of the morning, away from her guests, too tired and yet too awake to sleep. She had the odd feeling that she had been waiting for this all her life, before her life even started. Not a kiss. But this kiss, with this man, with the way this man felt and smelled and tasted.

She moaned in his mouth, and he gripped her tighter. She pressed herself to him. His tongue was exploring, and she arched her back so she could feel more of him. She fitted tightly against him, feeling the power in his chest and arms, wanting more of him, wanting above all to be closer. She wondered what he would say, how he would look, if she pulled him into one of those cubbyholes in the walls.

But then finally, some sense crept into her head, and she pushed him away.

They stared at each other for some moments. She felt—anguish. Of all things to feel. She walked away from him, pushed through the crowd, found the iron stairs and hauled herself up them before she had time to think about it.

She crashed out of the public house and stood there outside, gasping, letting the cool night air sweep over her. It was drizzling and she held her face up to feel the fine mist on her face.

And she felt that ache. The ache to feel Ivor Tristram's chest under her hands, to feel his flesh, to let her soul touch his. And to hide from the rest of the world.

12

Maisie was good as her word. She came armed with a basket of flowers so it would look as if Lila were looking at her wares and trying to select posies. The man with her, Sunil Mehta, looked painfully exposed to Lila. He no longer had the beard he had in his illustration in the dailies—Lila had found the original notice in the papers. And he didn't necessarily look like a lascar. He was dressed more like a farmer, in thick dark trousers and a linen shirt. But there was nothing he could do about the color of his skin.

They stood there, surrounded by people in the park, conspicuous as hell. There were children shrieking, nannies jiggling babies, couples riding together, mamas driving with their young eligible daughters, or at least the ones who hadn't been snapped up at the height of the season. It wasn't the height of the season now, at the end of the summer, but because it was unseasonably warm, some people were still hanging around and some families had returned from summering in Brighton. Lila sighed, turned her face up to the sunlight and tried to soak it in. She tried to dispel the fog that seemed to be lingering from the night before, and to focus on the young man and woman standing in front of her.

She was both frightened for Sunil and found herself bristling at the thought of Ivor Tristram jumping to conclusions instead of making any attempt to find out the truth. Except, of course, what was the truth? What if Ivor Tristram and his cousin were right and Maisie wrong? Doubts, eternal doubts. She felt a spark of irritation at Ivor Tristram's assurance. And a pang of envy. To feel sure about everything, to not worry if you were right or wrong.

"This seems an easier way to earn a living," she couldn't help saying to Maisie, eyeing her flower basket, feeling a little bit like the chit's mother.

Maisie's eyes flickered toward Sunil for a second. "Than doing laundry and cleaning houses, Miss Lila?" she said, louder than she needed to.

Sunil pressed Maisie's hand. "She was servicing sailors when I first met her two months ago. Cleaning and washing clothes is better than that."

He was well spoken. Clear and precise. Lila's head instantly latched on to the *two months ago*. Her eyes moved inadvertently to Maisie's distended belly. Had the man—perhaps—noticed Maisie's condition? She kept her face as straight as possible.

"The baby will be mine, Miss Lila," Sunil said at once. "Maisie's and mine."

The man was perceptive, and Lila had the grace to feel chastised. "My apologies, Mr. Mehta. It's just that the two of you won't have it easy." Her eyes moved to Maisie's face. Why was she sticking with Sunil if he wasn't even the father of her baby? He was in trouble, there was no way around it. No easy way, at any rate.

Clearly, everything she thought was visible on her face this morning. Because Maisie said fiercely, "He's my man, Miss Lila.

Father of my babe or not. He knows what I—did before." She said it defiantly. Almost challenging Lila to expose that she was still earning a living through—not to put too fine a point on it—whoring.

Lila smiled reassuringly. "I'm not judging you." Not that she had any right to. Maisie had been left to fend for herself when she was seven. Not one person in the Marleigh household had helped her. Those who tried to, like Lila, had failed, and most hadn't tried. She touched the lavender sprigs in Maisie's basket and selected one or two bunches. "You are in—let's say—a bit of a fix. What happened that night, Mr. Mehta?"

"Please call me Sunil," the man said. He had a thoughtful and sensitive face, she couldn't help thinking. The eyes were clear. Sensitive, yes, but steady. "I would like to work and support Maisie and the babe, Miss Lila. We want to be married. I can get work. I learned to read and write. I could find work. But no one will give me any if I can't leave the house for fear of discovery."

"Tell me what happened."

A couple of young women walked over and spent an age looking at Maisie's posies. Lila was seething with impatience at their dawdling. She noticed they were starting to get looks. They had to speed this up. She was conspicuous, spending such a long time speaking with Maisie and Sunil. She wished she could pull Sunil aside and hear his side of the story. But it would attract too much attention. And she didn't want to expose him any more than she had to. Finally, the young women, taking several of Maisie's bunches of flowers with them, left, giggling and talking about various young men of their acquaintance.

They didn't have too much more time. She could see people turning to stare at what she was doing. She bent to the basket again and urged Sunil to give a quick account of what had happened.

There had been some kind of social evening at Ivor Tristram's house. Maisie and Sunil went there to keep an appointment. At the appointed time, Maisie went to the rose garden outside the study. And Sunil tried to keep a lookout. Neither was admitted into the house—who would have let them in? Instead, they entered the back way, when the host and guests were occupied in the front rooms. Lila bit her lip. If nothing else, they had entered the premises illegally.

"I was waiting outside the windows of the morning room, Miss Lila," Sunil said. "It is around the corner from the rose garden. I heard sounds of a scuffle coming from the study and I was worried it was Maisie in trouble. I ran into the study from the garden door. It was completely dark. I heard thuds and groans and what sounded like two people struggling against each other. Someone groaned and then I felt someone run past me." He paused, as if he was trying to recollect exactly what happened. "I was pushed aside, but before I could recover, someone else was groping near me. I was trying to steady them so they wouldn't fall." He held out his hands, unconsciously mimicking how he was trying to steady the person he encountered in the dark. "But then there was light in the room and everyone was pointing at me. The young woman whose arms I was holding to steady her, she was screaming at me, saying I assaulted her. It was an obvious conclusion, Miss Lila." He wiped his face. Lila quickly looked around. Maisie was starting to look worried, restlessly looking about her at who might be watching them. It was time to wrap this up. "I ran for it. I didn't stop to explain myself. I don't know if this was a mistake. But I expected the worst."

Lila was frowning. Probably looking as worried as she felt.

He was right. It *was* an obvious conclusion for people to reach. Ivor Tristram's cousin Tiffany did not see her attacker. Yet, according to Sunil, there was someone else in the room who attacked her. Someone who ran out of the room, brushing past Sunil on the way out. If Sunil was telling the truth, until that other man was found, Sunil would not have his freedom, and it was only a matter of time before some enterprising Runner found him and arrested him. In fact, being out here like this, so exposed, was a terrible idea.

"I have to go now," Lila said quickly. She picked bunches of flowers and herbs and paid for them. "Come to my house at night. We must find a way out of this." She looked from one face to the other, the one serious and thoughtful, the other blazing.

Under her customary fire, Maisie looked both relieved *and* suspicious, Lila couldn't help noticing. Really, the chit didn't trust a soul. Though was that so surprising?

"Miss Lila," Maisie said, through her teeth, as if it was being forced out of her with a sharp pair of heated forceps, "thank you for your consideration."

Lila's lip quivered. "You're welcome, Maisie," she said gravely.

Maisie tossed her head. "You . . . I don't know if you understand. Just last night, when Sunil was alone, and I was at . . . work—there was someone, a Runner sniffing about the place." She looked over to Sunil for confirmation.

He nodded.

"A fat, ugly man he was."

"Stout," Sunil corrected gently. "Probably all muscle. It must be useful. In his profession."

"A fat, ugly man sniffing about the place," Maisie said. "Asking my neighbors questions. The thing with Whitechapel is, there's only one thing folks hate more than plaguey rats. It's the Bow Street Runners, miss. So, everyone shuts their door in this man's face. But he's asking questions. And too near to home." For the first time, Maisie looked desperate. She wiped her nose. "I've seen someone else too. Looks even cagier than the Runner. Skinny bloke, really tall, wears all black and walks about like the Lord of Death."

"And what makes you think he's after you?"

"I don't know that he is, Miss Lila. But he looks at me funny. And I can tell you, in my line of work—that *used* to be my line of work," she said hastily, throwing a quick reassuring glance at her beau, "you learn to see who looks at you funny. And I've seen him one too many a time, see? Anyway, I have what you rich folk call *instinct*."

Lila took a deep breath. "I will try my best, Maisie. Just be careful in the meantime."

Maisie gave Lila an address where Lila could send a note if she wanted to get in touch with her or Sunil. The pair strolled off, Maisie with her basket, Sunil with a steady hand on Maisie's back, murmuring thoughtful words to her. Lila's own words made her stomach turn. Weren't they the words she said to Maisie years ago, when Sarah Marleigh accused Annie Quinn of theft? Didn't she promise to help Maisie then, promise that nothing would come of it? She had a horrible feeling she had lived through this all before. That *then* and *now* were merging in a way that had a horrible ring of inevitability to it—inevitability and doom. She couldn't help feeling that the outcome would be the same. Annie Quinn's face—a second before the rope was put around her neck—rose in her mind, and she warded it away with her hands.

She squared her shoulders and turned to her groom. "Roger,

we must go to Berkeley Square to pay a call. But I will need to change and take a hackney cab."

Her groom made a slight adjustment to his black silk filigree eye mask and gave her a casual salute. He didn't remark on the strangely long conversation she had just had with a flower girl. You had to say that about her staff—they were loyal to the bone.

Back at home in Brook Street, she saw that Kenneth Laudsley had sent a note reminding her to keep herself free for Vauxhall in a few days' time and find a fashionable mask or a hood to wear, or something "a trifle mysterious, darling, because it'll be fun, but mostly so you're a credit to *moi!*" She scrawled a hasty response to say that she wouldn't miss it for the world, and wondered—though she didn't write it—if there was a certain someone Kenneth had his eye on whom he wanted to tryst with in Vauxhall, and that was why he was so eager to go.

An hour later, at hardly the most fashionable time of the day—or even the most appropriate—Lila Marleigh was admitted by a very surprised-looking housekeeper into Ivor Tristram's residence. She explained that she was there *on business*. And after the housekeeper presumably conferred with Tristram, she was shown into the man's study.

It was a surprisingly appealing room with teal walls and rosewood furniture. There was even a sofa or two, though the main furniture in the room was a large desk and chairs, and most of the room was lined with bookshelves. But Lila didn't take the time to admire the view. Unexpectedly, she found herself in the very room in which Tiffany Tristram was attacked. Only four nights ago. She lost no time in retracing the steps that Maisie and Sunil had outlined.

As you entered the room, you were faced with the large rosewood desk, with a chair behind it and two across. Sunil entered by way of the garden door and only made it to the center of the room, next to the large desk. Tiffany was not attacked there. She was presumably attacked closer to the inside door, where Lila stood now.

Lila had worked all this out and gotten her bearings, and so that could explain how, when Ivor Tristram walked into the room five minutes later, she was found crawling on the carpet on her hands and knees.

She felt him before she saw him. She sat up. At the sight of that self-assured and slightly sardonic face, the previous night flooded back into Lila's mind.

It would be going too far to say that she had forgotten what happened between them at the rat pit. It would be fairer to say that she had spent most of the rest of the night and this morning thinking of nothing *other* than the feel of Tristram's lips as they explored hers, and the expression in his eyes when he gazed at her, his face centimeters from hers. How had he looked at her? There was desire there, but also an intensity that took her breath away. She was sure of it, sure that he felt that draw that she felt too. The feeling of meeting something you had been searching for. Of two pieces clicking to form a whole. Of feeling a craving that you couldn't put a name to and someone unexpectedly rising to meet it. She could sense that he felt it too and didn't want to feel it. Maybe he was disgusted with her, or even with himself. But since her appointment with Maisie and Sunil, Lila had tried to push all her other thoughts into the background to focus on getting up the nerve to confront Tristram in his own home.

Now, though, she was seeing his face. His face that inexplicably seemed to be made up only of lips and eyes, though there was the jaw, not hard, not soft, but something in between, so that it expressed passion and stubbornness and an innate sense of fairness all at once. And the eyebrows that reflected a sense of humor, but also that remoteness, that keeping of other people at a safe distance. Right now, seeing him towering over her—and looking at her ironically—as she knelt on his carpet, she couldn't remember why she was here. The next thing she knew, he was holding a hand out for her. She took it with dignity and came to her feet.

"Hairpins," she said.

"Hairpins," Tristram said, his eyes on her face. He looked almost . . . resigned to see her. She supposed it was marginally better than repulsed.

"They are very useful in some ways, but then you lose one and all of a sudden, you can't find it at all. They . . . evaporate." She smiled brightly, her face a little hot.

"Evaporate."

"Poof. Like that," she said, to her horror, clicking her fingers to illustrate. "Have you noticed it?"

A slight pause. "Not especially."

"Shame," she murmured.

"What does it look like?"

"What?"

"The hairpin, Miss Marleigh."

"Oh, yes. Well, it looks mostly like a hairpin."

Neither spoke for some seconds. He looked at her hair. Then he said, "You have one in your hair that looks like it has an emerald in it. Like that one?"

"Yes, it must be, mustn't it?"

"I'll ask my entire staff to keep an eye out for it when they are cleaning and make it their highest priority."

"Oh no, it's not expensive and it doesn't have any sentimental—

you're joking, of course. Please don't worry about it. I will just have to pacify Hannah—my maid—with something or the other. I might tear a large hole in my skirt—that will make her forget about my lost hairpin."

He was watching her face, seemingly patiently waiting for her to come to the point. The heat rushed to her face. It suddenly struck her what it might look like, her coming here, cornering him in his home after their kiss. She put a hand on her throat. She wished more than anything that she occasionally stopped to think before she jumped into things. For some moments, she didn't know what to do.

He was looking at her almost with surprise now, scanning her face, noticing that hand at her throat. Really, the man sometimes looked as if he could read her mind.

"How can I help you, Miss Marleigh? You told my staff you had business with me."

She squared her shoulders. "Yes, I do. You offered to compensate me for letting your father go."

Lord, did his face transmit *all* his feelings, or was she sensitive to every single one of his expressions? She wanted, more than anything, to feel that ever so slightly rough cheek of his on hers. At her words, he looked . . . disappointed. As if she was doing exactly what he had expected, and putting a price on her relationship with his father. She cleared her throat. Tried not to watch his face like a fool.

"Yes," he said.

She couldn't help it. He was like a magnet, and she found herself taking a step closer. He didn't spring back. His eyes darkened as he looked down at her upturned face.

"I will let him go."

"You will?"

"Yes."

"A change of heart?"

"Something like that."

"For how much?"

"You have called the Runners to look for a certain lascar."

Now she had shocked him. He couldn't look more surprised if she had asked him for a baby elephant as a pet, in return for his father. She felt a deep sense of well-being at that shocked face. To her own intense surprise, she chuckled.

Now he looked even more astonished. She tried to school her face.

"My apologies, it's just your face. In any case, the Runners. I want you to call them off. I want you to give me time to find out who actually attacked your cousin four nights ago. In return, I will . . . expect nothing further from your father or yourself. I need a few days. That is all."

13

I vor couldn't be more surprised than if the Queen herself had shown up for a morning call. Not that it was morning. It was really not the sort of time to show up somewhere and ask to be seen without an appointment. But here she was, nevertheless. And he felt . . . unusually tongue-tied. It was odd, he thought. When you've spent all night thinking about someone's big eyes—the woman's eyes were like an owl's, all large and earnest and strange. Had anyone told her that? They made up half her face. And you couldn't stop looking into them. Hoping to see what you wanted to see. Desire, maybe. Or an answer to the question you were asking that you didn't even know you were asking. No, you couldn't spend all night thinking about someone and then have any idea what to say to them when they suddenly materialized in front of you the next day and became all of a sudden flesh-and-blood. He was half convinced he had dreamed up the rat pit. Or maybe he was dreaming now.

Here she was. In his own home. Crawling on his carpet. On her hands and knees.

He found himself not knowing what to say. An unusual sensation for Ivor Tristram. Why was she here? *Was* she here or was he still asleep? (The crawling about on the carpet and the strange conversation about hairpins—*hairpins?*—suggested the latter.)

Was she here because she wanted him—or because she wanted his money?

He didn't particularly care which, as long as he could reach out, grab her, and pull her into his arms. And maybe she would kiss him the way she kissed him the night before. Her body arching into his as if almost fighting him. As if it were completely open to him, willing to show him anything he wanted to see, all her longing. The way her arms clasped around him. The way she made little sounds in her throat. Made him feel big and powerful, yet at the same time completely helpless.

Bloody hell.

He rubbed his face. He had expected her to name a sum. In return for his father. A sum that he would pay, with some minor negotiations, and then he would never need to see her again.

Or maybe she would refer to what happened last night. And he would have to say the words he didn't want to say but which were the *only* words he could say under the circumstances. That nothing could ever happen between them. Even if she broke things off with his father—even if she broke things off with any of the men dangling after her—even then, it was impossible. She had been with his father. It was impossible.

But she wasn't asking for money. Or not yet. She was saying something about the lascar.

A wave of tiredness—and unreality, like a boat shifting at its moorings—hit him, and he abruptly gestured her to a seat and sat down next to her.

"Please explain."

She took a deep breath and launched into her explanation. She knew someone who knew the lascar, she said, the lascar who was supposed to have attacked his cousin Tiffany four nights ago. She related what she thought had happened to Tiffany. That someone else, some other man, had attacked his cousin in his study and then the lascar—she was careful not to name names, even the first name, he noted—had come into the room and been caught by the guests when *they* came into the room, making it *look* like he had attacked Ivor's cousin.

She stopped abruptly.

He was still feeling thrown by the turn this conversation was taking. Not to mention her being in his house in the first place. She wanted to talk about Tiffany and *the lascar?*

"Tell me where this man is, Miss Marleigh."

The words came out more peremptorily than he had intended. And sure enough, she lost that look that had come over her suddenly a few minutes ago when she clutched her throat, a look of uncertainty, like she wanted him to take charge of things. God, he *would* take charge of things if she kept on looking at him like that. But that was all gone now. Now the sparkle was back in her eyes. "I should, should I? Well, I won't."

"No, of course not. A dangerous man might be on the loose and you won't tell me where he is."

"I don't know where he is. It is perfectly true, so there is no need to look so disbelieving. I'm not asking you to trust me. I can see that would be too much to ask."

Wretch. He sat back. "What are you asking me to do?"

She instantly went back on herself. "Of course, I *am* asking you to trust me, but only for a few days. So I have a chance to find out what actually happened."

"And how exactly do you mean to do that?"

"We have to find out who actually attacked your cousin, of course." She looked like this was obvious.

"We?"

"I will do it myself, with the help of the lascar and my acquaintance. But if you helped, or your cousin, things might go quicker. I'm convinced it was not the lascar who attacked your cousin. He had no reason to, and he is not the kind of man who would. He wants to make a life for himself and—for my acquaintance. I can't see him jeopardizing the future they've planned together for . . . for, well, nothing."

"A future that would be easier if he had, say, a jewel or two that he could sell."

She scoffed. "And the easiest way to get a jewel or two is to attack some unknown woman in a completely dark room in an unknown house on the spur of the moment? Or did he plan this great robbery out in advance?"

"If it comes to that, Miss Marleigh, why was the man even here? I am guessing your acquaintance has a parent from the colonies and was dressed as a maid? My cousin saw her."

"Yes."

"I could make you divulge the whereabouts of this man, you know."

Her eyes glittered. "What will you do? Attack me in your study?" She was actually staring at his arms to see if he could make good on this threat.

"I don't make a habit of doing things like that. But I could hand *you* over to a Runner and tell him you know where this lascar is. Look, Miss Marleigh, I am not going to do any such thing. But wouldn't it be better to let the law take its course?"

Now she looked scornful. "The law? You think the *law* would protect someone like the lascar? Or my acquaintance?" She came to standing and was now pacing about his study. He stood up too, and leaned back against his desk, his arms crossed. "The law would not protect either of them. The law would take your word—that of a wealthy man with land, and your cousin's, the daughter of a wealthy man—over anything they said in a heartbeat. They wouldn't even need evidence. It might not even come to court. You *know* what would happen if the lascar handed himself over. All I am asking is for you to give him a chance to prove his innocence."

He was silent for a long time. She was still pacing about the room. Looking delicious. He had the sinking feeling that after she left he might sit there staring at the path she was tracing on his carpet.

"I'll help you," he found himself saying. "If you must do it, then I'll help. I will try to suspend my judgment and find out if an alternative set of events could have occurred in this room four nights ago. In return, you will let my father go."

She flinched almost like she had forgotten that that was part of the bargain.

He couldn't help wondering what his father gave her. Money? Jewels?

Yet.

Yet it was nearly impossible to imagine Lila Marleigh with him. It was nearly impossible to believe it. But he couldn't gainsay the evidence. This morning he had heard first from his mother's doctor who stressed that his mother was declining quickly and was unlikely to last beyond the end of the autumn season. And then from his mother. *Your father has said for me to stay away from Lila Marleigh. Perhaps I should, Ivor. What will I get from it now? When I am gone, he will do what he has always done anyway. I just wanted to pretend for a few short months that he cared for me. She is so young! Can he, for once, not throw his amours in my face?*

There was something pathetic about it. And he felt what he always felt for his mother, a mixture of irritation, impatience, and pity. He wanted her to have some dignity, to leave his father. But it was too late for that now.

"In return, you will let go of any claims on my father," he repeated. "And give me your word that at the end of an agreed-upon time, if we can't discover an alternative version of events, then the lascar will give himself up."

She didn't even dither. "No."

"No, Miss Marleigh?"

"That is, yes. I will of course let your father go," she said graciously. "That would only be a fair return for your help. *But* I can't promise that the lascar will give himself up. That's not up to me to decide. If he has to leave the country, then that is what he must do. I won't get in the way of that, and I will not give him up to you."

God, the woman was excruciatingly honest. She had character and moral fiber. Was she really so desperate that she had to put up with men like his father? He had done some digging, and seen that her finances were not comfortable, but she was not in debt either. She was living day to day, week to week, month to month, almost shockingly dependent on the success of her social evenings. Was that why someone like her, someone intelligent and warm, put up with a weak man—with someone like Ivor's father?

"Two weeks," she said. "Give me—or us, if you will help me—two weeks."

"A week, Miss Marleigh. I would be a fool to give you more. The man could be in Timbuctoo in two weeks."

She dithered now, thinking about it. "Very well," she said finally. "A week. I have no social evenings arranged for three nights at the beginning of each week. I have a week to devote to this. Do you?"

"Yes," he found himself saying. Did he have a week? Didn't he have a list of things that needed attending to at home? An endless list of things that always needed attending to and about which his agent lost no time in reminding him?

Yet he did need to get to the bottom of this. He couldn't let Tiffany get attacked in his own damned study and then do nothing about it. In fact, he had been searching high and low for the lascar himself. He had visited the docks several times and made inquiries, and in fact the sailors had been shamelessly quick at producing any old lascar for Ivor's inspection. But none of them was the right man. Ivor had seen him, after all.

Lila Marleigh was right. The lascar—whatever his name was—didn't have a chance if he was handed over to the authorities. They would judge him to be guilty. And if he hadn't attacked Tiffany, then wasn't it up to Ivor to find out the truth?

And if one tiny part of him wanted to spend more time with this woman, just for a few days, well, to the devil with that part of him. It could go to hell as far as he was concerned.

14

Nothing had prepared Lila for Whitechapel. There was nothing there that would normally bring a woman of her class to it. Even someone as far gone, she thought resentfully, as a society hostess. As her hired hackney cab pulled closer to Whitechapel, she couldn't help feeling as though she was entering a current that was sucking her in, a current that would never let her go.

Tristram would be waiting for her. And, more reluctantly, Maisie and Sunil—if they showed up at all. Lila had sent Maisie a note, told her she wanted Maisie and Sunil to meet with Ivor Tristram, and that they would be in Whitechapel that evening. Really, it would be a wonder if Maisie and Sunil showed up. There was no one like Maisie to take off in a huff. The girl always seemed to be halfway to the next county any time Lila managed to get half a minute with her. Maybe Lila shouldn't have told her that Tristram would be at the meeting in Whitechapel. But she couldn't go in there like that, she couldn't ambush Maisie.

It would take some persuasion (and more than some patience) to convince the girl that Tristram had promised to help; that, in fact, he was their best chance, as he was the accuser and they needed his cousin's account of events. She even said in the note that she trusted that he wouldn't hand Sunil over to the Runners right there and then.

She really hoped he wouldn't.

She felt she understood the man. He had faults. Too many to count. Obstinate. Used to getting his own way—which was an irritating quality in anyone, especially a man. And it was clear he couldn't peer into her soul, read her mind or see the real her. All major flaws. He was holding on tight to the tawdry image he had of her the first time he'd met her, and in fact, even *before* he met her. But she didn't think he was dishonest.

She really hoped it wasn't the memory of his lips on hers that was making her think that way.

It wouldn't be surprising if Maisie and Sunil didn't turn up. Maisie at least didn't trust a single soul (though maybe she trusted Sunil). Lila could hardly wonder at it. The household Maisie's mother worked at for seven years saw her hang for a crime she didn't commit. Even if somehow the crime had been proven, the Marleigh family could have intervened and prevented the hanging. That's how things worked. Jonathan Marleigh was an earl, the Earl of Beddington—he could have gotten Annie a more lenient sentence. But they didn't lift a finger. Why would Maisie trust the wealthy?

Lila got out of the hackney cab. Tristram had offered to drive her there in his carriage, but she'd said no. She looked all around her as though she was on a distant planet. The houses in Whitechapel were black with soot. The roads pockmarked. The devil's arsehole, Hannah called it, when Lila told her where she was going, and she had nearly tied Lila to the bed when she heard that Lila was going alone.

There were huddles of people whispering on street corners.

There were men and women quarreling. Prostitutes in torn stockings and grimy petticoats lolling against the walls of the gin palaces, lifting a skirt, displaying as many holes in their mittens and scabs on their legs as there were gaps in their teeth. Beggars lined the streets. And Lila couldn't help it. She couldn't help wondering what happened to other women in Maisie's condition. Seven months pregnant with one of her customers. Who knew which one? Maisie certainly didn't. She was lucky she had Sunil. Most women in her condition wouldn't have a soul looking out for them. And she might not have him for long, Lila reminded herself. If Lila couldn't prove his innocence, what chance would they have?

As Lila stood there, waiting for Tristram, a boy scampered up and begged her for a penny. He grinned, showing large gaps in his teeth.

Lila looked at him in surprise. "I don't have any coins to give you," she said. "But if you come back home with me, I can give you a bath so you can tell your arse from your face." The threat of a bath made the boy goggle, cross himself, and pelt down the road as if all the Bow Street Runners in London were at his tail. Lila shook her head, half imagining herself pelting after him. Give Hannah a bathtub and some cleaning cloth, and she would make short work of the lad. Lila's lips twitched at the thought of that urchin in Hannah's clutches. He'd rue the day he met Lila.

Next, a prostitute emerged from an alleyway after servicing her customer, her petticoats still bunched up around her hips.

Seeing Lila staring at her, she spat in the corner. "If you like what you see, missus, you can have some of it. I'll bet you have a sweet tongue on you." She jigged her hips and cackled, and so did a group of young men who were gambling under the light of a streetlamp. "What you laughing at, bone-grubbers?" she said to them, and dropped her petticoats though not before giving them an eyeful.

Ten minutes later, Lila and Tristram were sitting in a tavern across a rustic wooden table with Maisie and Sunil. Maisie was bristling. Her arms were crossed over her chest, above her belly. Sunil had a soothing hand on her back.

"I don't see how it's a good idea for us to be meeting with the very man who's laid the complaint against Sunil and set the Runners against us!" She was skinny, except for the belly, and every pore of her was seething with anger. "We might as well walk right up to a Runner, bold as you please, and say *please, sir, take us in right this minute.*"

"Maisie," Lila said soothingly—though her soothing tone wasn't having any visible effect on Maisie. "We could give this a chance."

"*I* wouldn't have come. It's only Sunil who made me," Maisie said, just to make this side of things completely clear in case anyone was stupid enough to think that she had come to this meeting willingly.

"We should hear them out," Sunil said, looking like a man who was verbatim repeating words he had already used several times over, probably several times in the last hour.

Lila glanced sideways. When he'd met her outside the tavern a few minutes ago, Tristram had frowned and asked her if she was mad, waiting in the dark like that for him. "I got here early," he said. "Just so you wouldn't be waiting alone. But you seem to be even earlier. Don't you care about what could happen to you in a place like this?"

Then, before she could scoff at his peremptory tone—who did he think he was anyway and what made him think she was any of his concern?—he told her she must pretend to be his wife when they went into the tavern, and when she glared at him, he amended it to fiancée.

She gave in and he put his hand reassuringly on her back and ushered her into the tavern. A warm hand, whose imprint she could feel even now, even though she was now sitting as far away from him as possible on what was not a very wide bench. He'd been right too, because she had shrugged off his hand, entered the tavern a few seconds before him, and seen the insolent up-and-down stare the tavern owner gave her before Tristram emerged from the door and put his hand on her back again. "My fiancée and I are meeting some farmworkers. We will need a table for four."

The man's manner toward her had instantly changed. She had glared at the tavern owner, though since he was busy bowing and scraping at Tristram who, understated though he might be, had an aura of command and wealth, he didn't notice and it probably didn't affect his health much.

Now Tristram sighed at Maisie's words and sat back on the bench, back to the wall, arms crossed over his chest, in a gesture that was already familiar to Lila. "I would say," he said to Maisie, with infinite patience, "that I would be the very man you'd want to convince of Mr. Mehta's innocence."

Maisie practically threw her ale in his face at that. "Why should I care about convincing *you* of anything?"

The tone was so scathing that Lila had to bite the inside of her lip to stop herself from grinning, or worse, winking at Maisie.

But the stupid man sitting next to her looked unperturbed. My God, she would like to see him rattled for once. "Because I am the one man who can call off the Runners," he said calmly.

Before Maisie could say anything more or spit at him, Sunil

intervened. "I did not attack your young cousin, sir." He said it in such a way that Lila couldn't see how anyone could doubt him. He had that sensitive look as if he wrote poetry or something when he wasn't tilling the land. She was sure he didn't do any such thing. But he did have that look.

"You were the only one in the room with her when the lights came on." Tristram was studying the narrow face.

"There was someone else," Sunil said. "Someone—your cousin must have managed to hit him because I heard a dull thump and a groan." He shook his head. "I must go in order. Let me start from the beginning. You see, I was waiting outside the morning room. I heard sounds of a scuffle and I feared it was Maisie. I entered via the door into your library."

"My study," Tristram said.

"Your study, yes. It was dark, but from the meager light of the window—which was curtained—I briefly made out what looked like two people scuffling by the inner door. I could hear the scuffle and I heard a thump and a groan, as I said. Then, before I could move much closer, it seemed in the dark like the struggling pair broke apart and someone brushed past me and nearly pushed me over. As I was recovering, I felt someone groping at me and of course there was screaming. Your cousin was screaming. I tried to steady her and myself, at which point the inner door opened and several people rushed in, two of whom had candelabra in their hands. You know the rest, sir."

"You would of course say something like that," Tristram said. "To suggest your innocence. What choice do you have, given the circumstances in which you were found?"

Maisie was instantly on her feet. "You—you cur! Why bother bringing us here if you aren't even going to *try*!"

Sunil didn't say a word, but just his hand around her wrist

seemed to have a mildly stabilizing effect. She practically had steam coming out of her ears but, under protest, she did sit down again. Lila couldn't help wondering if Tristram had ever been looked at with quite so much malevolence before. Lila took her hat off to Maisie. You had to hand it to her. If she were awed by Tristram's wealth or standing in society, she was hiding it admirably. Lila refrained from giving her a round of applause.

There was silence. Lila couldn't help glancing at Tristram, who was looking at Sunil. His words nearly shocked her off her seat. "Strangely, your account matches my cousin's."

For the first time, Sunil leaned forward. He had been nothing but the picture of endurance so far. Even Maisie looked gobsmacked. "What?" she said dumbly.

"What?" said Lila.

Sunil couldn't find any words.

"I've asked my cousin to go over the incidents of that night a few times," Tristram said. "Her first account, soon after the incident, was fuzzy, as you can imagine. The second was before I heard about you from Miss Marleigh. The third was this morning, and I quizzed her closely. She was attacked, yes, and then, after she kneed her attacker, he retreated—as though he meant to run out of the room. She even remembers hearing footsteps. Her account from here on is less certain and based slightly on conjecture. She thinks the man for some reason, instead of running out of the room, must have stopped in the middle of the room and she found him again when she was groping in the dark."

"It wasn't the man who attacked her!" Sunil said eagerly. "That was me!"

"I am inclined to believe you. The man who attacked her and then fled from her had no good reason to stay standing there.

He would either have continued his attack on Tiffany or fled the room before he was recognized. There would be no good reason to stop in the dark in the middle of the room and stand there, waiting to be discovered." He spread his hands in front of him. "When asked the make of her attacker's coat—which my cousin felt under her hands when she was struggling against him—she says it felt like silk. I daresay you were *not* wearing a silk coat?"

Sunil did not bother shaking his head.

Tristram continued. "There are some other little details. You ran nimbly out of the study when you saw us push into the room. I saw you do it. You climbed out of the window without showing any discomfort."

Sunil frowned. "Why shouldn't I have?" His wide brown eyes, with the very long eyelashes, looked confused.

"Tiffany—my cousin—seems convinced she kneed the man who attacked her in the groin." He stopped abruptly and glanced at Lila.

She smoothed down her skirt. "I will try very hard not to have a fit of the vapors, Mr. Tristram, at the word *groin*. A delicately nurtured female such as myself. Perhaps smelling salts would help, though. Or a reviving sip or two of brandy. I have never heard such language before. I am practically *dying* of—"

"Thank you, Miss Marleigh," Tristram managed. He didn't say anything more. Lila didn't look at him. She smiled at Maisie. Maisie actually gave her an encouraging look back.

Tristram apparently decided not to respond further, but instead looked at Sunil, the only person at the table who seemed to be giving him some respect. "I can't say that I am unequivocally convinced that you were not my cousin's attacker, Mr. Mehta. I can't say that, because everything my cousin said—it could still have been about you. But I would like to take a few days to be sure of the truth."

Sunil almost sagged on his bench.

Even Lila felt enormous relief. Whatever she had been expecting, it wasn't this. Not this easily. She had expected Tristram to be his usual suspicious self. Though this turn of events just showed that the man wasn't suspicious of everyone—just of Lila Marleigh. She frowned again.

Maisie leaned eagerly forward. "So, how?" she said simply.

Tristram looked thoughtful. "There were at least twenty guests in the house that night, at least half of them men, and that's not to mention the male servants. Though I could vouch for the servants."

"The silk coat rules out the servants," Sunil pointed out.

The three discussed it for a few minutes, but Lila didn't participate. Gradually, the others became aware of her silence. Maisie, who was watching her, shifted in her seat. Lila barely had to frame her question. The obvious question. She opened her mouth. But Tristram got in there first. He was looking at Maisie and Sunil. "What the devil *were* you doing in my garden in the first place?"

There it was. Lila crossed her arms. That was exactly the question. She looked from Maisie to Sunil and then back again. "You have to tell us, you know, who you went to meet. Unless we know the details, we're groping in the dark."

Now it was Maisie's turn to sit back and cross her arms across her chest. She looked mulish. It was a look Lila knew very well from when Maisie was seven and had no intention of telling anyone how she spent an afternoon or how many biscuits she ate when in the kitchen. Sunil was glancing sideways at her. "*Pyari*," he said soothingly. She glared at him, and he withdrew and shrugged man-to-man at Tristram, which only made Maisie glare more.

"Maisie, Mr. Tristram has a right to know what we were doing in his house," Sunil said.

"If you want to get to the bottom of this—" Lila began.

Maisie flicked her head. "Who I went to meet had nothing to do with what happened to your cousin, sir, Mr. Tristram. So what odds does it make if I tell you or not?"

"He or she may have seen who attacked Tiffany."

"Well, he couldn't have," Maisie said stubbornly. "*I* being the only soul that was in the garden at the time. *He* didn't show up."

There was silence again. "Maisie," Lila tried again.

The girl clucked impatiently. "It was your half brother, Miss Lila. So there you are. You said you wanted to know, so now you know."

"*Jonathan?*" Lila couldn't have been more surprised if Maisie said she went to Tristram's house to meet an orangutan. "You went there to meet Jonathan?"

Why anyone in their right mind would choose to meet and spend any time with Jonathan Marleigh, Earl of Beddington, Lila's half brother, was beyond Lila's comprehension. The man was boring, peevish, petulant, mewling . . .

"Why on earth?" Lila said, truly confused.

"Because a long time ago, he said he'd help me out with some dosh if I needed it."

Lila was even more surprised. "*Jonathan?* Are you sure? Doesn't sound like him."

"He was rat-arsed at the time," Maisie explained.

"Still," Lila said.

"I've never taken him up on it. He didn't lift a finger to help my mother. I couldn't see my way to going back to him and begging him for money. But, seeing as Sunil and I wanted to live an honest life, maybe in the country, raise this one," she glanced at her belly, "and maybe have one or two more, I reckoned it wouldn't hurt to have some money put by. I won't find work for long."

Lila couldn't help gritting her teeth. "And you thought to ask Jonathan over me?" She sounded as aggrieved as she felt. *Jonathan*, that good-for-nothing sniveling *brat*. "Why not me, Maisie?"

Maisie didn't answer.

Even now, Lila couldn't help wondering if the chit was telling the truth. She had no reason to lie about whom she had gone to meet. Did she? But the reason she gave for the appointment? It didn't sound like Jonathan Marleigh to promise anyone money. He was tight as a donkey's arse, and she was fairly sure he had little money to play with. He had lost most of it gambling. She had been hearing about him for years.

"The man has no money to lend or give," Tristram said to her surprise. "But we can at least knock one theory on the head. He couldn't have been the one to attack my cousin. I don't know if it is official yet or not. But I have good reason to believe they are more or less betrothed."

15

Before Lila could give full vent to the disgust she felt at the idea of *anyone* wanting to marry her half brother, her heart started racing. Her body caught up before her brain did because it took her a few seconds to realize what was putting her on edge. "Don't turn around," she urgently said to Maisie and Sunil, "but I think your Runner has just entered the room."

The pair went rigid. "Are you certain?" hissed Maisie.

"Stout and muscular, scar on his—" Lila started.

"Fat and ugly," Maisie corrected.

"That's the one." The man was walking around casually, but his eyes were keenly scanning the tables. He was leisurely making his way across the room. And Lila could see it. He was scanning the bronze complexions only, the bronze complexions of *both* the men and the women. She frowned. "How does he know you're here?" She couldn't help it. Her eyes swung around in Ivor Tristram's direction.

"If he does, it isn't because of me," he said imperturbably.

"We're going to need a diversion," Sunil said urgently. "Or—" He looked uncertain.

"No," Maisie said fiercely. "You give yourself in, you swing. So don't you say it again. I'm sick of hearing you say it."

Lila couldn't help thinking she was right. She was chewing on her thumb. The man was drawing closer.

Tristram looked calm as a daisy. "There is a door behind us." His face was calm as could be, but his words were sharp and urgent. "If Miss Marleigh and I create some kind of diversion, can the two of you make your way out as quick as you can?"

Sunil nodded. Maisie reached for his hand. He clasped it.

Lila and Tristram got to their feet and stepped out from behind the table. Tristram was keeping an eye on the Runner, so Lila did the only sensible thing.

She picked up a pitcher of ale and threw it straight in Tristram's face. Where it created a great, big splash.

He turned his face to stare at her. He looked—to her great satisfaction—dripping wet and thunderous.

Trying not to collapse in a fit of hysterics—he looked ridiculous and she was worried sick about Maisie and Sunil— she glared at Tristram. "How dare you, sir!" she screamed. And since that only attracted half the room, she threw the empty pitcher on the floor, where it made a loud clang, and then she followed suit with each of their mugs, one by one. "I am not a fool!" she screamed.

Now everyone was looking. Lila glanced in the direction of the Runner. He was looking resigned, and not worried, as though this kind of *domestic* was a nightly occurrence. Lila moved further away from their table, hoping it would give Maisie and Sunil time to sneak out of the tavern. She climbed onto a table. "How *dare* you!" she flung in Tristram's direction and stamped her foot.

She was looking down at Tristram's face, her fists on her

waist. He was calmly wiping his face on a handkerchief and now he was holding an authoritative hand up to her. She thought he would be—somewhat justifiably—livid, but she could swear, after the first shock was over, there was a glint of something else in his eyes, she couldn't define what.

"Come down at once, Lila," he said. "This is not the time—or the place."

She couldn't help a secret thrill at the sound of her name on his lips. "I will not come down, sir! If you're so afraid of making a spectacle you would not be looking down—looking down . . ." her chin trembled, "*another* woman's *bosom* when you are sitting next to your fiancée!"

Tristram's lips quivered. He gestured with his hand again. "Come on, now. Let's talk about this rationally."

"*Rationally!*" She was really getting into this now. She was reeling on the table—hoping she wasn't about to fall off. She was screaming. "Rationally! Oh, you like being *rational*, don't you? Oh, let's all be *rational*. Well, here's rational. I will *not* marry you, sir. I will marry someone who . . ." chin trembling again, "loves me."

There was a lot of noise now in the room. It sounded like the women were urging her on, and there were shouts of *you show him, you show the man he can't treat you like dirt, you show him!* The men were mainly shouting to Tristram to take her across his knee and whip her.

As a show of indignation, she took the opportunity to swing a glance around the room. The Runner was standing, arms crossed, nearby now, not intervening but also not looking at anyone else. She took solace. She dared not draw attention to the back door by looking that way. She hoped Maisie and Sunil had left or were making their way out.

Then Tristram shocked the life out of her. In a deep, sonorous tone that surely would make most women swoon, he said, "You're the single most important person in my life, Lila. Darling."

She stared at him. His lip was twitching, but his eyes were completely serious. He looked even more amused at the sight of her shocked face. She glared. "Don't darling me, sir!"

She then bent down, picked up the tankards on the table and started throwing them one by one—to an avalanche of cheers from the room, the women *and* the men this time—on the floor. This brought the harassed owner hurrying toward them—she was surprised it had taken him this long, or perhaps he had been hoping to start charging for all the extra entertainment. But then, and this was better, the Runner strolled up to them. He was a singularly unappealing-looking man. Muscly and squat with a scar running down from his left eye all the way to his jaw. He looked permanently mistrustful of humanity but in a resigned rather than actively hostile way. His shoulders were those of a bull and his hands were huge, thick and calloused.

"You're breaking the peace, miss," he said.

Her chin trembled. "I am not breaking them!" she said, pointing at the tankards. "They are made of *wood!*" She turned to Tristram. "Ivor, am I breaking them?" she asked, her voice trembling.

"No, darling. Come now. You may safely leave this to me, sir," he said to the Runner.

"Don't look like it," the Runner said lugubriously.

"Come on, Lila."

Lila finally consented to take Tristram's hand and then his hands were at her waist, and he lifted her down. To cheers of *kiss her, kiss her, you fool,* he clasped her tightly and did exactly that.

She leaned out of the kiss, gave him a sharp slap across one cheek, saw a great look of forbearance on his face, then wrapped her arms around him and kissed him until the people in the crowd were practically begging him to carry her off to bed.

He then apologized to the crowd, who were shouting for an encore, and escorted her out of the tavern none too gently and to great applause. The last thing she heard before they exited the building was *you show her how it's done, mister!* Lila was hiccuping, trying not to burst into hysterical laughter, but Tristram wanted to put more distance from the tavern. "You wretch," he took the time to say.

This was too much. She was giggling in earnest now. So, he dragged her into an alley, where she gasped and sputtered until the fit passed. Her eyes were streaming from it and Tristram too was chuckling.

"Did they make it?" she gasped in the end. Still hiccuping.

"I saw them make it to the door."

"God, you nearly killed me with the things you said," she said, still laughing.

"You owe me for a ruined cravat and shirt. Next time you want to drench me in ice-cold liquid, perhaps water?"

This sent her off again. He was laughing too. But then, brain still half-dazed, she noticed someone enter the alleyway. The smile vanished from her face. "Don't turn around," she said in a whisper.

She wrapped herself around him. And though Tristram's eyes sharpened at her urgent words, he complied. She could feel the tension in him—he must have heard the footsteps now—but he was giving every appearance of being oblivious.

And then she for a few seconds forgot about the man in the alleyway, as Tristram's mouth opened on hers and she felt she was sinking into him, letting go of a weight she didn't know she was carrying. She wrapped her arms tighter around him, feeling the rough cloth of his coat on her palms, and now she had his face in her hands. His arms were so tightly wound around her, he was practically lifting her off the ground.

A whisper of movement behind her. Lila abruptly drew back from Tristram. She giggled for good measure, as if she had no idea there was someone else there. Then swerved her eyes toward the man in the alleyway and gave an exaggerated start. Tristram was still holding her close, and she could feel the taut tension in his body.

The tall, skeletal man dressed all in black, his face narrow and long and pale as the tomb, gave them a sharp look. The Lord of Death indeed. Not the Runner this time, but the other man who seemed to be following Maisie and Sunil. Maisie was right. He was walking at a measured pace, and he didn't break his stride. He touched his hat. "Not so healthy to be out and about in a place like this, I reckon. Sir, ma'am," he said. "I'd not be wandering the streets if I was you."

His voice was low, and Lila couldn't help thinking his words sounded like a warning. Or a threat.

He passed on by and walked all the way to the end of the narrow soot-colored alley and turned the corner. Tristram placed his finger on her lips, took her hand, clasping it firmly in his, and walked casually in the other direction, to the mouth of the alley.

They walked quickly once they were out of the alley. "Let's talk in my carriage," he said. "If you don't mind me taking you back to your place?"

She shook her head. They reached the carriage, he handed her in and then settled himself in with her, his movements brisk, and asked his groom to be off. There was a beat, a mere breath of a second once the carriage started moving, then they instinctively turned to each other, her hands clutching at his lapels, his arms around her.

Her lips met his and she arched toward him, moaning softly into his mouth. One arm was firmly around her, the other first at her waist, at the lower swell of her breast, then moving down, drawing her leg closer. She was clutching him, his coat, his neck, his hair, and she felt there was something desperate about it. And yet he was holding her just as close, a little frown on his brow when she peeked at him from under her eyelashes.

But the distance was too great, and she hoisted herself onto his lap. They stared at each other for some seconds in the half dark of the carriage. He drew her close, adjusted her hips, and bent her face toward him so he could nibble at her lips. She pressed herself closer, opened her thighs wider, and she could feel him, just the tip of him at her warm, damp core. He swore under his breath. It was through layers of clothing, yet she could feel his hardness pressing against her, and she wanted nothing so much as to yield to him, open around him, feel him push into her. The ache, the ache was back, and it was beating like a pulse between her legs. She could smell him, taste his lips, the shape of them, the way they gripped hers, the way they drew her lips into his mouth, pressed his tongue into hers. She gasped as he bent down for a moment and put his open, warm mouth on the top of her neckline at the swell of her breast. He planted kisses there and then between her breasts. As he did, his hand grabbed her hip and pressed her closer still.

A large bump on the road drew them apart in shock.

They stared at each other in the darkness. There was a real

ache between her legs now and the yearning for him was so huge, she felt she might explode. They were both panting. Yet the interruption now seemed too much to bridge. She drew herself off his lap. He helped her off. And she sat down on the seat again. They were silent for some time. And the only sounds were the clip-clopping of the horses on the cobbles.

Then she turned to him in the dark, her hands pressed together in her lap. "That man." She wanted to sound purposeful, like what had just happened was only in the heat of the moment and meant nothing. But she couldn't help hearing the tremor in her voice.

"Have you seen him before?" he asked.

His voice was steady. As if he was determined to be calm about the whole thing too. Maybe he was calm? Maybe it didn't shake him the way it did her? Maybe it was nothing more than a warm, available body? He hated her, she knew it, she saw it in his face often enough. Hated her for being who and what he thought she was. She drew further into herself. It was as if the insides of her were blazing and yet she was shivering. What was she thinking?

She shook her head in answer to his question. "No, but Maisie has. She described him to me. She said she thinks he's been following her, keeping an eye on her and Sunil."

They were going along at a good pace, but the carriage was well sprung, and they hardly jolted over the cobblestones. There wasn't much light, but she could see Tristram frowning. His attention was well and truly back on that man now, the man in the alleyway. His breathing was no longer jagged. "That is as good an explanation as any for why the Runner was in the tavern."

"You think someone told him where he could find Sunil?"

He was thinking about it. "The Runner was looking about him, searching. Why the tavern? Why tonight? And if he had followed us in, why not take Sunil in right away? Why did he enter after we did? Someone obviously informed him of Sunil's whereabouts. Someone who must be keeping an eye on him."

She sat silently in the carriage, tired suddenly, after all the excitement of the tavern, and the yearning that was leaving her feeling sapped and torn. "Who could he be? It doesn't make sense."

Tristram was silent for a long time. "It only makes sense if this man, the man in the alleyway, is—or is connected to—Tiffany's real attacker. He would want to make sure the Runners arrest Sunil."

This made her sit up. "Is that not far-fetched?"

"Yes. It could be."

She gripped his sleeve. "What if it isn't far-fetched, Ivor? What if someone is actually after them, and not just the Runner?" she said with no conscious thought.

Then her hand stilled on his sleeve.

They both froze. More than the theatrics in the tavern, more than the kisses, more than what had just happened in this carriage, this gesture of hers, the tugging at his sleeve, the instinctive turning to him when she was troubled, the saying of his name, as though they knew each other, as if they were close to each other, seemed to paralyze them both. Tristram was looking down at his sleeve. He wasn't frowning. He was—nothing—his face was blank.

She tucked herself into the corner of the carriage, wanting all of a sudden to be anywhere but here. She drew away from him, looked out the window, though she didn't see anything.

They sat in silence for the rest of the journey.

At her house in Brook Street, Tristram walked her to her door. She felt horribly self-conscious. He too had lost the grimness of the carriage, and also the amusement on his face from the tavern. He was looking down at her, his eyes hard to fathom, as if trying to read her. Before she could say anything—even if she could have thought of something to say, which was doubtful—he took her hand and kissed it. A brief, cool kiss. Nothing more.

"Let's speak about it some more tomorrow," he said, and then, with no further words, he was off.

16

His man had made inquiries and, though Ivor was surprised at the speed of the results, he was even more surprised at what Hector had to tell him.

Hector—Hector McConnell, Ivor's valet—had been with him since they were both just twenty, so for the last eight years. Ivor felt that there was a trust between them and an easy camaraderie. Hector knew Ivor didn't like fripperies, but he was particular about the cut and comfort of his tailoring. He knew that Ivor didn't mind the odd flourish—a floral waistcoat, a silk handkerchief—but he didn't like a fuss and he liked to dress quickly and efficiently. Hector admired that Ivor was a regular at Jackson's—Hector himself had sparred with Ivor on occasion—and nifty with the reins. And Ivor liked that Hector was infinitely loyal and trustworthy. Moreover, he knew when to chat and when to be silent. He knew Ivor's moods, didn't press when Ivor was set on something, but didn't hesitate to speak his mind when Ivor was about to make a mistake. And it turned out, the man wasn't a bad detective.

"Are you sure?" Ivor asked.

Hector was sorting out clothes for the afternoon, brushing

the shoulders of a coat with a lint brush, smoothing a sleeve, polishing a button. He didn't bother answering, and Ivor knew he didn't need to.

"He's conspicuous, ye might say. Tall fella. A good few inches over six foot. Not to mention, he looks mighty like a cadaver with that pale face and sunken cheeks. Don't see them that skinny usually."

"Yes," Ivor said.

The trouble was why? *Why* was the man following Maisie and Sunil? What was underneath it all? Maisie Quinn had seen the skeletal man—whose name Hector said was Ezekiel Pritchard—following her and Sunil a few times. He had not attacked them, approached them, or spoken to either of them. But taken with the fact that the Runner seemed to be good at sniffing out Maisie and Sunil's whereabouts (though not yet their lodgings, it would seem, so they must be good at hiding their tracks), it looked like Pritchard was following the pair and then informing on them to the Runner.

And now the man—Pritchard—was on to Ivor and Lila Marleigh. Would he inform the Runner about them too? And given that it was Ivor himself who lodged the complaint against Sunil, would it count in Sunil's favor that Ivor was now friendly with him? Or would it in fact count against *both* Sunil and Ivor—Ivor, after all, would be seen as covering a crime, not handing Sunil in even though he had evidently attacked Ivor's cousin. Ivor frowned as he did his cuffs.

He was reasonably sure if the Runner arrested Sunil, the consequences would be severe. Lila Marleigh was right about that. The law would almost inevitably judge against him, especially since they didn't have any real evidence that Sunil was telling the truth, that his version of events was the correct one.

It was mostly just his description of what happened that evening in Ivor's house. Yet Ivor was almost completely convinced that Sunil was telling the truth. Not only did the man have no reason to attack Tiffany—*and* his account matched Tiffany's own in minute detail—Ivor was a pretty shrewd judge of character. And he couldn't see Sunil Mehta attacking a woman. The man didn't have any reason to, and he wasn't the kind who would do it on the spur of the moment. It didn't fit.

Ivor was a pretty shrewd judge of character, but not—apparently—in Miss Lila Marleigh's case.

He heaved such a great sigh while doing his other cuff that Hector, who was brushing lint off his riding coat, looked up at him. But then he casually went back to the coat. After a few moments' silence, he said, "Escorted Miss Marleigh back all right, sir? Last night, that is?"

Ivor jerked so hard that the cufflink fell from his hand and onto the carpet. Curse the man. "Damn you."

Hector kept on brushing Ivor's coat.

Damn the groom too, Simon Barlow. He must have told Hector about last night, about Ivor driving Miss Marleigh back to her house. And Hector was much too sharp for his own good. He was walking out with the maid, Carly Simmonds. He was slim and lithe and not very tall. He had dusty brown hair and arched brows that made him seem cheeky, which he was. He had rescued Ivor from a good few scrapes down in Oxford. Though, for the most part, he had helped Ivor get into those scrapes in the first place.

Ivor felt a sudden nostalgia for those uncomplicated days.

He had done exceptionally well at Oxford and then let go of everything he learned there almost as soon as he graduated. He took the reins of his father's estate once most of it had been run into the ground and he turned things around, by sheer force of will and by staying up half the night working for months and years on end. Staying fair to the farmers on his estate and at the same time not bleeding money was well-nigh impossible, but he managed it by the skin of his teeth and with nothing but pigheadedness and a determination not to fail. Uncle Arthur's advice on investments eased things off finally. But fun, he had forgotten how to have fun.

He remembered suddenly the way Miss Marleigh—Lila—had thrown the ale chock full in his face. He grinned, bending to do up his shoes now.

"Had a good evening then, sir?"

The grin vanished from Ivor's face. He sighed. "Will you lay off me, man?" he said mildly to Hector.

"That bad, is it?"

"It isn't bad at all." His boots done up, Ivor straightened.

"Been wondering why you're looking so moon-faced."

Ivor gritted his teeth. But didn't think the remark merited a response. Then he said, "Don't you have enough on your hands with running after Carly? She puts you through your paces, as far as I can tell. And good on her. Though why she puts up with you, is more than I can understand. If she gives you a hard time, it's less than what you deserve."

"A fella likes his woman not to be too easy. Just easy on the eye." Hector winked. "But you see, ye love a woman and all of a sudden you get the nose of a hound, you do."

Ivor frowned. What was the man talking about now? He didn't want to ask. No doubt Hector would enlighten him. He did.

"Ye can all of a sudden sniff it out when other fellas love other women, so to speak."

Ivor almost laughed. Whatever he felt for Lila Marleigh, it

wasn't love. "Don't be foolish. I have no interest in the woman at all."

"Which woman?" Hector said, the picture of innocence, his eyes wide as if he had been talking in complete generalities, so what was Ivor talking about?

Ivor ignored him. "Love is far from my mind. She is one of the most aggravating women I have ever met. She throws things you say back in your face. She loves to challenge you. She laughs and talks in such a way and with so many people, that you have no idea if she is being herself or hiding herself completely so you can never see the real her at all." He stopped abruptly and, walking over to the side cabinet, riffled through some files he had to send to his agent. He had been looking through them peacefully in his bedchamber two nights ago and had completely forgotten about them since then.

"Reckon you don't like her at all, sir," Hector said. "Complete indifference, as far as I can tell."

Ivor flung the file with a thump on the cabinet so that it fell, and the pages scattered all over the floor. He cursed. "She is the one that ruined my shirt and cravat last night, so *that* should teach you to be championing her."

"Dear God, the woman is a fiend. They are ruined, sir, utterly ruined."

Hector sounded serious now, frown in place, distinct severity in his voice, Ivor was happy to hear.

"A woman like that," said Hector, his cheeky voice back on again, now that he had given himself a few seconds to assimilate the information about Lila Marleigh and the ale, "you should never see again, sir. I expect you don't mean to?"

Having gathered all the loose sheets from the floor, Ivor closed the file and then quickly retied his cravat in the mirror.

"Be so good as to ask Mrs. Manfield to bring in tea and biscuits, will you? I am expecting guests."

Hector looked accommodating. "Of course, sir, at once, sir. And who might we be expecting, if I may ask?"

"Go to the devil," Ivor said, before banging the door of his bedchamber behind him.

17

Twenty minutes later he was sitting in the rose garden with Lila Marleigh, Miss Quinn, and Mr. Mehta.

"Please call me Sunil," the man was saying.

"Do call me Ivor," Ivor said.

Sunil looked very surprised, and Ivor was irritated to see the look of surprise that Lila Marleigh tried to hide. She looked . . . ridiculously beautiful today. Her curls were half down her back. They were so dark that they formed a nimbus cloud around her creamy complexion. She was wearing muslin the color of clotted cream, with purple and indigo flowers all over it. And she was mostly refusing to meet his eyes, unless he spoke directly to her.

He spoke directly to her. "This will come as a surprise. But the man—the man in the alleyway . . ." She looked up with that eager, direct gaze of hers. She was nothing if not curious and inquisitive, annoyingly so. And those large owl-eyes: no one needed such large eyes. He wanted to place his lips on each of her eyelids.

"What man?" Maisie said. She had grudgingly asked Ivor to call her Maisie, in the manner of someone granting a favor that they really didn't want to grant.

"When we left the tavern last night, there was a man following us."

Maisie gurgled. "It was all I could do to get out of there. I couldn't take my eyes off you, Miss Lila, swaying about like a drunken sailor on that table. And the ale, all over Mr. Ivor's face!" She went off into a peal of laughter.

"Yes," Miss Marleigh said smugly, "I know." She sounded proud of herself. "I do hope I didn't ruin your clothes," she said politely, looking at him for only a second, before taking a sip of her tea and ignoring him again.

"You've ruined your standing with my man," he said.

She placed her teacup down on her saucer and crossed her hands demurely in her lap. "I wouldn't have thought I had any standing with your man at all, Mr. Tristram."

Jade. Ivor fought with himself. "It must be because I come back in a towering rage every time I see you," he said, matching her politeness.

She inclined her head. "Yes, it must be that. Though of course he may know me from . . . well, because your father knows me? From my visits to him?"

He gripped his teacup so hard he was afraid he was going to break it. How like her to throw that in his face when he was trying his damnedest to forget about it. But then he saw Maisie looking from one to the other.

"Visits to Mr. Ivor's father?" Maisie's eyes were wide. "Whatever for?"

"Oh, in the way a mistress visits her . . . man," Miss Marleigh said innocently.

Maisie nearly choked on her tea while Sunil calmly drank his. "*You* would choke someone to death before consenting to be his mistress."

Ivor looked sharply at Maisie and then at Lila Marleigh's casual face. Was she right, Maisie, or just deluded about Lila Marleigh? Was he surprised? *Was* he? Or had he already come to the same conclusion? He would deal with this later. Oh, he'd positively enjoy dealing with this later. "Would anyone here like to know who the tall man is who has been following Maisie and Sunil?" he asked, with a great effort at calm. "Or is no one interested? If not, I have a long list of other things we can chat about."

They all quickly assented. He told them.

To his satisfaction, they all gaped.

"The—the cadaver is *Jonathan's* man?" Miss Marleigh was the first to recover.

"But why?" Maisie looked astonished. "Why would Mr. Jonathan—I mean Lord Beddington's man—follow us?"

Sunil was frowning.

Ivor opened his hands in front of him on the garden table. He was happy to briefly notice that Mrs. Manfield, though she would undoubtedly have been surprised at some of his visitors today, wasn't the kind of woman to embarrass him with inferior china or stale biscuits.

He picked his words. "My first thought was that only someone who either attacked Tiffany or was hired by the man who attacked Tiffany would be interested in following the two of you. Following you and informing the Runner about your whereabouts." He looked up at the three faces. Even Lila Marleigh had forgotten not to look at him. He remembered suddenly the way she had put her hand on his arm and clutched his sleeve last night in his carriage. He thought for a second that she had forgotten to be a salon hostess and just been herself instead. He imagined that didn't happen a lot. He suppressed a sigh. He had had another sleepless night.

"But why would *Jonathan*," she said the name the way she always said Jonathan Marleigh's name, with great disdain, even loathing, "or his man, attack your cousin, Mr. Tristram? Didn't you say he was betrothed to your cousin?" She shuddered a little. "You know, I can't imagine why anyone would betroth themself to Jonathan. My apologies if I offend you."

"He's in debt."

"Oh, he would be. And I suppose your cousin—she could help him with that?" She wasn't teasing or being ironic. Simply asking him for the facts.

"I don't know enough about him. To tell you the truth, Tiffany falls in love so often, I was expecting it to pass. I can't help thinking she's only adamant about your half brother because she knows he's so unsuitable and her father will hate him."

"Oh, I don't know about that," Miss Marleigh said musingly. "That was always the thing about Jonathan. He is a worm through and through, don't get me wrong. But there was one thing that could make him turn on the charm. And that was when he wanted something—or rather, needed something—for self-preservation. Jonathan was always good at self-preservation."

"Tiffany is an heiress. She could certainly help him out with his debts, yes. Though *not*," his mouth tightened, "if I have anything to say about it."

Miss Marleigh took a careful sip of her tea again. "I can't say I have much time for Jonathan, but I have to say I'm a little sorry for him," she murmured. "And I'm *so* glad I'm not your cousin—or, say, your sister."

"I can assure you, that's a mutual feeling," he said before he could stop himself. He gritted his teeth—it would be better not to throttle a guest at the garden table—before he carried on. "The trouble is, even if he wants to marry my cousin for her fortune, he would have even less reason to attack her. He would want to keep her happy. Not jeopardize things. It doesn't add up that he attacked her—yet, if he didn't, then why is his man following Sunil and Maisie?"

"Your cousin, sir, Mr. Ivor, she didn't break things off with Mr. Jonathan, or anything like that? I mean, could he have attacked your cousin because she broke things off with him?" Maisie asked.

Ivor flicked his head. "No, she was very much still with him, even after the incident. They are not officially betrothed, but she thinks they are as good as. Tiffany had made no connection between Jonathan Marleigh and her attacker. There is, however, something else." Lila Marleigh leaned forward on the table. My God, she was intensely attractive when she forgot to be the hostess. Actually, she was intensely attractive no matter what. "I asked my staff to more thoroughly clean and search my study. They are usually thorough, but I thought more was needed." He put a hand in his pocket. And came up with a large button covered in prettily embroidered cloth. "They found this, as if it had been kicked under the desk."

They stirred. Lila Marleigh fingered the button, tracing the embroidered flower with her thumb. Maisie was leaning over to inspect it.

"It could belong to anyone who's been in my study," Ivor said. "But it could also belong to the attacker. Tiffany says she was struggling with him for some time and clutching at his clothes. She could have broken something off without either of them realizing it."

"So, now we have to find out if the button belongs to Jonathan Marleigh, my lovely half brother."

Ivor turned to look at Lila Marleigh. "Yes, I gather that,

but how? I could send my man Hector to try, but the odds of him finding himself in Jonathan Marleigh's bedchamber to look through his clothes are practically nonexistent. He could have found out from Beddington's man, but the man seems somewhat sinister and is unlikely to help Hector."

"He has an ugly gob," Maisie said succinctly. She was frowning. "I could go and pay him a visit, couldn't I? Mr. Jonathan, I mean. I mean, he did ask me to see him at your place that night since I told him it was urgent, and he said he had social engagements every night for a week. And then he didn't show. So, I could go knocking at his door, ask him for that missed appointment he promised me."

"And be handed over to the Runners?" Miss Marleigh said. "No. We can't take the risk. His man is following you; we know that much. It can't be for any benign reason. He'll have you in for harboring a wanted man before you can blink. He's a nasty little boy, Jonathan. Never grew up. He used to egg us on—me and my sisters—to do all kinds of naughty things—like I said, he could be charming when he wanted—and then he'd rat on us as soon as our backs were turned. And he was so good at acting as if he was our best friend—oh, and I suppose we were so desperate for even one friend in the house—that he got away with it for years before we started catching on. Though of course by that time we were also really good at only looking out for ourselves and no one else. He is a good ten years older than me. But he's one of those people who never grow up."

Something twisted in Ivor's belly, sudden and sharp. She spoke unconsciously and with all the aggravation she still felt at her half brother. But the wistfulness in her face, and the hurt, he expected she didn't know that the hurt was there. She had had no friend in the house where she grew up. He knew what that was like. But he thought it natural in an only child who felt he had nothing in common with his parents. But someone with siblings? He was staring at her. She looked up and caught him staring. She blinked and stared back, not her usual challenging or ironic look, but something else. Something full of unexpected yearning. And he felt that thing again—a part of himself, a secret part that he didn't let other people touch—reaching out to a secret part of her and clutching on to it for dear life.

"If I can't go and Mr. Ivor's man can't ask around—" Maisie broke into his thoughts.

Lila Marleigh answered. "Then I have to go."

Ivor frowned.

Her face was matter-of-fact now. "He's my half brother. What could be more natural? I mean, other than that I've told him often enough if I never see him again it'll be too soon." But she brushed this away with a hand. "No matter. I'll find a way. I will have to go. There is no other way."

"I'll come with you." Ivor said the words before he had time to think about it.

All three of his guests looked surprised. "Why would you, sir?" Sunil said. And then said, "Oh, I see. To meet your cousin's betrothed. That has a ring of truth."

Lila Marleigh frowned. "That's all very well. But you would hardly go there with *me* if you wanted to vet the man and talk business."

"Let's work on the reasons," Ivor said. "But let's not delay it. That Runner isn't going anywhere. Let's go today."

Sunil and Maisie took their leave, promising to be careful. "He's not going to rat out where we live, that's for sure," Maisie said with determination. And they walked away hand in hand.

As they stood at the threshold of his study after Maisie and

Sunil left, Ivor, before he could stop himself, clasped his hand around Lila Marleigh's wrist. She turned around and stared at him in surprise—and something else. That sudden awareness, that spark of desire that he thought was so near the surface that just a glance could call it up.

"You aren't and you've never been my father's mistress." He was surprised at his own words. He hadn't known they were about to pop out of his mouth. And yet. Hadn't he known this for days, even from when he first met her?

She looked—to his slight amusement—a little resentful. "Figured that out, have you?"

"Lila—"

And she was in his arms. He clasped her, held on to her like he wouldn't let go. Her lips met his.

"You could have just told me," he said.

"Told you what, to go to the devil?" she murmured on his mouth.

"I've no doubt about that. But you could have told me the truth, that you weren't my father's mistress."

"Why should I? I don't care what you think."

He smiled at her words and her tone. But he had to ask, had to know more. "You didn't want to have to deny it? Is that it?" He searched her eyes.

"I didn't have to deny it." Her eyelids fluttered.

"There's something else, isn't there? Some other reason you didn't deny it?"

She flicked her head. "I don't know what you mean."

But he thought he was coming to know her signs, signs that no one else would notice. He was coming to know her. "Lila—"

"It's nothing," she said firmly. "It's nothing important. I was never your father's mistress. Isn't that all you need to know?"

He wasn't sure about that, but he didn't want to probe, not right now.

He bent his lips again. She instantly arched up to him, met his tongue with hers. That sound she made in her throat. The look on her face. It kept changing, her expression. From resentment to pleasure to almost pain as a frown of yearning fluttered on her forehead. He could see everything there. Her face was a glass window, through which she let him in. He couldn't help feeling that it was a great privilege, that she didn't let everyone in. Maybe she didn't even know she was opening up to him, under his lips, his hands. He held her tighter.

He half carried her and gently backed her against his desk. He lifted her up onto it and she opened her legs to accommodate him.

"We should go soon," she said breathlessly, leaning her head back to give access to her neck. He wrapped his mouth around the blue vein there. "We have to catch him before he's off on some engagement."

"Five minutes. We'll go in five minutes."

He nibbled at her throat hungrily; he'd always been hungry until he met her. She gasped as he gently pulled her dress down and flicked her hard nipple with his tongue. He had been imagining doing that for some time. She held his face, arching to give him more access, her legs opening wider. He wrapped his mouth around her, drinking her in, feeling the hard nipple on his tongue, the soft velvet of her, the way the nipple hardened as he flicked it, in a way that reached and coursed through his own body. She was moaning now. She edged nearer, pressing herself to him, unerringly finding his erection, letting him feel that hot core of her that he had felt all too briefly the night before. She was shaking as he licked and sucked her nipple—or was it he who was shaking? He lifted her skirt and, moving away the layers, and nudging her thighs further apart, placed just a finger where his erection had been seconds before. He lifted his mouth from her nipple and gazed into her eyes. A question. Her face answered it. He inserted just a tip of his middle finger. She gasped so loudly and clutched him so hard, he had to place his mouth on hers.

She was looking at him with so much desire, so much trust and so much need he thought he would die, just from looking at her face. Or maybe the hot dampness of her would kill him. There was so much yearning there, it was almost pain. And he felt his own pain meet hers like it had been waiting to do that all his life. He inserted his finger deeper and rubbed the silken contours he found there, the ridges and valleys. She edged yet closer to the edge of the table and opened wider.

Then she reached down with her hand and placed his thumb where she wanted it. He smiled on her mouth. And bit her lower lip. But she was past caring about that, was almost impatient with it, focused as she was now on one part of her body. He kept his mouth gently on hers, feeling her breath mingle with his, as he worked his middle finger and his thumb—gentle as the trickle from a mountain spring—until she tightened so much, he thought she would burst. And then she did burst. She convulsed around his finger, gasped, almost crying, and moisture dripped down his finger onto his hand, beautiful, warm moisture. She was trembling, sitting there on his desk. And he had to do it again, and one more time, just to feel it once more, that great need of hers that he could satisfy, that he could soothe. He had his forehead on her shoulder now. He was shaking too. But she had recovered enough to reach her hand down to him and find him through his trousers.

But he placed a hand on hers. "Not now, Lila. Later. We should go. If we have any hope of catching him before he heads out for the evening."

"Let me, now," she purred. "Please."

And it sounded as though all she wanted to do was touch him, feel him in her hand, like she longed to feel him.

Dear God, how was a man supposed to refuse that? Was she trying to kill him? But he couldn't. He didn't want to, not right now. He wanted to savor it. "Later." He sealed the promise with a kiss.

18

To say that Jonathan Marleigh looked surprised to see his visitors would be an understatement.

Lila looked at him with all the loathing she felt. He was just as weak-chinned, his eyes uncertain and wavering, his mouth as petulant as it had always been. She shuddered.

Clinically, he wasn't completely unappealing. He had white-blond hair, overstyled, but not completely awful. Reasonably proportioned features. He looked a little soft all over, and he had the habit of taking his handkerchief out and blotting his nose with it. But he—no, no, Lila couldn't see his appeal. She wondered what kind of woman was Tiffany Tristram that she had agreed to marry *this* man. And yet, *yet* she couldn't forget—didn't let herself forget—the countless times that he had taken the sisters in, charmed them into thinking that he was their friend. He had a way of making you feel seen and heard—it was only after years of it that Lila and her sisters had realized that he only did it when he wanted something. And he only did it when no one else was looking, only his victim. Despite appearances, he wasn't stupid.

Jonathan had kissed Lila once. A long time ago, when she

was nineteen, he ten years older. It was hard and brutal and soft and wet all at the same time. She not only slapped him, but also looked at him with so much open revulsion that his face twisted, and he said, "You think anyone would want to do more than kiss you? You think Robert Wellesley ever would? You smell like the colonies."

"Why did you kiss me then?" she raged, wiping her mouth on the back of her hand, wondering if she would ever be able to wipe that fish nibble from her memory.

"To find out what it felt like. Robert says it's sweeter than a whore's mouth. I wanted to see if he was right. I've tasted sweeter whores, me."

She spat at him. But then not being happy with that, she raked her fingernails down his face so everyone could see what he was like. Oh, he hadn't liked that. The trails down his cheek didn't heal for days. She grinned now, remembering it. "Jonathan," she said sweetly, "how wonderful to see you. It's been too long. I've been *dying* to see you."

She saw Ivor glance sharply at her. Damn the man. Weren't they here to put on an act? Why did he have to look at her like that? As if she was betraying him somehow by putting on an act? She tightened her lips, but then made sure to keep her wide smile in place.

Her half brother looked pale, more so than usual. But then the man gambled half the night away, drank more than he gambled, and did nothing useful with his time. He was probably not used to the light touching his flesh. A bit like a vampire, Lila couldn't help thinking.

"My apologies for this call," Ivor said.

"I must admit, I was surprised to see your note," Jonathan said, ushering them in. "Pleasantly, of course."

Lila had been expecting to feel some revulsion at seeing

Jonathan Marleigh, but the shock she felt at stepping into the Marleigh House in Grosvenor Square was physical and it paralyzed her as they stood in the foyer.

For a few seconds, she struggled to get her breathing under control. She felt damp patches in her armpits. She felt as though she was suffocating. She had felt nothing but small, utterly small and powerless in this place. For many, many years. At the injustice of her birth, at not having any choice about who she lived with, because grown-ups she had no respect for had decided she should live with them. She had felt powerless with rage. Rage at the people around her, and yet it felt like corrosive rage against herself.

All the old feelings rushed in on her now and they shook her to her core. She clenched and unclenched her hands, trying to steady her breathing.

As Jonathan ushered them into the saloon, the violence of the sudden feeling seemed to pass. Ivor gave her a questioning look, gave her arm a quick and reassuring squeeze as he followed her into the room, perhaps sensing some of her feelings. She was surprised and grateful that he noticed. She was left feeling a little drained by the shock of this encounter, but at least she wasn't going to be sick on Jonathan's overtight boots. At least, hopefully not. She swallowed.

Once they were seated and tea was brought in, Jonathan pointedly turned to look at them.

Ivor looked calm as could be. "Tiffany told me that you have an understanding."

Jonathan, the idiot, looked a little nervous for a second, but then straightened and lifted his chin and smiled in that way he used to smile when he wanted something from one of the sisters. "I see."

"I am a sort of guardian to her," Ivor said. It was said amicably enough, but there was a hint of danger in it, which made Lila thankful she had no love lost for Jonathan. "As you can imagine, I was surprised you didn't think to speak with me—if not Tiffany's father."

Jonathan, who was older than Ivor by a few years, looked even more defiant. God, he was a weak, weak man. "Tiffany—Miss Tristram—wants to marry me. She knows her mind. And it was a secret betrothal for now. A man doesn't like to be rushed, you know."

Ah, the petulant look. That he had when he was a little rattled but wanted to brave it out so no one would notice. Lila's nausea vanished and she felt a certain sense of well-being settle in her belly. If she hadn't already been half in love with Ivor Tristram . . . wait. What? She frowned.

"I am not rushing you in the least. I thought we could speak, man-to-man. It is hardly surprising, after all. Tiffany is an heiress," Ivor said. "And strange though it might seem, my word carries some weight with her."

Lila glanced sideways at him to see if this claim was true. What he had said on the way here was how often Tiffany Tristram fell in love and how there was never any point trying to convince her that the man was inappropriate because it only prolonged her feelings.

"Of course, I see why you think you should speak to me," Jonathan said. His eyes wavered and he blotted his lips. He didn't *look* convinced. But then he pointedly turned to face Lila. "Still, I am at a loss to understand why my lovely half sister is here. Don't get me wrong. I couldn't be more ecstatic to see her, it's been too long. But I still don't see—"

Lila smiled brightly. "Oh, Mr. Tristram really didn't want to bring me along. He would rather have done this alone. But when I heard he was coming *here,* to this dear old house," she almost choked on the words, "to see *you,* I begged him to take me." She turned to face Ivor. "Didn't I, Mr. Tristram? And you felt that you couldn't say no, you're so good!"

Ivor looked as if he would like to say no to a good many things she asked. He was pitching it perfectly. He wasn't doing anything so crass as exchanging significant glances with Jonathan Marleigh, but with hardly any expression on his face at all, he was making it clear that he had no hand in bringing Lila with him, that Lila practically forced it on him.

It was a world-class performance, Lila thought admiringly, but Jonathan looked intensely polite. "Yes, but you see, I still don't understand. I mean, I didn't even know you were acquainted."

And yet. His eyes said different. Jonathan's man Pritchard would undoubtedly have filled him in on the events of last night. Of what had happened in the alleyway. Of course, Jonathan knew they were acquainted.

So be it. Lila glanced at Ivor, blushed slightly and looked overcome. "Oh, we all have our secrets, don't we, Jonathan? Do spare my blushes!"

Jonathan looked from one face to another, looking politely incredulous, as if he didn't believe it, or couldn't imagine anyone would consensually want to spend time with his oldest half sister. "Well," he said finally, "perhaps we can talk business man-to-man in my study, then, Mr. Tristram." He looked pointedly at Lila.

"I would *love* to look at the old portrait gallery, Jonathan," she gushed. He looked so skeptical at this claim—well he might since she once told him she'd come back to this house in a coffin, though she'd try to prevent even that—that she said, "I used to hate you, Jonathan, I admit it. But you know, as I get older, I'm getting sentimental about family. Perhaps I simply have better judgment. We silly women," she added, knowing his low opinion of the female sex.

He gave a half smile.

"I would love to see the portrait gallery, and all Papa's ancestors, if you don't mind. It would give you two men the time to be private."

He didn't look suspicious now, or at least no more than he did habitually. "Of course," he said. "I am afraid I am expecting other callers. But I can give you twenty minutes."

"That should be plenty," Ivor said.

As the men made their way toward Jonathan's study, Jonathan's footman escorted Lila upstairs to the portrait gallery. Up the marble stairs, down the long hallway, past the door to a spare bedroom, and then finally to the portrait gallery. There was a maid—a young woman with pretty curls and a bow-shaped mouth—cleaning outside it. Lila gave her a quick smile, hoping she wouldn't take it in her head to pop into the gallery to clean in there, not for the next fifteen or so minutes, at least.

And there she was, standing outside a room she hated above all others, full of pictures of Marleigh ancestors. Portraits, yes, of her father's ancestors, and yes, she had loved her father. But a reminder of her place—which was no place at all—in this house. Can a bastard have ancestors?

She braced herself for it as she entered it now, but realized that—after that first shock downstairs—she was ready for it. The smell assaulted her, a familiar cloying smell, the stench of betrayal and darkness, swirling guilt and fear. The room looked the same. It was long and narrow, clothed in dark-red curtains that had faded almost to a dull rose now, the portraits half in shadow, as if no one wanted to look at them and they knew it—or perhaps they were biding their time, waiting to pounce. Lila had often thought so when she was a child, that they moved and spoke in whispers when no one was looking and would come to life if you weren't careful. All the ancestors looked pale and resentful, like Jonathan. There was a portrait of her father at the far end, but it was more than she could bring herself to do, to look at it. Not to mention that it was hung next to a portrait of him with Sarah Marleigh. Of course, there was nothing of Naira Devi in the room, the Earl's second wife—or rather, his mistress—and certainly nothing of their daughters. There never would be.

Except, Lila thought, in the coldness and distance that seemed to ooze from the pores of the portrait of her father, Nathanial Marleigh, and his first wife, Sarah. In that coldness, in what looked like a complete lack of understanding or empathy, in the gaps, you could see Naira, and you could see her daughters. Lila was not tempted to walk to the far end of the room and confront the ghosts.

At first, the footman showed a tendency to linger, but then quickly got bored and left. She didn't have a minute to lose.

19

The smell of Jonathan's bedchamber assaulted her, and it was as though she could feel his lips on hers again. This she hadn't been prepared for.

She had to take a few seconds to steady herself. The room was decorated in salmon and cream, but she couldn't help noticing that the wallpaper and furnishings were fading and looked threadbare. There was a distinct smell of damp—no, not just a smell. There were mushroom patches, expanding in a corner of the ceiling, creeping out from behind an armoire, decay taking over. The entire house had that look. Of something suppurating. Lila imagined it, the damp, spreading its tentacles, destroying this place where love had always died.

Jonathan Marleigh didn't have a lot of money to play with. He wasn't sparing too much of it, though, when it came to his clothes. There was silk, sateen and tapestry aplenty, coats for every occasion—not perhaps the best cloth or tailoring, but good enough to pass the knowing eye of the *ton*. But his bedroom, that hadn't had a farthing spent on it in years. He would spend what was needed to maintain his front, but beyond that, it seemed he spent as little as possible on the parts no one would see. That was Jonathan all over. Look beyond the façade and all you got was rot.

She rummaged quickly through his wardrobes. She focused first on the coats. She frowned, her movements getting more frantic. There were silk coats, a good few, and they had ornate buttons, some bronze, some golden-hued, some embossed, but not one with floral embroidery. Damnation. She checked and she checked again. She had pictured finding the coat so clearly in her mind on the carriage ride over to the Marleigh residence that she couldn't believe it wasn't here. Just when she made the transition from wondering why on earth Jonathan Marleigh would have attacked Tiffany Tristram to being convinced that he did it, she wasn't sure.

She looked quickly through the other wardrobes, just in case it was not with his other coats. Of course, the button, though it looked as if it belonged to a coat, could at a stretch have come from a waistcoat. But it seemed not. An increasingly urgent search through the waistcoats, but no floral buttons there either.

She had the floral button in her pocket. She took it out now, walked over to the window and in the light studied the design again, the coral bud, the grass-green stem and leaves. A little faded, but not yet falling apart. She cursed. Where was the damned thing? Were they barking up the wrong tree and did it not belong to Jonathan after all? Of course, Jonathan could still have attacked Tiffany Tristram, and this could still be someone else's button. Or it could belong to Jonathan and the coat could be downstairs for cleaning. She was already nearly at the end of the twenty minutes' grace, and she still needed to make her way down the stairs again and back to the portrait gallery. She could hardly ask to see the steam room or the laundry.

The clock was ticking. She couldn't help another look through all his coats and waistcoats, and she couldn't help going on her hands and knees and searching the floor of the wardrobe, in case something had slunk down there. But there was nothing. No coat. No coat with floral embroidery on the buttons.

She straightened. She had better get down there. She stuffed the button back in the pocket of her skirt and, closing the door of Jonathan's bedchamber behind her, she quickly crept down the back stairs. As before, avoiding the door outside which the pretty maid was cleaning, she entered the gallery through a back door. She was out of breath and slightly sweaty from the hasty search and the dash downstairs.

"I was wondering where you had got to."

She stopped dead. The soft voice with that thinly veiled sneer had always had that effect. There he was. Jonathan, looking suspicious, and smirking slightly at the same time. No Ivor. Where was Ivor? The sunlight glinted through Jonathan's white-blond hair.

She smiled brightly, trying not to pant. "Oh! Gosh. You startled the life out of me!"

"Enjoying a little reconnoiter of the old house?" The smile was weak, but the eyes, she couldn't help noticing, were alert and set on her face. God, those blue, almost white eyes. She could never escape the feeling that she was looking into a void, that there was nothing there, and that she wouldn't want to see what *was* there if she could.

"Oh, I couldn't help it! I couldn't help it! It's *so wonderful* to be back." She was going to make herself sick.

"Where did you go?"

"Hmm?" She turned wide eyes toward her half brother.

"Which room, I mean? Just now. What—uh—made you feel so sentimental?"

He was watching her. Unblinkingly, like a reptile. What made him attack his own fiancée? *Did* he attack his own fiancée? What was he hoping to get out of it? Jonathan was a big believer in self-preservation. Something about it didn't fit.

"Oh! Everything really. But really, I just wanted to—race down the entire length of the gallery, up the back stairs, down the back stairs, and race through the gallery again. Just like the old days." She couldn't ever remember racing about like a mad hare in the house. In the grounds of her father's estate (now sold) in Essex, yes. Many times. In the garden at the back, yes. But in this house? No. She could only remember long hours of restless pacing, like she was afraid something would eat her if she sat still, like the walls would close in and crush her. The silence was oppressive, the way people steered clear of one another, yet, when they spoke to you, singled you out, it was that much worse.

She could of course remember one happy day in this portrait gallery when she had taken a knife to one of Jonathan's portraits and ruined it beyond repair. But that was the only one.

"How . . . curious," Jonathan said, still watching her face. "I never knew the place brought so many joyful memories. I, for one, don't remember that many good times. Hardly any before you and your sisters came to live here. I never saw my father. After all, *you* had him all to yourself." He smiled slowly. "And, to tell you the truth, I remember the good times even less *once* you moved here."

Her smile was frozen in place. She had never stopped to think what it must have been like for him to live with his mother, the ever-resentful Sarah Marleigh, all by himself, waiting for a father who never showed up, who chose to live on the other side of an ocean. And then, out of the blue, to have three sisters thrust upon him, evidence that their father had forgotten all about his first family in his new home. Had lived a life of luxury, parties, sunshine, hunting, and pleasure with other Company members and local Indian royalty, while his wife and heir lived in a house that was starting to come apart at the seams. Forgotten all about his son whom he never saw.

"If you had given us a chance . . ." she blurted out before she could stop herself.

He tapped his snuffbox with a single fingernail. "I am glad to have been the source of so much pleasure today. I never thought you liked me that much."

"Of course." She cleared her throat, swallowed hard. "Aren't you . . . family?" There, she thought, *there* was a hateful word if ever there was one.

He was smiling that weak smile of his. He was standing near a window, and she was still just inside the back door. But then, to her shock, he peeled himself away from the window and walked nearer, until he was within touching distance.

He stood there, completely still, arrested like a gecko in the heat of the desert. And then he reached out a hand and touched her arm.

Before she could stop herself, she flinched as if she had been burned.

He drew back his hand. She was staring at him, she knew, with loathing. She couldn't school her features. His lip curled as he saw the look on her face. He drew nearer and she held her breath. He was leaning forward now and, though he couldn't have been moving especially slowly, it felt as if she was watching it unfold trickle by trickle, drop by drop. He touched her lips with his mouth.

She growled and pushed him so hard he nearly fell over.

He straightened and was looking at her with open hatred now. "Not so sentimental now, darling sister."

She was panting. "Take your nasty little kisses somewhere else, Jonathan. To someone who wants them." To hell with keeping him appeased. To hell with sympathy for the lonely boy he must have been. She had spent as much time in the house as she needed. And she couldn't prove that the infernal button belonged to him. "Though it must be hard to find someone that does."

His lip curled some more. "If you think Tristram will offer you anything more than his bed—if that—you must be barking mad. Sister."

Her face froze, cold fury rising inside her. And of course, when she was this mad, she had nothing to say. She was frozen.

"Cat got your tongue, darling sister? He comes from a respectable family, Lila. I'd stake not a bastard amongst them. Certainly not the half-breed from some native slut—"

She cut him off not with a hiss, a growl or a snap, but by launching at him and punching him in the face.

He fell backward against the wall and cursed. She held her fist in her other hand, breathing hard now. "You swine. *You* should know when you talk of sluts. Given it would be difficult to get a woman to spend two minutes of her time with you for anything other than money."

The words were lame, but she was too much in a rage to be clever. He was wiping his lip, where there was a flourish of blood. A spurt. He looked as if he was going to charge at her and beat her senseless. Just as she was looking around for a weapon to defend herself—the poker at the fireplace would do—the door opened and startled them both.

It was the pretty, curly-haired maid. She looked just as

startled. "Oh, sorry, sir, miss. I forgot you were in here. It's only the housekeeper asked me to darn that curtain, sir, miss. I was collecting laundry and darning." She tapered off, red in the face now.

They were both staring dumbly at the maid. Lila recovered first. "Not at all. I'm sorry for keeping you from your chores. I was just leaving."

"Get on with it," Jonathan said viciously to the maid.

Oh, yes, this, the casual rudeness to the people who worked for him, unless there were guests in the house—guests that mattered, that is. Lila didn't. She looked at him with disgust but he wasn't looking at her. They both moved in the direction of the door.

Then Lila's heart started pounding and she turned around, her profile to both Jonathan who stood at the door and the maid, who stood in the room. "What's your name?" she asked the maid.

Jonathan frowned. Waited at the door. Now there were footsteps coming up the stairs. It was Ivor. He reached the head of the stairs and stopped. Lila looked at him, trying to convey she didn't know what. He looked at the tableau, from Lila to Jonathan, at the droplet of blood on Jonathan's mouth, the rapidly swelling lip, and his face went rigid. He was staring fixedly at Jonathan's face. Lila saw the fist clench on the banister and she hastily intervened. "Oh, there you are, Mr. Tristram! I have had a wonderful time in the gallery. I was just speaking to—" She looked at the maid again.

The maid blushed again. "Ellen, miss."

"Ellen, are you very good at darning?"

"The housekeeper says I'll pass, miss."

Lila put her hand in her pocket and came up with the floral

button. Jonathan looked merely impatient, nothing more. Lila held her hand out to the maid, her heart thumping painfully hard. "I found this just now. I think I should hand it to you, in case you are missing it."

Ellen took the button in her hand and her face brightened. "Oh, yes, miss. It's from my lord's best coat. I've been looking for days, thinking we'd have to replace all of them nice buttons with some plain ones." She looked genuinely pleased.

And it would all have been fine. Jonathan looked nothing but disgusted at this interchange between Lila and a mere servant, except . . . except that Lila couldn't help it. Before she could stop herself, she turned her face and looked triumphantly at Jonathan. It was gone in a second, but the damage was done.

His face froze. His eyes flickered to the button that was in Ellen's hand and then back at Lila's face. Lila had the time to school her face now, but it was too late.

Ivor was holding out his hand. "We should go."

"Of course," Lila said.

She walked to Ivor. They walked down the stairs together, Jonathan following. In the foyer, he gave them a little bow. "Pleasure, Mr. Tristram. Lila. Do come back any time." Then he stood watching them leave, as if he wanted to make sure they were gone.

20

"It's his button," she said as they walked away from the house, both walking fast, not pausing.

"Yes."

"He knows we know."

"Yes."

They walked down the familiar street, a street Lila had consciously avoided for some years now. Lined with pretty terraced houses. A fashionable street, not so much in the heart of the city as to be bothered with its hustle and bustle, but near enough that it gave access to the best parties. Not that there were any parties when she was growing up. She remembered days sitting in her bedchamber upstairs, staring out of the window at this very street, the rain curling teardrops down the windowpane. She would place her palms on the inside and look out, wondering how soon she could escape, wondering, planning, thinking things out, making sure she knew how to get by in the world alone.

She had gotten into this habit when she first went away to school. She suddenly remembered it viscerally now. The stagecoach would drop her on the main road when she came back for the holidays. She would walk up the street toward the Marleigh house, portmanteau swinging in her hand. She imagined that people watched her from behind the windows, gawked, whispered behind their hands. "The Earl's bastard," they whispered. "Looks like him. Or do you think she looks like— you know—the slut?" She imagined that was what they said about her and her sisters. She pictured the twitching curtains.

She would walk all the way up to the house, head held high. She would climb up the steps to the front door. There, she would stop, set down her portmanteau, turn her back to the door, and make a flourishing bow.

To the imaginary gallery of watchers. To no one in particular. Or to the entire neighborhood. A bow that thumbed her nose to the world and its expectations. She suddenly remembered it now, that mocking bow. A bow, perhaps, that she had never stopped making.

Ivor handed her up to his carriage. Then climbed in after her. "That was hard for you," he said abruptly, almost coldly.

She was surprised at the harsh voice. "Yes." He was searching her face, so she added, "Old memories. They can feel like festering wounds sometimes."

"Yes."

They stared at each other in silence for a few seconds. It was as if his fingertips had reached out and touched hers, even though neither of them had moved. She broke the silence, feeling slightly breathless for some reason. "Would you take me to my house, Ivor?" She felt self-conscious using his name. But she didn't take it back. She hoped she wasn't looking at him too defiantly. In any case, he didn't seem surprised.

The carriage moved away from Jonathan's house. She felt she breathed easier once they turned the corner from that street. The air seemed lighter.

"You'll come back later?" he asked. "To my place?"

She couldn't help looking a little surprised, not at the question, but at the slightly diffident note in his voice. She could swear she felt a trickle of wetness just at that voice. She had never seen him look at her like that. She wondered if many people had. Or anyone, come to that. The assured, imperious note was gone—for now.

"Yes." Maisie and Sunil were coming back later, and of course, she would have to be there, to discuss what had just happened in Jonathan's house. But that look on his face, it would be easier to stick pins into the balls of her feet than to resist that look or to deny it. The eyes that lingered on her face, they had their usual thoughtful, slightly preoccupied, expression, as if he had a lot to do and think about, but they had something new, a questioning look that was likely as new to him as to her.

But then she remembered. "Oh no!" she said suddenly, placing a hand on her cheek. "In a fit of madness, I promised Kenneth that I would accompany him to Vauxhall Gardens tonight. At least, it wasn't a fit of madness, but my life seems to have turned on its head and I don't know where I am from moment to moment. I shall have to cry off. He will hate me, because I am almost certain there is someone he has his eye on who will be there." She was genuinely distressed. Normally, she had the kind of mind that remembered appointments—dates and times—with no need for an appointment diary. If she had five different engagements in a day, she could keep track of all of them. But not at the moment, it seemed. And Kenneth, though he was never ill-bred enough to be angry, would be bitterly disappointed. She *did* promise him. "I had better tell him I can't make it," she said abstractedly.

"Don't do that," Ivor said, somewhat to her surprise.

She looked inquiringly at him.

"I've been thinking that it's a risk for Maisie and Sunil to come to my house again, so soon after their first visit. We don't know who will be watching their movements and put two and two together. Especially after what happened in Whitechapel." He had that thoughtful look that he had when he was working things out in his head. "Vauxhall Gardens could be a neat solution. People will be dressed for a social evening, many in masquerade, not to mention that we are likely to mingle with all classes in the pleasure gardens. A Runner is unlikely to disturb us. Would you mind too much if I sent them a note to ask if they could join us there?"

There was that slightly diffident note again, as if he would be sorry if she said no, as though *he* wanted to take her to Vauxhall Gardens. She had forgotten all about Vauxhall in the recent whirlwind, but now, at the thought of spending the evening with Ivor, wearing masks and hoods and losing themselves in a mass of laughing people, she shivered. "I wouldn't mind," she said simply.

He looked pleased at her answer. They drove in silence for a minute or two, then he asked about her salons. She thought he was being polite and keeping up the conversation—after all, however irascible he could be with her at times, no one could deny that the man had manners—but to her surprise, he asked her if she enjoyed them, if she found them wearying, if she was used to the strange hours she kept or if they bothered her. It was as though he really wanted to know.

She was surprised to see that she wanted to tell him; she also reflected that no one else ever asked her about what she liked or didn't like. To the people in her salons, she was just a hostess—a glittering one, a sociable one, but hardly one whose feelings mattered. Even men who had a passing *tendresse* for her and could occasionally be considerate, like Henry Alston, didn't think to ask her about herself. Even someone she thought of as her friend, someone like Annabel Wakefield—she did sometimes remember to ask how Lila was, but even she, Lila could not help thinking, probably had her reasons to be kind. It was a new feeling, and she didn't know exactly what to do with it. She found herself taking on her sociable mantle, because to tell him how weary she sometimes felt with the constant pressure to be a social—and therefore professional—success was unthinkable.

She entertained him with stories of her guests' exploits instead. Lady Crowther's expanding menagerie was always a good topic for conversation. Lady Crowther, who lived only two streets away, owned a blue-faced monkey, brought all the way from the Far East to be her special pet, second only in her estimation to her cockatoo procured for her from the Amazon and the ruby necklace gifted to her by the maharajah of somewhere. Lila chippered on about them all. He was listening.

She found herself asking him in turn about his work, his estate, and he told her about some of the modern ideas he was trying to implement on the land. When he saw that she wanted to know more, he went into more detail, and she was happy to note that he didn't give her superficial or watered-down explanations. She couldn't help thinking that they hadn't spent such an easy twenty minutes in each other's company before.

"I'm sure any modern innovations will cause a sensation," she said.

"You like to cause a sensation, don't you?" he asked, looking a little sardonic. "Amateur theatricals, riding astride in the park, driving with a groom who wears a silk eye mask in broad daylight?"

She bit her lip. She hesitated, then almost defiantly, she told him something most people didn't know. "My groom, Roger. He has burn marks around his eyes from an old injury. He was used to hiding them as he was growing up. But . . ." She shrugged. "I've learned from Kenneth not to hide. People are good at ferreting out secrets and they almost invariably hold them against you—or so Kenneth says. Kenneth and I have been friends for so long—ever since we met in Vauxhall, in fact, when I was twenty and very stupid—and I have learned over time that though he is wrong about all manner of things, he is almost always right about how society works. It is perhaps better to wear your secrets with style, if not pride. I try to follow that maxim where possible. And I teach my staff the same."

He looked a little surprised. "Your other staff too, not just your groom?"

"Some of them. It's nothing really. My maid—Hannah—has a slight limp. She never thought anyone would hire her, not as a lady's maid, not where the household, let alone a guest, could see her. One of the maids—Bettina—has never been able to see properly but finds her way around magnificently with her hands and her hearing, which is better than anyone's I've ever known. I swear sometimes she knows someone is about to knock on our door when they have barely turned onto our street. And Walsham, he would freeze me out for a month if he knew I was telling you that his knuckles are permanently bent with arthritis, but the things the man can do with just his right eyebrow—let's just say, he makes people *quake*. Especially me."

He was quiet for some time. She couldn't help watching the side of his face, wondering what he was thinking. She felt strangely exposed. As if she had turned herself inside out and now didn't know how to turn herself back the right way again. And wondering if she should not have told him. She didn't normally tell anyone. Not that anyone ever thought to ask about the people that worked in her house.

"No one else would hire them," he said plainly.

"They are excellent at their work," she said defensively.

"Good of you."

"No!" she said quickly. "There is no good reason these people should not have work. They are loyal to the bone. And work harder than most other people. Harder than I ask them to." She was pressing her hands together. She wanted him to understand. "It isn't that I am kinder to them than anyone else. I just care less what people think. Or I'm selfish and do it to look even more eccentric. Please don't make it out that I—"

He stopped her by placing a hand on her hands, which were clenched in her lap. He didn't say anything. Just kept his hand there. They sat in silence again. They weren't exactly looking at one another, but Lila had the strange feeling that he was glancing at her when she was looking down at their hands, and when she looked up at his face, at those times he wasn't always looking at her.

Lila had the time to think that no one should have to sit in a carriage alone, that sitting with someone who held your hand, that was the only way to sit in a carriage at all.

"I must disentangle Tiffany from Beddington." Those were his next abrupt words.

His face was so grim, she instinctively untangled her own hands and squeezed his. Now it was his turn to look surprised. He stared down at her hands as if no one had ever given him a reassuring squeeze before. For heaven's sake.

"Not used to someone looking out for you, Ivor?" she murmured.

"I'm used to looking after myself." His voice was a little stiff.

She couldn't help a spark of irritation at that tone, so insular and sure, his usual Ivor Tristram tone. She withdrew her hands.

"I will see you in a few hours then," she said, trying to keep her tone light, "and we can think what to do next. For now, I have to get changed and keep an appointment with Kenneth to drive in Hampstead Heath."

He was frowning. "Don't tell me you plan to run that race to Brighton."

She had forgotten all about the infernal race. But she bristled at the tone. Really, just when you started to mellow under the man's warmth and perception. "Why shouldn't I?"

"To make that much of a spectacle?"

He may as well have added *even for you.* Her brow creased. Why shouldn't she make a spectacle of herself if she chose? And in any case, just because there was—something—between them, a growing closeness or just a passing warmth, didn't mean he had the right to tell her what she could or couldn't do, or the right to get affronted if she made a scandal of herself. "Kenneth is my old driving teacher. He taught me all I know about driving a curricle. We try to practice at least twice a month. He says it's the only way to keep me from getting *cack handed.*" She smoothed her skirt. "I admit I am rather good at driving."

He smiled abstractedly at the cheeky and slightly challenging look she gave him. But he didn't say anything. She felt that the easy mood between them had broken. As if he had withdrawn. Because of the damned race? What was making him look like that, like he had backed off and disappeared somewhere where she couldn't follow? She wanted to get it back, the warmth between them. But she was irritated with him too.

"Do you have a lot to do this afternoon?" she asked, watching him from under her eyelashes.

He mentioned some letters he had to write to his mother and agent. She asked—hesitantly—if his mother was very ill. He nodded and said that she was and that he meant to spend a few months down at the estate to be with her at the end, once his business in town was over.

She couldn't help it. Her heart twisted at his words. His business. The business with Jonathan, with Sunil, his cousin Tiffany and his other interests. And what of Lila Marleigh? Was she business too? Or was she not even that? And when he was done with her, would he turn around and go home where he belonged? She shivered a little at what had happened between them in his study, earlier today. The way he looked at her, as though he didn't want to miss a flicker of expression on her face. The way he sometimes seemed to sense things behind her casual words that she didn't think anyone could read. She wondered if she would miss those annoying probing eyes when she couldn't see them anymore. She wondered if she would miss the imperious way he asked her not to make a spectacle of herself.

Maybe, when he was done with his business in town, he would be done with her too. He would come back next month or next year, another season, and hardly know her. Or even see her. She felt suddenly that it would be easier not to see him at all, than for him to be a stranger.

He didn't seem to be aware he had said anything odd. *Had* he said anything odd? Why would he stay in London just for her? He found her desirable, lots of men did. She had an awareness in her, an awareness of her femininity, her sexuality, that drew men to her, she knew that. Or maybe it was her vivacity or that she was genuinely interested in people. But more than that? No one seemed to feel more than desire. As if there could be more to her beneath her laughing voice and ready smiles. No one asked to see the heart or the passion, and certainly not the vulnerability, not the unspoken longing to be held and cherished. No one asked to see her soul.

She withdrew into her corner. She stole a glance at him.

He was just sitting there, silent and frowning, still far away from her, and then startled her with his abrupt question. "Did my father—was he—did he—?"

Abrupt, yet he couldn't think how to complete it, it seemed. Her heart broke with that half-uttered question.

"He has never bothered me. I know how to take care of myself, and I know how to handle men like . . ." She stopped. It seemed a half question could only evoke a half response.

He flinched slightly, involuntarily, but he didn't say anything.

That thing twisted in her chest again. She turned her face away and looked out through the window, wondering how they had gone—within a few short minutes—from being completely at ease with each other to . . . this.

At her door, he said goodbye. And he looked abstracted. As though his mind was already on other things. He didn't linger. Just as he was turning away, she said, "Thank you so much for the ride, Mr. Tristram! You are so kind!"

He looked in surprise at her cheerful tone. Loud, resonant, her hostess voice. He looked for a second as if he might say something, but then he merely nodded and left.

And she turned to go in, wondering why thunderous clouds had come galloping into the afternoon now. And how she would dispel them, not just for the curricle drive with Kenneth, not just for the evening at Vauxhall Gardens, but in a few days, when they might have sorted out the mess that Maisie and Sunil were in, and Ivor would be free to leave town.

21

The visit to Jonathan Marleigh's home had brought back old memories that Lila normally kept safely tucked away. That she was good at suppressing. Only in her nightmares, when she tried and tried to wake up but couldn't, did she sometimes feel the terror of lying awake in the Marleigh house in the dead of night and feeling utterly and infinitely alone. Only in those dreaded hours did she ever go back to her childhood. But the visit to that house had done something and a heavy gloom hung over her. What was it about that place? She had turned up there at age seven, having recently lost her parents. She turned up there with two of her sisters.

She stood at her window twenty minutes after Ivor Tristram had left her at her door, clutching her throat at the memory. And Sarah Marleigh with those strange, glittering, resentful eyes looked the girls up and down and curled her mouth. "Look, Jonathan," she said, "this is what kept your father so busy for so many years." Jonathan was seventeen at the time, but in that moment, Lila had thought he couldn't be more than thirteen or fourteen. The hair was pale, the face cold, the eyes expressionless. "Oh, cheer up, darling," Sarah Marleigh said to him. "Greet your sisters with a kiss." She made him kiss each of their cheeks.

Lila squeezed her eyes shut now at the memory. At all the memories of those lonely years. If only, if only she and Mira and Anya had teamed up, worked together, even just spoken about how they felt living there. But they already had a bond sealed by guilt that wedged itself between them. Grief and guilt.

Lila flicked a hand harshly away from her. Lila had walked into a room once, when she was about fourteen or so, and Mira just twelve. She had walked into the room and Jonathan was in the bedchamber. Mira was sitting on the bed, at the edge of it and Jonathan next to her, his hand on the inside curve of her thigh. Lila didn't say anything, didn't kick him, punch him or kill him. She stood there, mute with loathing, until he nonchalantly got to his feet and left the room. Lila never spoke to Mira about that.

And the one question that often plagued her. Why did Sarah Marleigh bother? There was not one bit of Sarah that could have wanted Jonathan Marleigh's bastards living in her house. And yes, she had gotten rid of the girls as soon as she could, sent each one off to boarding school when she turned eleven. But why had she invited them to London to live with her in the first place? Sarah was dead now, and Lila didn't know if she would ever find the answer. Sometimes she wondered if Anya or Mira might know, or guess what was behind it. Oh, she and Mira and Anya had a lot to talk about. A lot to discuss. But there was never a good time. The chasm was too deep.

TWO HOURS LATER, after a spanking ride in Kenneth's curricle, looking flushed and happy, she handed the reins back to her teacher. Thank goodness for friends. And thank goodness for horses. The distress of the morning, the horrible memories of the Marleigh House, weighed less heavily on her shoulders.

Kenneth was nattily dressed in a lavender coat and buff trousers, looking neat as a pin. *Her* hair was everywhere after that drive but his looked hardly ruffled.

"You drive beautifully," he said graciously. He couldn't help giving her a tip or two, which she accepted, quizzing him on one or two points but resolving to do better.

He maneuvered the curricle and his matching chestnuts into a sun-dappled path lined with sessile oaks and tall beeches, and they drove much more sedately. Lila felt she could curl up in a corner and go to sleep in the sunshine like a cat. She yawned.

"Not sleeping?" Kenneth asked, lifting an eyebrow.

"Not much."

"Did you find the person you were looking for, in the rat pit, by the by? I never got the chance to ask. You disappeared without a trace that night."

"I left a message with your groom that I was leaving by hackney cab!"

"Yes, very thoughtful. It would have been more thoughtful if I had found that out *before* I spent half the night looking for you in the tavern, wondering if I would find your remains in the rat pit or in some forgotten alcove, having been nibbled to death by one of the terriers. Or worse, one of the men." He shuddered. "It was not at all the thing. I found the whole event gory beyond belief. But *did* you find the person?"

"Yes." She frowned so hard that he was moved to ask her more.

"I can't remember the half of what you told me. But you wanted to help her. Did you?" he asked lazily, as if he probably wouldn't bother listening to the answer.

"I let her down once a long time ago. I'm damned if I let

her down again." She repeated a little of Annie Quinn's story. She had told him the other day, the morning after Maisie first came to her house. But she was sure he hadn't been listening. He was probably not listening now. But he surprised her.

"Her mother was hanged for a crime she didn't commit," he said thoughtfully. "And now her fella seems as though *he's* going to be hanged for a crime he didn't commit. The girl seems to have rotten luck."

She frowned. "Yes, she does, doesn't she?"

His words troubled her, but she couldn't place exactly how. Maybe it was because of her own guilt. Because she couldn't save Annie Quinn and now, now—what if she couldn't save Sunil either? Was that what was troubling her?

"What is that thing that repeats over and over in your life? I'm almost sure it comes from the name of a Greek goddess—most things do."

She had no idea what he was talking about. She mostly didn't. He was right though. Wasn't it too horribly ill-fated what was happening to Maisie?

"You know, there are bets being placed about your chances of winning a race you haven't fully entered yet." Kenneth's words broke into her thoughts.

Not the dratted race again. "It'll pass. People will get over it. You're the one supposed to be racing whatever his name is—Herrington's nephew—not me."

"Hmm, if only people were convinced of that," he murmured. They passed by a bunch of kids racing each other and holding bunches of string above their heads. They yelled and giggled, and Kenneth waved at them as if he was the Queen. "I say do it. Set everyone's tongues wagging. You could do with creating a scene like that to pick up numbers in your salons."

"I hate the salons."

Kenneth was used to her thoughts on the salons and didn't say anything, but let her have a rant about the guests, the permanent ringing in her ears, the wide-awake early mornings.

"You're so good at them," he said languidly, niftily moving the curricle, with hardly a break in speed, around a bend, "that one must ask, *do* you hate them so much—or are you simply in the habit of thinking you hate them? A bit like the *ton*—one can't help loathing it, yet one can't live without it. One almost thinks one would miss it like an old wound that one is used to scratching."

"Of course, I hate the salons."

"Yes, but do you?" he persisted in his indolent voice. "In any case, that is neither here nor there. We were discussing a small matter of a race to Brighton. Stop trying to distract me. I swear there is no one whose mind runs in as many different directions as you. It is not at all relaxing."

"I don't need to distract you since you're so good at doing it yourself. Ivor—I mean, Mr. Tristram—said I'd make a spectacle of myself if I ran it, that it would cause a sensation with Roger standing behind the curricle with his eye mask on." She bit her lip, hoping he hadn't noticed the slip. She glanced in his direction. It seemed that he hadn't.

"As I say," he said, "don't hide. Flaunt instead. You can have an enormous dowry or a title and then it doesn't matter how you look or what you do. But if you have neither—and not even birth—then there is no hope but to be outrageous. And, let me tell you, you are good at *that* too. Quite subtle about it, as if you really don't care what people think. I envy you sometimes. I feel as though other people's opinions are *all* I care about. Especially in the middle of the night when I feel like I am drowning in my own bed. It must be nice to be like you and not care about other people."

She glanced sideways at him. She couldn't help thinking that his life couldn't be easy. That other people's opinions must hurt him much more than they ever hurt her. But Kenneth wasn't one to pick apart and discuss his life, not even with his closest friend. Despite the easy garrulity, there was something intensely private there. She opened her mouth to say something, but he interrupted, as she had half known he would. "I am talking, of course, in complete generalities, Lila," he said, looking casual, yet sounding firm, "so do let's not make a thing of it."

She accepted this—she knew him—and sat looking ahead. She let out a sigh. But didn't know exactly what she was sighing *at*, so didn't follow it up with any words. Whatever he implied about himself, was Kenneth right about her? Did she really not care what people thought? Not *anyone*? And yet what of love? Did she care that there was no love in her life? She sighed again.

They were driving at a steady speed. "Ivor?" he said, so casually that she nearly fell off her seat.

She sat straighter, looking indignant, and primly placed her hands in her lap.

He was glancing sideways at her. But he didn't say anything. She pursed her lips. She didn't need to say anything nor defend herself. She really didn't.

"We have met once or twice," she said angrily. "What of it?"

"Why, nothing, darling. It is interesting, that is all."

"Why, because why would someone like him want to spend time with me?" she flung at him.

"Lila, darling, don't bite my head off just because your drawers are wet for a *man*. *I* have always said some man would be lucky to have you. It is only you who thinks that no one will. Has he?"

"Has he what?"

"Had you."

"Take care that I don't punch you and topple you off your seat!" She looked fiercely ahead. "I know what men think when they look at me. And to tell you the truth, I don't care." She was glaring now.

He was glancing at her. She could feel his glance.

"What?" she said irritably.

"Lila, m'dear. Do brush your prickly bristles away. I am not trying to tease you. But now and again it doesn't hurt to let your barricades down and let someone enter."

"I don't have my barricades up, thank you very much."

He let it go at that and went back to trying to make casual lighthearted conversation and didn't seem to mind too much when she answered him in curt monosyllables for the rest of the journey.

22

"Are there any particular cakes that Miss Marleigh is partial to, sir?"

"How the devil . . . ?" He stopped himself. He lowered the glass of brandy that he had been about to sip from. "My apologies, Mrs. Manfield. You were saying?" Though he knew damned well what his housekeeper was saying. It seemed the entire household was saying the same thing.

She sedately repeated the question about the cakes. Ivor honestly said that he didn't have the blindest idea what cakes Miss Marleigh liked, or if she liked cake at all. He was about to add that he didn't *care* what cake she liked, and then found himself wondering if she would like a solid fruit cake. A crumbling ratafia biscuit? Or something moist like a rum cake?

Good God.

He glanced a little crossly at his housekeeper. She was clearing away the dinner things—he had asked for an early and light dinner so he could be off to Vauxhall immediately after. He couldn't help it. He couldn't help feeling—excited wasn't the right word. Anticipatory. Curious. Mildly interested. Yes, more like that. He was in a mild state of vaguely pleasurable anticipation at the thought of seeing Lila at Vauxhall.

Cakes! How the devil was he to know if Lila liked cakes? As it was, he couldn't seem to spend ten minutes with her without them bristling at each other like cats. If he made a cake of himself asking what kind of pudding she preferred, no doubt that would turn into a full-scale battle too.

Mrs. Manfield took some things out of the dining room.

He couldn't help it. Sitting there, at the dinner table with his brandy, he couldn't help hearing again the little noises Lila was making in her throat earlier that day, when she was perched on the desk in his study. He stirred at the sudden, visceral memory, as if she was there in the room with him now. Perched on the dining table, her legs apart, her hips open and inviting, her head thrust back. The animal noises of pleasure, pain, and longing that she made. Noises he felt would live in his very cells for the rest of his life, and noises that he would never tire of hearing. The way she looked at him—the way she *was* looking at him when she was sitting on his desk—a look of abandon, yet a look of yearning that tugged at his heart.

He took a shaky breath. He couldn't wait for the evening to be over—it hadn't started yet, it was true—so he could place her on that desk again. Or maybe the sofa this time. Or maybe even . . .

But then he frowned. The carriage ride. They were talking to each other easily, hardly self-conscious, not at odds, without their usual misunderstandings and mutual lack of trust. And then something happened to break that. What happened? He had to search his memory, because the feeling of discord had left more of an imprint than the conversation itself. What was it they were talking about? The damned Brighton race?

It was his father. Of course, it was. No, even before then. It was Jonathan Marleigh's swollen lip. He gripped the dining table. It was all Ivor could do not to launch himself at the man when he saw that thick lip. *What* did he do to Lila that had made her punch him? He had meant to ask her. Yet, instead, an awkward and impertinent question had popped out, about his father.

Why in hell did he ask her that? *What* was he trying to ask? Did his father force his attentions on her?

Dear God, did he want to know?

Even the thought made him violently nauseous. And she answered it just as the question deserved, by informing Ivor that she could look after herself. Which only made him madder. Mad at himself for asking the question, for putting her and himself in that horrible place again, and madder still at his father, or maybe at himself, and maybe at Lila, because even though he was sure his rage was directed mainly at men like Jonathan Marleigh and his father Benjamin Tristram, yet, *yet* he couldn't help feeling some rage at Lila, for being quite so—quite so desirable. What man *could* look at her, the way she spoke, the way she looked, her independence, the stubborn pride, the hiding of any vulnerability, the yearning in her, *how* could anyone look at her and not want her?

Mrs. Manfield came back into the room as he was sitting there staring somewhat blankly, yet ferociously, in front of him. She instructed the footman—George—to clear away things from the side cabinet. George did as he was told and left the room, tottering under a load of silver platters.

And then it turned out that she—Lila Marleigh—employed people who limped, or couldn't see, or had scars. She would do that. It was exactly the kind of thing she would do. Employ people others didn't employ, stand about talking to street urchins and prostitutes in Whitechapel, run races that no one would allow their sisters or daughters to run—would find it scandalous if their sisters or daughters even considered it. Yes, Lila Marleigh would do exactly those things.

"It is as you said," he said to Mrs. Manfield, apropos of nothing. "As you *and* Tiffany said, I am hardly known for . . ." Now he had no idea what to say. He sat there frowning. What was he trying to say?

"Known for what, sir?" Mrs. Manfield prodded.

Her gray curls were neat as ever, and hardly a crease in her black dress, yet the woman had a motherly twinkle in her eye. Why could his staff not mind their own business?

He flicked his head irritably. "For my relationships with women."

Mrs. Manfield hid a smile—which irritated him even more. "Most men are waiting for one woman, sir. You don't need twenty. Most men don't, that is."

He was a little startled. "What?" he said stupidly. He cleared his throat. "I mean, I beg your pardon, Mrs. Manfield?"

George came back in and she handed him some more platters. Told him off for a scuff mark on his shoe and told him that—once he was done with the platters—he could get a bowl of soup in the kitchen. He grinned, touched his forehead toward Ivor, and then scurried out of the room.

Mrs. Manfield turned back to Ivor. "Some men have a series of women, sir, if you don't mind my being blunt. Others have one now and again in their life, thinking that that is all they want. But they are really—without knowing it—waiting for one woman. The right one, sir." She was looking almost kindly at him, as if she was talking to someone a little stupid. "They're waiting for the one who makes them . . . find their own place in the world. And stop fighting."

"Fighting?"

"The world, perhaps, sir, or perhaps even fighting themselves."

"Fighting themselves!"

"Strange how many men do that, sir. Themselves, their emotions, anything that can make them feel." She was looking kindly at him. "Sometimes it takes a woman, sir, if you don't mind me saying, for a man to stop running away from himself."

Dear God.

23

Despite the afternoon at Jonathan Marleigh's house, despite the anxiety she felt about Sunil's precarious situation, Lila couldn't help a shiver of delight. It was a mild evening, yet there was the whisper of a cool breeze that tickled the warm dampness of her neck, the top of her breasts, and her bare arms. She wasn't wearing a mask. She wore a sea-green dress of silk embroidered in gold thread, tied with a gold sash, and a short light summer cloak made of red lace that was so fine it was almost not there.

After the awkwardness of the carriage ride earlier in the day, she had chosen to meet Ivor in Vauxhall, instead of accepting the offer of a ride. But now she was glad that she had. Meeting him like this, in the spangled lights of Vauxhall, both dressed for a social evening, it was secretive and special and exciting, and they both grinned when they saw each other. She couldn't help impulsively putting her hands in his and he lifted them to his lips. The awkwardness evaporated like mist.

They headed to the rotunda. She couldn't help feeling they were a couple of children who had been given an unexpected treat. There were people everywhere, and the gardens were studded with a jeweled sea of lights, and Lila heard laughter, the shrieks, the sudden puffs of people who fell out of bushes and alcoves, but she was aware mainly of Ivor, the backs of their fingers brushing each other, sometimes entangling, making her shake, not with the cold, but with something else, something that filled her body and made her forget why she was really here. She felt as if every cell in her body was aware of him. She was tingling when he touched her, or glanced at her. He grinned suddenly again, and she couldn't help laughing.

"You know, I wasn't sure you'd come," he said.

"I said I would."

He was laughing. Lila couldn't help a shiver at the sound of that easy laughter and the face that rarely relaxed like this.

Kenneth Laudsley met them in the rotunda. The two men eyed each other a little warily.

"I suppose you intend to steal my date right from under my nose and not even apologize for it," Kenneth said mildly.

"That is exactly what I intend to do," Ivor said, good-humoredly enough, but there was no mistaking the proprietorial tone.

Lila was sure she should resent that tone—how dare he?—except she felt instead a shiver of pleasure. She was hoping she wouldn't giggle. Or beg Ivor Tristram to haul her over his shoulder and carry her off to the nearest alcove. As it was, Kenneth handed her a glass of ratafia, and she gulped down most of it. She giggled.

Ivor gave her his smile, the one she was already starting to think was hers alone. She turned to Kenneth. "Don't tell me you want me to hang on your arm half the evening. It will cramp your style."

"Well, no, Lila darling, but as one knows, if one is seen

with one eligible person, the other eligible people only want one more. No one wants someone who is alone and lonesome."

"I am a mere prop then! How dare you, sir." She hiccuped. She placed her fingers on her lips.

"I am about to steal your companion for a dance, Mr. Laudsley," Ivor said. "Hopefully your credit will stand it."

Kenneth mock bowed. "Save a dance for me, minx," he whispered in passing. "And don't do anything I wouldn't do."

"If I did only *half* of what you would do!" she said, crossly, as she was almost pulled into the throng.

The oaks and elms that circled the rotunda were lit with lanterns. But the rotunda was a cram of people. It was so bright and so full of laughing, dancing people that it was blinding. There was a band playing at one end and couples dancing. She was in Ivor's arms, and they were dancing the waltz. She had no idea if it was the ratafia or the lights or the noise but as she twirled and swayed in his arms, all she saw were his eyes. She was a river of light, a universe of feeling.

After the dancing, everyone flocked outside to watch the hot-air balloon, and Lila, after another glass of ratafia that seemed to magic itself out of nowhere, with Ivor on one side, and Kenneth, with his friend Jeremy Ashton on the other, felt as though she would lift with the balloon and fly away if she didn't watch out. She eyed Kenneth and Jeremy Ashton. The man was as dark as Kenneth was fair. In fact, she was sure he had some Mediterranean or even African blood in him. He was medium height, and powerful-looking—not powerful like Ivor, with his muscles and stern look, but easygoing. Kenneth looked older than his twenty-six years. She thought Jeremy was about the same age, but had such a relaxed, *peaceful* look that he looked younger. She couldn't help noticing the way the two men stood close, yet not too close to each other, their hands almost touching. She glanced to her other side at Ivor and hoped, really hoped, he wouldn't be offended by Kenneth and Jeremy. But he didn't look offended.

"Now that Laudsley has found a friend, maybe I can whisk you off."

"To one of the bushes?" she murmured. Then she blushed. She hadn't meant to say that.

He laughed. "Later. For now, let's go and find that pair of no-goods before they get themselves into any more trouble."

She bit her lip guiltily. She had almost forgotten about Maisie and Sunil.

They turned from the crowd that was still watching the balloon. Ivor had asked Maisie and Sunil to meet them in the tent near the balloon ascent. There was, if possible, an even larger and noisier crowd of people inside the tent than at the rotunda. She complained that there was no way they would find anyone in the mass. Ivor gave her hand a squeeze. "Look, can you stay here for a minute and don't move? That way you could keep an eye on the entrance, and I shall make a round of the tent."

"Of course."

He was off. She stared in a daze all around her. There was an aquarium at the other end of the tent, and just between the shoulders of people she caught glimpses of a tiny acrobat who wore a scaly, glittering costume. He was performing impossible contortions in the tank, his scaly costume shimmering, the audience nearly fainting at the sight.

Then there was someone at her elbow. It was Henry Alston. She blinked stupidly a few times, trying to reconcile him with this moment.

"Oh, Mr. Alston! It's good to see you. I'm too mesmerized to notice anything in particular at the moment. And," she leaned toward his ear, "I may have had a glass or two of ratafia."

He smiled in pleasure. He looked very nicely turned out. With those chestnut curls of his and those wide-open hazel eyes. "I am delighted I spotted you, Miss Marleigh. Don't tell me Mr. Laudsley has deserted you."

"Oh no, he's around," she said absently.

She was still scanning the crowd, almost automatically, keeping an eye out for a sight of Maisie and Sunil.

"Miss Marleigh, you know I have been waiting for an opportunity to speak with you."

She turned to look at him in surprise. It was as if she had already forgotten he was there. She had—in the madness of the last couple of days—forgotten Henry Alston altogether. He was just like a boy, with that painfully eager look on his face. Painfully eager and dreadfully determined.

"Dear Mr. Alston," she said quickly, "let me stop you right there."

"Don't stop me," he said, just as quickly. "I can't help thinking you know what I want to say. Miss Marleigh, I am sure you will have any number of objections, the chief one being my age, but I want you to give me the opportunity to show you . . ."

She made herself focus on him. As it was, she was intensely distracted by everything going on around her. It was overwhelming. She felt that parts of her were drifting off into the noise, the lights, the crowd, the chatter. "Henry," she said gently, "if I said something about your age, I would be right. You know—"

"I know my mind," he said, his mouth tight. "Please, Miss Marleigh, give me a chance to speak to you." She didn't think he was totally conscious of what he was doing, but he clasped both her hands in his. It was hardly a violent grip, but it was surprisingly firm. His voice was full of passion. "And I—I am wealthy, I don't gamble. It isn't simply that you are the most beautiful woman I have ever met. It isn't just that. When I look at you, I see someone full of life and vitality, so strong, who doesn't need anyone!"

She almost laughed. "Henry don't put me on a pedestal. I'm hopelessly weak. I will squirm myself to death from needing— needing I don't even know what." She desperately wanted him to understand, to stop talking nonsense, to find someone his own age. Most of all, she thought, with some sad self-reflection, she didn't want to have to think about him at all. She managed to squeeze her hands out from between his and instead held his hands. "Henry, listen to me, you *think* you like me. It's natural at your age. I quite understand! But . . ."

She was conscious of something, someone next to them. She turned her head and saw Ivor, with Maisie and Sunil behind him. She pulled her hands away from Henry Alston. Ivor's face was hard, his eyes glittering. And he was looking not at Lila but at Henry Alston.

"I must go and join some friends, Henry, Mr. Alston," she said, keeping a bright smile on her face. "I will see you tomorrow at my salon, I hope?"

He was looking defiantly at Ivor. "Of course, Miss Marleigh," he said, giving her a stiff little bow. "I wouldn't miss it."

He took his leave. Lila greeted Maisie and Sunil, and the four of them made their way out of the tent, leaving the crowd to sigh over the contortionist in the aquarium. Outside, Ivor pointed them in the direction of some lanes bordered on both sides by lantern-lit elms and the group turned in that direction, Maisie and Sunil walking a little ahead and Ivor and Lila a few steps behind. Lila glanced at Ivor's set face.

"He's very young," she started.

"You encourage him."

She bristled at once. "Just because I'm *nice*—"

"Is it so wrong of me to suggest that you don't give false hope to a boy who—"

"You're jealous!"

He stopped. So abruptly that she nearly tripped over herself. He caught at her arm and briefly, stunningly, kissed her hard on the lips. "Yes. I am."

She stared at him. He was staring right back into her eyes, searching she didn't know for what, but strangely, she had never felt this near him. "Ivor . . ."

He placed a hand for a moment on her back and looked down into her face. "Let's not fight."

"Then don't be annoying," she said, half teasing, half yearning.

His mouth relaxed at her words. "Come on," he said.

They were at one of the paths on which many couples and groups strolled and there was no opportunity to say any more. She found herself shivering a little at that fierce light in his face. What would she do when he left London and she couldn't see him anymore? She felt it would break her in two, and she wished for a second, futilely and yet desperately, that she had never met him, never set eyes on him. That he had never reminded her that there was no one in her life who minded—or cared—whom she spoke to and how she spoke to them, what she did with her time and how she did it. That he hadn't cracked her in two and reminded her of all her missing parts.

24

The four of them fell into place. It was obvious there was a mismatch, of course. Ivor and Lila dressed in their silk and lace and Sunil and Maisie in their homespun. But in the mad bustle of Vauxhall, which seemed to brim and simmer with secrets, Ivor hoped it wouldn't matter, wouldn't make them too conspicuous. If people they passed—of all classes—gave them curious looks, then their group wasn't the only curious sight in Vauxhall. Sunil and Maisie were wearing eye masks, as were many people in the gardens. Maybe that would give them some anonymity.

Quickly and succinctly, Ivor and Lila filled Maisie and Sunil in on what had happened at Jonathan Marleigh's residence earlier in the afternoon.

When the story was told, Maisie as usual saw no reason why they were all here in Vauxhall, pretending to have a nice evening, when they knew who attacked Ivor's cousin. Why weren't they clearing Sunil's name? Why were they walking here, casual as you please, like gape-eyed gudgeons of the first order?

Ivor couldn't help a glance at Lila. She was wearing a dress the color of the sea and a lace cloak so fine it was more tempting than if she weren't wearing it. He felt the strong desire to peel everything off her, layer by layer. A dreadful urge to claim her and possess her so that stupid boys like Henry Alston wouldn't dare touch her. Did she have to look at everyone, *everyone* with that wide, clear-eyed gaze? With so much warmth and sympathy that no one could help wanting to stay in her glow forever? The gaze he sometimes found defiantly independent and other times so full of need that he couldn't resist it. He resisted the need to pull her roughly to him again.

He lifted his eyes to look at Maisie. But before he could answer her question, Lila spoke.

"What can we do?" she said urgently. She looked at Maisie, then Sunil on one side of her, and then turned her head to Ivor. "We have nothing. No evidence. That button . . ." There she was again, the clear-eyed Lila, desperate to help Maisie and Sunil. He could swear she had forgotten about them for a while when they were dancing. He made her forget for a little while. He was afraid she would make him forget just about everything if he wasn't careful.

He looked at her now. "Your half brother was in the room when the lights came on."

"Yes," Lila said seriously. "He was in the room. It would be our word against his. I see that. He could have lost the button when he came in with the others—"

"Well, he didn't, did he! If you believe that . . ." It was Maisie, of course, looking outraged.

"It's not what they believe," Sunil said peaceably. "It is what will stand up in a court of law. Lord Beddington could have lost the button when he came in with the others."

"And Tiffany—my cousin—will hardly say that it was Jonathan Marleigh who attacked her," Ivor said.

"And Jonathan himself . . ." Lila said, then stopped.

"Lord Beddington has only to say that he saw *me* when the lights came on, attacking Miss Tristram. He is an earl. His word counts for more than anyone else's." Sunil looked apologetically at Ivor.

Ivor flicked his head. "Absolutely right, Mr. Mehta—Sunil. I'm afraid it does. Earls and dukes, people with titles, can simply claim clemency and they cannot be prosecuted for their crimes. Jonathan Marleigh's word will count for more than any of ours, I'm afraid."

"We have to do something!" Lila said.

They discussed the matter as they walked. They turned at the end of the lane, walked back through the tunnel of trees and lanterns, and then turned yet again when they were back at the mouth of it.

As they were walking, deep in conversation, a halo of straw curls materialized out of nowhere. "Ivor! You naughty man! You never said you were coming here! If I had told Papa, he would have given me his permission to come so much easier!"

"Tiff!" Ivor said in surprise.

But even as he was wondering how exactly to introduce his cousin to the group he was with, before he had time to process this unexpected meeting, Tiffany's face froze. She clutched at her throat as her eyes rested on Sunil. "How—what—you!" she stuttered, her face white as a sheet. "*You!*"

Ivor hardly had time to react. "Tiff," he said again. "Listen to me."

She was staring. Not at Ivor—she hardly registered what he said—but at Sunil Mehta. Sunil took off the midnight-blue eye mask he was wearing and looked in a clear-eyed way back at Tiffany. Even Maisie Quinn was fidgeting, looking awkward.

But Sunil looked steady, trustworthy, if only Tiffany could see it. Lila was staring at Tiffany. "Miss Tristram."

But Tiffany barely glanced at Lila. Or Maisie. She was still staring at Sunil. But then she slowly turned to look at Ivor, as though she'd never seen him before. Before anyone could react, she was fleeing from them down the lane. Ivor cursed and followed her, holding his hand up to stop anyone else from following, though he doubted that anyone would. Tiffany was running toward the mouth of the lane. He had to walk fast to stop her. "Stop, Tiff, will you? Listen to me."

She whirled around and stared at him. "What was that man—what *is* that man doing here? With *you*! Is this some kind of horrible joke, Ivor?"

"Tiff, if you'll stop running and come back with me—"

She looked at him in horror. "*Nothing* would make me go back there! Nothing! How dare you even suggest it! Do you know I have nightmares about that night! Have you any idea? And do you know that in my nightmares no one comes into the room when I scream?"

He cursed under his breath. She was enraged, her eyes blazing, her yellow silk dress swishing and whipping as she moved. He held a hand up and didn't try to touch her again. "Tiff," he said in a gentler voice, "I know, Tiff."

Her eyes widened. Her pupils were wildly dilated, glittering with the light of the lanterns all around them. She was slightly out of breath. "Have you ever been violently attacked in a dark room—or in *any* room for that matter!—by someone much stronger than you and you knew you couldn't resist, that he could do anything to you—and no one might ever know? Have you, darling Ivor, because if you haven't, then forgive me, but you *don't* know what you're talking about!"

Ivor shook his head. "No, that was a stupid thing for me to say. It's just that I think you might be mistaken about who attacked you. If you come in—"

The color rushed to her face. "I am mistaken about who attacked me? Perhaps I am mistaken that the attack happened at all!"

"I didn't—"

"Poor woman that I am, what do I know! If I say a man attacked me, I must have the wrong idea. If I say he was violent and it felt like—it felt like he hated me, wanted to hurt me, then what do I know? I must be mistaken!"

Ivor frustratedly shook his head. It was true that he often only heard half of what Tiffany said, and she accused him of being interested in nothing but work, of being aloof and distracted, but he didn't normally feel so out of his depth when speaking to his cousin. She was right. What did he know about what she had experienced? Helpless rage filled him again at the absent Jonathan Marleigh. He wished he knew what to say to Tiffany, but he couldn't seem to find the right words. Guilt flooded him, inexplicably; guilt that the world seemed to be full of men like Jonathan Marleigh and Ivor's own father.

He had to say it. What else could he do? "Tiff, I think it might have been Jonathan Marleigh who attacked you."

She laughed in his face, a wild, maniacal laugh that made him realize with numb shock that though she seemed as though she had gotten over the attack last time he had seen her, it was clear today that she hadn't gotten over it at all, that she was haunted by it. "You know I expect Papa to use all kinds of strategies to try to get me away from Jonathan. But I didn't think you would."

"Why, though, Tiffany? Why do you think your father doesn't

want you to be with someone like Jonathan Marleigh?" His voice sounded weary. He wanted her to see Beddington for the man he was, but he also knew that it would only set Tiffany's back up more. And he was right.

"Papa doesn't want me to be happy. He has never wanted me to be happy. It seems you don't either." She looked more, not less stubborn.

Before he could answer she had fled.

25

Lila sat in the little parlor. It was beautifully decorated in mushroom and teak and there was a fire roaring in the hearth. She watched Ivor's face.

She marveled at the fact that it was late, after midnight, and here she was, sitting in a man's house, not wondering what she was doing there. He didn't seem to be wondering it either. He looked deeply troubled.

Maisie and Sunil had left them at the gardens, not long after the encounter with Tiffany Tristram, all of them deeply shaken. By mutual and silent consent, Ivor and Lila had ended up here, in Berkeley Square, at Ivor's house.

Before they left the gardens, Lila pressed Maisie's hand, said that they would figure something out, plan what they were going to do to find justice. She felt like a fraud. How was she going to help Maisie?

She told Maisie it was salon night the next day, and she could find Lila at Brook Street. And Maisie said, "I might see you there tomorrow night, Miss Lila. I doubt that's where I'll find you tonight." The cheeky girl. Lila had lifted her chin and said she was sure she had no idea what Maisie meant. Maisie gave her a saucy grin, but Lila could see the fear lurking not far under the surface.

"I'll go and see Tiffany in the morning," Ivor said, treading into her thoughts, looking troubled. "Even if we can cast doubt—even if she can see that she has no real idea who attacked her, only who was in the room with her when the lights came on—then it might help."

Lila didn't answer. She slipped off her shoes, curled her feet on the sofa, drew near him and, placing a hand on his chest, kissed him. There was stubble on his jaw and she wondered for a second why men ever bothered shaving it off. With the stubble, his top shirt buttons undone, his shirtsleeves folded and no sign of a jacket, he looked like a pirate.

He was taken a little by surprise—his mind was firmly on the matter at hand—but he recovered quickly and drew her nearer.

"I made a mess of it," he said ruefully. "Not one thing I said was the right thing to say to Tiff."

She couldn't help finding that look endearing. She didn't think she had seen that rueful look before. There was a vulnerability in it that was more delicious than his usual self-assurance. She wondered how many looks he had that would keep surprising her. She murmured something soothing, her fingers on his cheek, her thumb gently tracing his lower lip. He reached his head down this time and kissed her, making her arch toward him, eager to lessen the distance between them.

When he pulled back again, he was looking seriously at her. "I'll sort it out with Tiffany, I promise."

She looked questioningly at him. "Why? Why do you want to? An innate sense of justice?"

He looked at her for a long time, his hands on her back, his eyes studying every millimeter of her face. "If they arrest Sunil,

it will end badly for him. And as long as Jonathan Marleigh—
or his man Pritchard—is feeding the Runners information, as
long as an earl is interested in the case, Sunil will not be free."

"Yes."

"So, we have no choice but to try to save him. And to get
justice."

She felt like she was drowning in those direct eyes of his.
"But those aren't your only reasons?"

"Those aren't the only reasons. I don't want to let you down."

Her breath left her in a whoosh. And she found she couldn't
think of anything to say. She just wanted to sit there, her legs
curled under her, her face heartbeats away from Ivor's, staring
at him, feeling his warm, sure hands on her back, feeling a
terrible ache between her legs that she wanted him to soothe.

"I wanted to knock him out cold when I came up the stairs
in his house today and saw his bleeding lip."

"It was nothing," she said quickly. "He didn't do . . . much.
I just always want to punch him."

He gave her an abstracted smile.

"Ivor, I've never been with your father. I have no idea why
you thought I had. I have never—"

He leaned his head down and, planting his mouth on hers,
harshly took it into his own. He seemed to drink from her
mouth, almost angrily. When he let her go, she was dripping
freely, the pulse between her legs nearly driving her to dis-
traction. But there was more to say. "I've never been anyone's
mistress, Ivor. There was never any transaction. But—but you
wouldn't be the first man—"

"I haven't asked you, Lila. I don't need to know. Will you . . . ?"

That diffident look was back in his face. He didn't complete
the question. But then he didn't have to. "Yes, Ivor. Please."

He took her hand and drew her to her feet. He placed a guard around the fire. He blew out the candles in the room and grabbed a candelabra to carry in his free hand.

The walk up the stairs and to his bedchamber was not long but, by the time they reached it, Lila felt like she was having trouble breathing. When he reached for her, drew her to him, she didn't know if the tremor she felt was in her or in him.

She pressed the length of her body to his. It was more than she had ever felt of him, the hard length of his body, the warmth, the encircling of his arms securely around her, the press of his chest on her breasts, the roughness of hair on her hands, but it wasn't enough. It was not nearly enough.

She was pulling off his shirt. She sank her face into the hollow of his neck, breathing him in as if it was essential for life itself, then reached up to kiss him again. Between them, they undid what felt like a million buttons on her dress. There was no finesse, only speed, and their fingers kept getting entangled. The dress finally fell around her in a whisper. But there were other layers to get through. Hurrying now, tearing, scrabbling, they finally managed to get out of their clothing, and they were in bed and she felt with a cry the entire length of him and he groaned in his throat at the feel of her.

She wanted to wrap herself around him and never let go. His mouth was everywhere. On her sternum, the hollow of her neck, her armpits, between her breasts, and then, mercifully, on her nipples. And he stayed there, lapping her up as if he had been waiting all his life just for this. She wanted him to hurry, but then with his mouth on her nipples, she wanted him to stay there, exactly there, for the rest of time. She was moaning and writhing now, and he had his fingers twined with hers, pinning her to the bed. His mouth was back on hers now.

"Now, please, Ivor, now," she said, opening her legs, drawing her feet up to make room for him.

He released her hands and braced himself. She reached down and felt him with her hands, the velvety silk of him, the hardness beneath the silk. She moaned at the feel of him, before drawing him closer and then into herself. They both gasped.

He started moving, slowly, just the tip at first, and then sinking more into the wetness of her that clung to him, drawing himself deeper. But he took his time, feeling step by step, bit by bit, how much she was ready for him. She clutched him with her legs.

He was so deep now, it was as if he was opening yet another layer of her, layer upon layer, opening and unfolding, reaching deeper parts of her, opening wells that gushed all around him and helped him sink in deeper still. His mouth was on hers, they were gasping, their breath mingling.

"I want you," he said, "all of you. All of you, Lila."

And he reached down a hand, a thumb between the press of their bodies, and rubbed a circle that shattered her. She was almost crying now. Because he shattered her again and again, until she was gasping, making noises in her throat that she didn't know she was making.

Just at the last second, when she was still convulsing around him, he withdrew and came on her belly. They lay together for an eon afterward, not moving, breathing each other in.

26

And then, oddly, they got a reprieve. Days passed without incident. The day after Vauxhall, Ivor went first thing in the morning to see his cousin. Tiffany agreed to see him—and that surprised him—but when he was let into the formal parlor (instead of the saloon in which she might normally meet family), she was cold as ice. The chin was raised, the eyes distant, and even her shapely nose seemed pointier than usual. He had never seen her like that before. Tiffany's feelings flowed easily. They were always near the surface. He tried again to explain his position, tried to ask her to imagine an alternative version of events, but she seemed to hold this against him. She held it against him that he was trying to refute her version of what happened. In one way, he could hardly blame her.

He tried to sound as reasonable as he could and show her his sympathy. He couldn't help thinking that his new feelings for Lila had sharpened his sympathy, given him a keener need to soothe Tiffany's hurt. But it had no visible effect on his cousin.

Just for a second, just for a fraction of a second, there was a point where he thought he might have a chance. Instead of arguing about the attack, and the identity of the attacker, he asked her to think if Jonathan Marleigh loved her.

She gritted her teeth and assured him that he did.

"And do you love him?" he asked gently. Lila had told him that Jonathan Marleigh could be all charm and attention when he wanted something, but Ivor couldn't help thinking that there was something coldly reptilian about the man.

That was the only time he saw Tiffany hesitate. He saw a flicker of doubt on her face. But then she squared her shoulders. "I know what it's like to hanker after someone's love. To think you need it in order to live. To toss and turn all night for wanting it. I don't have to do that with Jonathan."

He wanted to press his advantage. "You're young, you—"

It was the exact wrong thing to say. "A child, you mean. Yes, that's the general consensus, isn't it?"

He left after half an hour, desperately wondering what to do next.

But then Hector stopped in his study to see him as he was sitting there brooding over the question, while holding some correspondence from his agent in his hands that he hadn't glanced through. "The blighter's gone out of town," Hector said. He explained that Jonathan Marleigh had left town just this morning, apparently gone to some friends in Yorkshire. "Reckon he's there for the start of the hunting."

Ivor was surprised at this news. Just yesterday, in Beddington's house, he was sure Lila and he had given the game away. Beddington knew that they knew what happened in Ivor's house on the night of that party, they knew who attacked Tiffany. Yet, the man had left town.

He was frowning, when Hector added, "If he's out of pocket, he can't miss the start of the hunting, can he?"

Ivor couldn't help thinking that Hector was right. Bedding-ton was deep in debt, deep in the pockets of moneylenders. He had to try to keep in with as many members of the *ton* as he could, or at least make a show of carrying on with life as usual. Especially if he planned to turn his fortunes around by marrying Tiffany, he might think time spent cultivating his acquaintances—or at least trying to show them that everything was normal—was time well spent. Still, Ivor was uneasy.

The next time he and Lila saw Maisie and Sunil, two nights later, they too said that they had had neither sight nor sound of Ezekiel Pritchard, Beddington's man. The Runner was still after them, but no longer seemed to find them as easily as before. This made sense. If the Runner was mainly reliant for information on Pritchard, and if Pritchard was out of town with his employer, then the Runner might not be able to trace them so easily. Maisie and Sunil were living in a series of brothels, and their lodgings at least were not easily traceable.

"Maybe he has got tired of it and left." Sunil was the only one who gave this optimistic view.

Maisie looked openly scornful. "He's up to something," she said succinctly. "Or at least he's not giving up his normal life to go after us because he thinks he has us."

Or his need to sort out his debts was greater than his need to go after Sunil. Ivor was uneasy, so was Lila. Though they wanted to believe that Sunil was right, that Beddington had simply given up, believing himself to be safe, neither deep down really believed it. The temporary reprieve should have felt like a relief, but felt instead like the calm before the storm. It felt like a ticking clock.

And yet. And yet Ivor had hardly any thought to spare. He and Hector compared notes every day. Ivor consulted with a barrister in anticipation of needing one if Sunil were caught. Ivor also dealt with estate matters, visited his bankers for a loan for some equipment and expansion, met with coffee investors with whom he did business. He spent some time in Jackson's salon once or twice.

His thoughts, though, were consumed with Lila.

It was as if half of him was always with Lila, even when he was doing other things. It felt as though he was waiting all day for the time that he could visit her. If it was on a night when she didn't have a salon, she visited him. He let the staff go early and Ivor and Lila sat in his parlor, curled up on his sofa. She was soft and pliable on those nights. And if it sometimes felt like they were both trying to steer clear of controversial topics, well, so be it. They were feeling their way. And what was wrong with that? They spoke of all kinds of things on those nights. He found himself telling her more about the estate, some of the farmers who lived on it and their personalities, his agent whose main job seemed to be to play devil's advocate and argue against any innovation Ivor wanted to make—and if Ivor backed down, then the agent would start arguing against *that* and accusing Ivor of being too nonchalant and old-fashioned. He told her about his Oxford friends and professors. About a cousin of his from his mother's side who had three-year-old twins who were the most horrendous little monsters in the world and who twisted him around their little fingers when they saw him.

She in turn told him more about the salons, more about her guests. Not only that. She told him about the business side, how she planned things, how she made things work, and he couldn't but be impressed. He learned the business side partly from his agent and partly from Uncle Arthur. He had support, bankers, backing, advice, and a social standing that lubricated his way—and he had the confidence and self-belief that went with generations of good social standing and relative wealth. She had nothing and no one to guide her, or even support her.

She did it all herself, learning as she went, through trial and error and sheer doggedness. He was more than impressed. He wanted to know more about her staff too. She was shy of talking about them, but gradually told him a bit more. He asked her about Annie Quinn, Maisie's mother, and she told him about it, not just with bitterness and resentment against the Marleighs, but a deep and abiding guilt that he couldn't shake, that he wanted to soothe away, but that he could do nothing about. She talked about herself freely, and that in turns delighted him, filled him with wonder, and also scared him out of his wits because he had never felt this close to anyone before, never let himself get so close. It was frightening, like no longer being able to feel boundaries he had spent years constructing. It was at times overwhelming to feel this much closeness and his instinct was to back off.

But she wouldn't let him off easily. If he was superficial in anything he said, or if his customary remoteness kicked in, she would probe, ask questions, want to get to the heart of things, she wouldn't take easy answers. It was as if she wanted nothing less than his soul.

It was as if his soul was what he wanted to give her.

And yet she seemed to hold some of herself back. Just as he did. If he couldn't bring himself to talk about his parents, she didn't speak about her sisters. When he brought up the subject, she said, "Oh, you know, we were—we are—just like sisters. Like any other sisters."

"Do you see them often?" he asked, searching her face for clues.

She tossed her head and said, "Life is too busy. Everything gets in the way. Anya has a busy life in court. And her voice is so heavenly that she gets other offers for work too. She is quite a favorite with Queen Charlotte, as far as I know. And Mira writes. Society gossip. She has a ready wit—not cruel, but getting to the heart of things. She has a way of seeing things as they really are, getting to the heart of the matter. And she is busy with that. And I have my salons. Who has the time?" She said no more. Even that was more than she customarily said about her sisters.

There was something there, more shared guilt, some kind of darkness that she wouldn't let him into. Something, he felt, that pre-dated even their childhood at the Marleigh house. But he couldn't imagine what it was, or decide if he was imagining it in the first place.

He didn't probe; it wouldn't have occurred to him to try. He took greedily all the morsels she gave. He took the softness, the nights she came to him and sat on his sofa and half dreamily told him about herself. He liked listening to her, but he thought with mortification that sometimes he didn't listen, sometimes he just watched. The way she talked, the way she'd forget herself, the way she shrugged or got impatient. He even enjoyed the way he irritated her, and the spark returned to her eyes. He cherished those nights at his house. And yet there was something even more intoxicating about her salon nights, when it would get too late for her to visit him, and he would see her instead, at her house, in the early hours of the morning.

She wasn't soft or pliable or talkative then. There was something nervy and agitated about her and she wanted nothing so much as a frantic silence. An anguished coupling that splintered his core. Where there was no slow tenderness, but instead a shattering, pounding fire that was almost pain.

Those days after that encounter with Tiffany in Vauxhall Gardens, Ivor felt they were living on borrowed time. Any day now Jonathan Marleigh would return; any day they would have to confront what to do. Lila aired the possibility of Maisie and Sunil leaving the country while Jonathan Marleigh was away and while the Runner was being less of a busybody. But Maisie and Sunil wouldn't hear of it.

"Why should Sunil be the one to leave?" Maisie said hotly.

"No, ma'am," Sunil added, "I will not run away. I did nothing wrong. Running away will simply prove that I am guilty. Just like any common lascar, people will say."

There was no point Sunil leaving the city and moving to the country. He would be conspicuous with his darker skin, much more so in the countryside than in the city, and as long as there was a stain on his name, as long as he was a wanted man, he couldn't live anywhere in peace. Maisie and Sunil were unwilling to settle for anything less than clearing Sunil's name. Ivor sympathized with the sentiment, but was afraid that they would regret this missed chance if things went awry.

Yet every night with Lila, he could keep the fears at bay. He could forget that this brief time must come to an end, that one way or the other time would settle Sunil's fate, and that Ivor himself would leave for Sussex.

Lila made time stop. Ivor often thought that life seemed to be a series of responsibilities and challenges, or else, things to run away from or protect himself from, things that would consume him if he didn't keep working or running.

Yet, with her, there was quiet.

There were moments where everything else was suspended, time shut down, and there was a pool of wonder. She seemed to lose herself, leave the world out, and because of it, *he* could lose himself too. And in losing himself he could find a tether.

When he was inside her—her face, one of abandon, as if she had found the one thing that could fill her and complete her—that face. If he could lose himself in that face—the way she wrapped herself completely around him, the way she felt every anguished second, if he could wrap himself in her silence—then everything else could be blocked out. He didn't know how it was possible to find so much peace inside the passionate and explosive storm it always was when they came together.

27

T he thunder shattered the night.

Lila tossed and turned, not finding a comfortable spot on the hot bedsheets. There was that crack of thunder again. She was fighting, aching to open her eyes. Her mouth was parched. There was an unbelievable peace in her body and yet a dreadful urge to wake up, to find some light. Another crack and her eyes popped open. She was shocked to see Ivor standing next to the bed. She sat up. "What?" she said stupidly. "Thunder?"

"Someone at the door."

"At the door?" That didn't make sense. She was sure she was dreaming. Except for the terrible thirst. She looked around for a tumbler of water. Oh, what had possessed her not to get some the night before? But of course, she hadn't been thinking at the time.

"It's four in the morning."

Her eyes snapped to Ivor now. She quickly climbed out of bed, bedsheet around her. He gave her arm a reassuring squeeze. "Don't be alarmed. I'll see what it is. The household will be up now, anyway, curse whoever it is. Stay here, Lila." He gave her a quick kiss on the temple.

But once he left the room and she heard him rushing down the steps and then some people talking, she realized it was impossible to lamely get back into bed and go back to sleep or even peacefully wait for Ivor to come back. And the knocking. It was starting to make her anxious. She walked around the room, discovered another dressing gown hanging on the back of the door. Ivor had been wearing one—a burgundy one. This was navy and too long for her. She threw it on.

It seemed intensely foolish to leave the room and display herself in front of Ivor's staff in his dressing gown. That wouldn't do. She crept out of the room and onto the landing. She stood at the top of the stairs, overheard some talking between a few people: Ivor, Mrs. Manfield, who was his housekeeper, and someone else—a footman perhaps. There was another male voice, perhaps a gardener or groom. Or Ivor's valet? She listened. The front door was opened.

"Mr. Ivor!"

Dear God, it was Maisie! At four in the morning. Was she in pain, was she in labor? It was a few weeks since Maisie had turned up at Lila's door. She had been about seven months gone then. The baby would be early if it was coming now, but it could be on its way into the world.

Lila almost clattered down the stairs in alarm. But then some grain of sense broke through and she stood suspended on the top step. Of course, most of Ivor's servants would know that she was there, in the house, in the middle of the night. They must know everything that went on. She was here half the time and Ivor was at her house the other half. Yet, appearing in his dressing gown, showing herself like this? She couldn't do that to him. She had no idea what his staff were used to. But he wouldn't want to give the appearance that she was someone important, or heaven forbid, that he had to make her an offer now because everyone knew she was spending the night with him. Yet, it was Maisie. All of Lila's senses were alert, her heart thudding.

"What is it, Maisie? What's happened?" It was Ivor's voice.

"Sir, it's Sunil. It's Sunil!"

And then she heard a gasp. Dear God. What now?

"She's swooned, sir!" Mrs. Manfield's voice, sounding urgent.

Lila clattered down the stairs. Forgetting about all of it now, what they would all think. It didn't matter. She had no head for it. She ran up to the group. Ivor was supporting Maisie, who had fainted.

"We have to get her into the parlor," Lila said.

No one questioned her or gawked at her. If Mrs. Manfield was startled at her appearance, she hid it admirably. Ivor at one end and Hector McConnell, Ivor's valet, at the other, carried Maisie through into the parlor. Mrs. Manfield seemed to have gotten rid of the footman by the time the rest of them reached the parlor. The men laid Maisie down on the sofa. Lila sat on the sofa next to Maisie. Her brow wasn't feverish, though there was a sheen of sweat on it.

"Maisie, Maisie," Lila said urgently.

Mrs. Manfield was making the girl more comfortable, adding a cushion, moving another one away to give her space.

"Hector, brandy please," Ivor said to his valet. The man instantly found a decanter and glass.

Maisie was already coming to. She woke up, whimpering a little, a hand on her belly, but then she tried to jerk up to sitting as soon as she saw Lila. "It's Sunil, it's Sunil, Miss Lila!" Her eyes were frantic.

Mrs. Manfield was standing next to them. "Miss Quinn, do

you have any pains?" Her voice was quick and efficient. "In your back or your belly? We can call the doctor."

"No, no!" Maisie cried. "No pain! Miss Lila, Mr. Ivor—"

"Mr. Tristram," Mrs. Manfield said, "I think the doctor—"

"Please," Maisie cried. She was actually crying now, great heaving sobs. "Just listen to me first."

Lila and Ivor exchanged glances. Hector was holding out a thimbleful of brandy. Lila practically had to force it down Maisie's throat. Ivor turned to Mrs. Manfield and his valet. "I think we'd better hear what it's all about. If the two of you could be on call . . ."

They both left the room, assured Ivor that they'd be back in a second, if needed.

"What is it, Maisie?" Ivor said. "What's happened to Sunil?"

"The Runners have him!"

Lila gasped. "No!"

"Yes, Miss Lila. We went out to get some air—he gets ever so tired of being cooped up. And we've got careless, I admit it, we've got careless! Half the time I kept forgetting he was still a wanted man. He was taken when we got closer to where I'm living. It's in a brothel, miss. And no one there would give him away."

Lila was holding Maisie's hands, trying to soothe her, trying to warm up her ice-cold hands. Ivor's face was serious. Lila talked to Maisie, tried to soothe her, but it was impossible to calm her down. And Lila didn't think the situation could be any worse. If the Runners had Sunil, then he was in deep trouble. How stupid, how stupid! She had wasted so much time. Her head had been clouded with Ivor for days. Once Jonathan left town, they had all become complacent. How could they have forgotten the danger?

She could have and should have done more. Lila was clasping Maisie's hands, trying to say soothing things. She wasn't sure Maisie could even hear her.

As Maisie sat there on the sofa sobbing, Ivor looked at Lila. "There's nothing we can do right now. It's not yet five in the morning. But I will go and see what I can do first thing. In a mere few hours," he said for Maisie's benefit.

Lila pressed her lips together and nodded. She turned to Maisie again. "Maisie, did you hear that?" she said in as firm a voice as she could. "Mr. Tristram will go and see what he can do first thing in the morning." When this led to further helpless crying, Lila said, "Maisie, they won't even let him in at this hour. There is nothing to do but wait. You must stay . . ." she was about to say *here* but then realized that this was not her house, "at my house. We'll go back there now."

Maisie was so far gone that she didn't even look surprised that Lila was here at this hour. In fact, it looked likely that Maisie had run straight to Berkeley Square and not Lila's house first because she fully expected to find Lila here. Maisie wasn't stupid. And she knew which nights Lila held her salons.

"It's too late an hour for either of you to go anywhere," Ivor said. "Mrs. Manfield will find a bed for Maisie."

Maisie didn't protest and Lila couldn't help thinking that moving a very pregnant woman at this hour when she was already deeply upset would be cruel, if not downright dangerous. She assented. Mrs. Manfield, when she came back into the room, at once took charge of the situation when it was explained to her what was needed. Then Ivor had a quick word with his valet and came back into the parlor.

Lila quickly gave him her hands. He held them tightly. "Don't worry now. I'll be able to do something. In the morning."

She looked frantically at him. "I'm so sorry about coming downstairs when the staff were all about." She wanted him to understand. "I didn't want to make things awkward for you. But when Maisie fainted, I couldn't. I'm sorry!"

He kissed her hands. "If anything, it might compromise your position, Lila, not mine," he said gently. "And it's not as though they don't know."

She snatched her hands away, her chest heaving. "If you think I was trying to get you to—get you to—"

"Offer for you?" he said in that maddeningly calm voice. He gave her a curious look. "No, Lila, it's never occurred to me that that's what you're looking for. Now, will you stop trying to claw my eyes out and we can both try to get some rest? I imagine there are a few busy days ahead."

She was looking frantically at him. Anxiety about Sunil and Maisie, the situation, Mrs. Manfield looking at her as if it weren't strange that she was in Ivor's bedchamber in the middle of the night, the lack of sleep—all of it was making her feel as tight as a string.

He rubbed her knuckles with his thumbs. "Bed, Lila. We'll talk in a couple of hours."

28

The next day felt like a week. Since it was the second half of the week, it was one of her salon nights. Wafting through her salon at midnight that night, Lila couldn't help thinking that she had entered a different dimension. The salons that she was more familiar with than pretty much anything on this earth felt strange to her today, as if she had never entered such a place, not even in her dreams—or was it nightmares? They had felt like that in the last few weeks, since she met Ivor. But tonight, knowing what had happened to Sunil, they felt like an alien land, in which people spoke a language she was not familiar with. Too loud, too busy, and too . . . unimportant.

Anything, anywhere, she thought desperately. She would rather be doing anything, just about anywhere else. Yet, it seemed she was never too far gone to be a hostess. She drifted from table to table, group to group, smiling, speaking automatically. Lady Crowther stopped her to tell her that she was soon due a mysterious shipment from Africa. "I am almost certain it will turn out to be a snake or a chameleon!" Her eyes sparkled. She was wearing a purple turban today. "Do you not think, Miss Marleigh, that it will be just the right addition to my menagerie?"

"It sounds . . . just the thing," Lila said lamely. Her dress was turquoise today, the skirt taffeta, the hem of the underskirt and the neckline embroidered in silver. It was fitted, rather than full like a ballgown, but strangely she felt overdressed in it.

Lady Crowther peered at her. "You look peaky," she announced in her voice that was loud at the best of times, but today, to Lila's shattered nerves, sounded like a personal attack. She stopped herself from backing away from her guest. She must try to get more sleep one of these nights. "You keep nervously looking at the door, Miss Marleigh. You are not thinking of running away, are you?" She made a moue at her own joke.

"No! Of course not!" Lila bit her lip. She sounded like someone who had never spent more than two minutes of her life in company. Gauche and uninitiated. But she was jumpy, no doubt about it. She promised Lady Crowther a glass of her special champagne punch—with orange cordial and a finger of ginger ale today, not one of her better days, not very original, but she was lacking in creativity. She had done one with elderflower and the tiniest pinch of cayenne recently that was a big hit, another with cardamom, apple, and nutmeg. Tonight, it was not a night for flair.

Next she bumped into her friend Annabel Wakefield. Annabel was slim, blond and pale, but had a quiet dignity about her. She looked with concern at Lila's face too. "Are you all right? Shall I find you something to eat?"

Lila made an effort to shake her head. Annabel was always kind. "No, thank you. Just tired."

Annabel smiled reassuringly, then said, "You don't really mean to run that race, do you, Lila? I keep hearing rumors. I keep thinking even you wouldn't do something so scandalous."

Lila sighed. She was getting tired of this question. "Why, Annabel, don't we all want to defy society sometimes?"

Her friend bit her lip. And Lila realized it was a cheap shot. Annabel was a married woman but had a lover outside of her marriage, and it wasn't fair for Lila to rub it in her friend's face. Lila gave her a quick smile. "I'm tired. That is all." She squeezed her friend's arm. She backed away, trying desperately not to keep looking at the damned door.

She and Maisie had returned to Brook Street bright and early in the morning, Lila looking as if she hadn't slept in a month—which was more or less the truth—and Maisie looking like nothing so much as a rag doll with not a sliver of life left in her: her hair lank, her face blotchy, and even her expression lacking its usual ferocity. They had made a sorry pair—to cap it all it was raining and left the two women wilting—and Walsham had nearly murdered Lila at her own doorstep. He looked so personally affronted that she hardly dared meet his eye. He was too much of a true professional to ask her something as crass as where she had spent the night—or where she spent half her nights—and why she had brought the *young person* with her or what she expected him to do with the person. But the questions were throbbing in the air.

Hannah showed no such reticence. She gave Lila a speaking look which didn't bode well. Betty whisked Maisie away and Lila gave her a grateful look. As she was heading downstairs, Maisie said defiantly, "Don't you be thinking, Miss Lila, that I'll not earn my keep."

Walsham ominously swayed on the spot at the tone. Betty looked shocked at this way of speaking but uttered nothing more than a minor squeak or two. She had both hands clasped around Maisie's arms—she liked to touch people, especially when she was trying to get a measure of them, and Lila was thankful Maisie didn't seem to be trying to bat her away like she was a gnat.

"Can't you just rest, Maisie?" Lila had uttered, in the full expectation that she was going to be completely ignored. She was right.

"If you think I'll be sitting on my arse—" Walsham's urgent throat-clearing silenced Maisie but made her look ferocious. "Do you have a cold?" she barked at the butler.

Lila said feebly, "Maisie, if you want to find work, Betty will help you. But I wouldn't put Walsham's back up. As it is, we are in his bad books and will remain there for months to come."

Walsham did not dignify this with a response. Though his eyelid flickered.

Then there was Hannah to deal with. Lila was lying— drowning—in a very hot bath fifteen minutes after sending Maisie into the nether regions, and Hannah was moving about dealing with Lila's discarded clothes. "I'm in the suds," Lila said mournfully.

"Well, seeing as you're in a bath—"

"Hannah, did you *see* Walsham's face?" She should have been horrified, but then to her utter despair, she found herself sputtering, crying and laughing all at the same time. She didn't even know at *what* exactly, given that the list of things that could be leading to hysteria was long. It was some time before she could utter another coherent word, but Hannah placidly let her get on with it.

When she showed signs of being done, Hannah said, "I don't know what you expect, Miss Lila, if you show up wilted as a winter flower, having not slept a wink in your own bed, and—pardon me, Miss Lila, but what do you want us to *do* with Maisie Quinn?"

Lila had sighed. She rested her head back in the bath. Hannah went on for some time about the perils of Miss Lila's impetuosity. She even said something about how Lila seemed set on housing every one of the city's lame and destitute. "Not that I can complain, miss, seeing as I'm one of them."

"You're not lame or destitute. *And* Maisie will stay here," Lila added militantly, in case there was any doubt. "She could work as a maid." She looked doubtful even as she said it and Hannah wasn't about to miss that look.

"I reckon someone who makes a living as Maisie Quinn makes her living—I'll not mince my words, if you don't mind—I reckon she will not want to be on her hands and knees all day scrubbing anyone's floors."

Lila had a distinct suspicion that Maisie herself would say much the same. Maisie had no wish to work as a prostitute. She found the life unsavory and at times unsafe. Lila knew that. She wanted to live with Sunil on a small farm where they could make a life for themselves. She didn't want to work as a maid in someone's house, working all hours of the night and day, having an afternoon off once a month if she was lucky, being groped by her employers when they felt like it, and worse.

Yet. Sunil was now in Clerkenwell Prison, and there was a good chance there would be a noose waiting for his neck when he came out of its walls. Without Sunil at her side, it was almost impossible that Maisie was going to have any option but to go back to—not to put too fine a point on it—whoring.

"If she could read or write," Hannah said, "it might be different."

The rest of the day had passed in a fever of waiting for news. A note arrived in the afternoon from Ivor saying he was doing all he could. That it was unlikely he would see her before nightfall.

And now here she was running her salon and no sign of Ivor Tristram and no further notes. It wasn't a hot night, the storm had cleared the closeness of the last few weeks, but Lila was still fanning herself. How was she supposed to get through this night?

Lord Herringford was standing at her elbow, much too close. "Whose racers will you ride in the Brighton race, Miss Marleigh? I like to get these things straight in m'head."

She looked irritably at him. "Lord Herringford, whatever you are looking for, I doubt you'll find it in my cleavage." She gasped at her own words. She placed her closed fan on her lips and swallowed. She felt nauseous.

Herringford looked like he had frozen. Shockingly, he was the first to recover. "Miss Marleigh, you are not yourself tonight. I will not hold it against you. We are old friends, are we not? Never one to hold anything against a woman. It's not as if you can help your megrims—only makes you more desirable to us poor old sods."

She gurgled hysterically at the thought of what he *had* held against many women in the course of his life. She blinked rapidly. Dear God. What was she going to say or do next? "You are gracious, Lord Herringford." *Old friends.* For the love of God. In a way, they *were* old friends. Herringford eyed her up and down every time he saw her, but the dirty old man had never crossed a line, not with anything more than his eyes and words. She placed her fan on her lips and gulped. She didn't know what she was thinking. Yet, there was something pitiable about him. She couldn't help smiling weakly, mostly to stop herself from batting at him with her fan.

He inclined his head. Leering some more, his face alarmingly red and sweaty and his waist ominously creaking whenever his nose reached closer to her chest, he repeated his question about the horses she was planning on racing. Ah, the Brighton race again. It seemed that throwaway remark a few weeks ago would never leave her alone.

She found herself clicking her tongue in impatience. She placed her fingers on her mouth. "It seems everyone believes I am going to run that race. Nothing I say convinces anyone that I don't mean to run it."

He winked. He clearly didn't hold a grudge, that much at least was true. He was swaying dangerously close. "Whose racers would you use, theoretically speaking, if you *were* running the race?" he pressed.

"But I—"

"Let's pretend for a moment." His lips were practically at her hair.

"Kenneth Laudsley's, I suppose," she said faintly.

She caught Henry Alston's eye. He glanced at Herringford and at once read the situation. He walked calmly over. "Miss Marleigh, you promised to show me that French cabinet you acquired."

She was so tired she had to think: what French cabinet? It took a few seconds for the fog to clear. "Oh, yes, of course, Mr. Alston. The *very* French cabinet. How French it is! Do come with me."

In the antechamber a minute later, she sagged in relief. Pitiful old man or not, Herringford was an ordeal at the best of times, and this was not the best of times. But before she could sit down, Alston was clasping her hands. "Let me talk to you now!"

"Mr. Alston—Henry!" He couldn't be serious. Having rescued her from Herringford, he surely wasn't going to start his own campaign?

"Don't deny me, Miss Marleigh. You don't know how much I am in agony! Every day I wait only for it to be time to see you. Every morning you are the first person in my thoughts. And every night, the last. I am unable to focus on anything else. You must know that. Please do not dally with me any more; do not, I beg you, keep me in suspense!"

His eyes were frantic. She had never seen them like that. It was not that he held his liquor that well. But he knew when to stop. But today there was a flush in his cheeks and his pupils were madly dilated. How much had he had to drink? She couldn't help thinking she'd stepped out of the frying pan into the fire.

Yet his chin was trembling. This was costing him an effort. He had probably been drinking all night just to get the courage to do this. Poor, poor boy. She could hardly hate him.

"Please, *please*," he said. "I wish you wouldn't think of me as a child. I can show you—"

"You are a child, Henry! A sweet, *sweet* boy. This will pass, I promise you. This is nothing more than a—"

And then he lunged. He groped for some seconds and then he was kissing her. He wasn't forcing her, not holding her violently, but desperately kissing her. As if he really wanted her to see, wanted her to see that he wasn't some stupid boy. It was all she could do not to fall backward with him on top of her. She was desperately trying to steady herself.

It was only for a few seconds but, before she could push him away, there was a dull thud and Henry was lying on the ground, turned onto his side and clutching his face.

Ivor. It was Ivor who had knocked Henry over.

"Ivor!"

Henry was getting to his feet, shaking a little. "Mr. Tristram, if you want to call me out—"

"Don't be ridiculous," Ivor said firmly. "And get out."

Henry glanced nervously at Lila. There were tears in his eyes. He was blinking hard. She tried to give him a kind smile. He set his mouth and looked at Ivor again. "I want to talk to Lila—to Miss Marleigh."

Now Ivor's hand was at his throat. "I said get out." He wasn't shouting. He was growling. Yet his face. Lila had never seen this face either. An almost ugly face—contorted with pain.

"Stop it, Ivor!" She managed to pull Ivor away from Henry's throat. Though it wasn't easy. Ivor's face was rigid with anger. She turned to Henry. "Henry, please go home and try to sleep it off. You'll feel better tomorrow." The words were kind, yet she couldn't help thinking she sounded like a nurse speaking to her ward. "And," she couldn't help adding, "it will never work in your favor to force your attentions on a woman. Never." She really felt like a nurse now, like she was trying to teach a child how to behave.

Apparently, Henry saw it too. He sputtered and went a dreadful pink. "I—I wasn't forcing . . . I wasn't—"

"Yes, Henry, you were," she said as gently as she could. But, really, what a stupid boy.

His chin was trembling now and she couldn't help pitying him. He looked as though he was going to say something but then, instead, he straightened his cravat, absently brushed a shaking hand through his hair and headed to the door. There he stopped. He had enough dignity not to look at or apologize to Ivor. He was looking at only Lila. "All your friendliness—you're saying now it didn't mean anything?"

Guilt filled Lila. "Henry, am I any friendlier to you than I am to . . . my female guests?" This was something Lila never understood. Why was it women never mistook her animation for a warmer feeling, for an invitation? Never thought that she must be desperately in love with them? The mind boggled at what men chose to see. And how they chose to interpret what they saw.

He didn't answer. His eyes, she saw with dismay, were red-rimmed and full of tears. He gave a funny little jerk of the head and then he turned around and left.

Lila was again ready to collapse on a chair.

"How you can encourage every dandy in town to dangle after you like that!"

She turned her face to Ivor in shock. "Are you blaming *me* for that?"

"Who else, Lila?"

His face was thunder, it was full of anguish. His face, almost contorted with pain. She instinctively reached a hand toward him, but he batted the air as if flinging the hand away. She drew the hand back and clutched it with her other.

"Who else, Lila?"

"He's a child, Ivor. He's just a child. I would have got rid of him. But I didn't want to hurt his pride more than I have to. He's not even twenty!"

He curled his mouth. "His pride! Herringford's too? My father? Is that how you treated him too? That's what you do, isn't it? Everyone's friend. Everyone's hostess. You have smiles for every man, no matter how much he thrusts himself on you. You're fair game for every man who crosses your threshold. Anyone can have a piece." He wiped his mouth with a hand that was shaking.

She was trembling with shock now. And as usual, with the shock setting in, with the heat filling her body and settling in the most secret parts of her like a furnace, she didn't know what to say. She was frozen. At the injustice of it. At the wrath in his face.

His mouth twisted. "I suppose it feels like love?"

She gasped and something uncorked in her. She was shaking. "How dare you! How *can* you? How dare you blame me? A man—a *boy*—forces his attentions on me and you blame me! How damnably predictable, Ivor, and how . . . how disappointing!" She was shaking.

And he looked—strangely—in pain. "Every time I think I've got the measure of you, every time I convince myself you're worthy of admiration—"

"Get out!" she yelled, her hand pointing at the door and shaking. "Just get out!"

"I need to tell you about my day, about Sunil." He rubbed his face. "But I cannot right now. I will make sure you know by tomorrow." He turned to leave.

"Ivor . . ." Her voice broke. She stared at his back, numb with shock.

And he did stop, just for a moment, at the door to the antechamber. But then he didn't turn around. He left the room and, a minute later, she heard Walsham seeing him out of the front door and wishing him a good evening.

29

The next morning, after a measly breakfast of coffee and a bite of toast, Lila was lying flat on her back in the back garden. Maisie Quinn—though she kept swearing that it was the devil lying on your back when you were enormous with child—was lying next to her on the grass. The sky was a clear blue, as crisp as could be, a cloud in the shape of a high perch phaeton drifting by, as if heading to a chariot race. There was a fat bee buzzing in the late roses nearby, and the old pear trees, which dutifully burst open every spring and turned overnight into a cloud of clotted cream, were fraying into a yellowy-green now as they headed to an unseasonably warm start to the autumn. They were in the back garden, but it was still possible to hear the bustle of London from the main road—carriages, carts, street callers, shouts, runaway horses. If she really listened, there were sounds within sounds, and she fancied—though it was highly unlikely—that she could hear the barges on the river, their horns splintering the morning.

How many times, wondered Lila, had she and Maisie lain just like this, when Maisie was a little girl, and Lila home for the summer holidays? When she was regretting again that none of her friends invited her to their country estates for the holidays, and how the ones who *would* get to spend part of the summer together would come back better friends than ever; for weeks afterward Lila would feel shut out from their closeness and their chat about their summer adventures. How many times would she wonder if her friends shut her out of their life because she was a bastard, or because her mother was Indian, and Lila had mixed blood. She never talked about her life in India or her mother, just to fit in. She never spoke Hindi. She hid away that side of her, shut it down, tried to become like everyone else. Pretty, empty-headed, frivolous, with not a care in the world. How many times did she think that no matter how much she tried, she could never be like everyone else? Her real self, the obstinate, headstrong, willful self (had she inherited that from Naira Devi?) always crept out.

How many times, on days like this—when the sky could be pierced with a shard of glass and a world revealed through there that was more peaceful and still than anything Lila knew in real life—would she feel grateful that, though the house was silent as a sepulcher, though she and her sisters looked at each other resentfully, there was Maisie at her side? Sometimes it had felt as if Maisie and Annie were the only ones who loved her. Yet even they had loved Mira and Anya too, not just Lila. Why was it she never seemed to be the most important person in the world to anyone?

She stared up at the early autumn sky now and felt deeply sorry for herself. Always on the periphery of love.

If any of the people who worked in her house could see her now, lying in the grass like this with Maisie, they would probably walk out en masse. Overnight, Maisie had taken on the self-appointed role of keeping Lila's clothes clean, and Hannah had said this morning that she had rarely met such an intelligent girl. But if Maisie had no idea of the dignity due to herself or her mistress (according to Walsham's rulebook), no one would have sympathy for her. Hannah might even feel supplanted by a stranger, Lila thought guiltily. However easy Lila was with Hannah, Hannah wouldn't dream of plonking herself on the ground beside her and staring dolefully at the passing clouds. The idea was so ludicrous, Lila gasped back a choking laugh.

They were behind the dip in the garden. She sighed. She didn't care. She didn't care if they all left. If she lived all by herself, then she wouldn't have to worry about paying anyone's wages or maintaining a large establishment. Maisie and she could live together in some little cottage and Maisie could mind the house and Lila could rear . . .

"Chickens," she muttered.

"Mutton," Maisie answered.

"Rear mutton?" Lila said in confusion.

"You're a mutton-head, Miss Lila, if you don't mind my saying. Who lies here like that with their servant and talks of *chickens?*"

Lila didn't have the energy to protest.

"When will Mr. Ivor come back?" Maisie said for the hundredth time.

"Will you stop whining on about that?" Lila snapped, before she could stop herself.

"Don't bite my head off," Maisie said, mildly for her. "*I'm* not the one who quarreled with you."

"He didn't . . ." She bit her lip. "I don't care what he thinks of me. The insufferable, arrogant man."

"That's all right then."

Lila ground her teeth.

She hoped he *would* be back soon. Her brow knitted. Did the man not realize that whatever *his* feelings about Lila, Maisie was waiting for news of Sunil? Lila and Maisie were both waiting.

What *were* his feelings about Lila?

Surely, he would see sense in the clear light of day. He had to. He was a rational man, when all was said and done. She had never seen him unfairly blame a woman for a man's attention. He had never done that with Tiffany. Why with Lila then? Were there different rules for her? She was a hostess. She was used to some degree of aggravation from her male guests. But it never came to anything. Her footman Johnny was always alert to signs of trouble, while Walsham . . . Walsham could get rid of any guest who was troubling her with just the twitch of one nostril. Why did Ivor have to make such a meal of it? Her brow creased some more. He had looked as if he was in pain. She remembered the rigid look on his face when he had seen her with Jonathan Marleigh that day in Jonathan's house. And the same when he saw her with Henry Alston at Vauxhall. She'd put it down to jealousy—she hadn't minded a bit of jealousy. But to *blame* her for Henry Alston's behavior last night, or . . . or Herringford's! That was too much! Not to mention the fact that Henry, though he was being really stupid last night, was just a child. She could have managed him. She *was* managing him, in her own way. Young boys didn't need to be humiliated. And the boy had sent her a note of apology first thing this morning. Admittedly, it still proclaimed his love, his worship, but it also begged her forgiveness, and hoped that she would over time see him as a mature and eligible man. Still pushing his suit, but at least he had had the grace to apologize, that was something. She felt like the boy's school teacher.

She squirmed.

Maisie was squirming too. Lila eyed her uneasily. She just knew it. With Sunil gone, Maisie would end up staying here. Lila had no problems with this scheme, none, except that Maisie would need somewhere to give birth and raise a baby. And with every bit of goodwill in the world, Lila couldn't see how a baby would fit into the odd, skewed life of her salons, where she—and in fact the people who worked for her—went to bed in the early hours of the morning for half the week, and often remained in bed until noon. Not today. Because, yet again, she hadn't gotten much sleep. It was barely eleven now. But normally.

Everyone, even Walsham and Mrs. Williams, had adjusted to the hours they kept in this house. It was the only way to do it. How on earth would a baby fit in? And, she thought with deep misgiving, Walsham was tolerant of Hannah's limp, and everyone found Betty endearing, and well, he wasn't quite reconciled to Roger's eye mask, thinking it foolish and unbecoming, but he tolerated all of them, just as they helped him when his fingers were too stiff to do his chores, but a pregnant woman—a pregnant *prostitute*—and then, in a mere few weeks, her baby? She covered her eyes with her hand.

"Don't you be thinking I'm going to let myself become a burden to you."

Dear God, everyone could read her mind now. She clicked her mouth impatiently. "Do not be ridiculous. As if I'm going to cast you onto the streets!"

"No, of course you're not. It makes complete sense to have me here, and the babe, and if he—or she—crawls into one of your fancy salons, or . . . or someone says why have you got a slut working for you, or the babe keeps waking you up when you've barely gone to sleep, or your fancy guests can hear a baby crying . . . ?"

Lila muttered something rude under her breath. "You'll stay here and that's it. If you think I'm going to let you run away again . . ." She opened her eyes and stared into the fathomless sky. Her heart was beating painfully now, as if she had run and run for miles and had now come to an abrupt standstill at the brink of a fathomless precipice. That's how she felt this morning, as if she was standing at the edge of a cliff. "Where did you go, Maisie? Why? Why didn't you stay? For years, I kept looking for you for years. I didn't know where to look."

There was no answer for a long time. Lila had given up expecting one when Maisie spoke. "I couldn't stay, Miss Lila. You were here, it was true, and you were like a big sister to me."

A lump formed in Lila's throat, but she didn't say anything.

"But you see, even you got punished for looking after me."

Lila frowned.

"If you gave me a treat—a cake or something—to eat when you shouldn't have, or you were caught playing with me, or climbing a tree, heaven forbid, you were punished for it. They used to shut you in the portrait gallery with not a speck of light allowed, not one candle, not a fire, just to punish you. When Ma was around, she could look after me, and she could look after *you*. But with her gone . . ."

Lila flicked her head. She had forgotten that. The pain in her throat was worse now. "I'm not such a mouse as to be afraid of a dark room, Maisie, or whatever punishment Sarah or Jonathan liked to dish out. I was old enough to bear it. You were . . . just seven."

"Ma had a friend who lived by the river. Her name was Prue Timmins. She was a whore. I went to her. I lived with her. I learned her . . . trade."

A pain in her chest now. "You were only seven." She could barely get the words out.

"Oh, I didn't—I didn't start then. It wasn't until I was thirteen or fourteen."

Lila viciously batted her eyes. "I could have helped you. I could have. I had no idea where to look for you. Thirteen or fourteen, Maisie!"

"You were a young lass yourself. I thought you'd get married. I had a stain on my name. I couldn't put that on you. The daughter of a thief."

"She wasn't a thief."

"I know."

It was on the tip of Lila's tongue, almost blocking her throat completely, to tell Maisie that she had seen Annie hanged. Yet, she couldn't bring herself to do it. That was her secret to bear, not anyone else's. What would she get out of telling Maisie? Perhaps a measure of relief, perhaps sharing one of her worst secrets. But Maisie would get nothing out of it. She swallowed the words. All the missed years, all the wasted time. All the years when Maisie needed her the most, Lila had failed her, not tried hard enough. "You know I never figured out what happened with that jewelry box. I keep thinking that Sarah herself must have had it in for Annie."

But Maisie shook her head. "Oh, she was a nasty one. But you girls were off her hands as long as Ma was living there. I doubt Lady Sarah was that keen to get rid of Ma. I always thought one of the servants. It wasn't a happy house. And many didn't like that Ma got to keep me with her and they couldn't do something like that."

Lila hadn't thought of it precisely like that before. Was it one of the servants, after all? It was the most likely explanation. Yet. Yet it seemed vicious and targeted.

And Lila could hardly bear it. The thought of Maisie working as a prostitute when she was not much more than a child.

Her mouth tightened. "I have been working for myself for four years at least, Maisie. If you had come back to me all those years ago, you wouldn't have had to . . ." She wiped away tears, hating herself for crying when it was Maisie who had suffered.

"Don't you go crying for me, Miss Lila. I'm happy enough." Maisie's voice broke a little. "I just want Sunil back. No one . . ." She struggled with herself for a second. "No one puts up with my temper like he does. Do you think most men put up with a shrieking banshee like me? Sometimes I throw things when I'm mad. The other day I broke a little chair. He was making me barking mad, Sunil—it's his calm face, see? I don't see why a man has to sit there calm as a daisy when there's spit coming out of *my* mouth. So I took this little chair—ugly as sin it was—and bashed it hard on the ground."

Lila could picture it, clear as day. "What did Sunil say?"

"He said it was a good thing I chose the ugly one."

Lila giggled. Then Maisie did too. They were both laughing hysterically and wiping tears, when Lila heard the distant dong of the doorbell. She sat up, straight as a rock. Maisie had heard it too.

They were up on their feet without a word and running straight for the house before either of them uttered another word.

30

Walsham was standing at the back door. Lila was about to brush past him, Maisie hot on her heels, but Walsham wasn't budging. One of his hands was on his lapel and the other arm behind his back. He was in full butler mode. He was looking significantly at Maisie.

"Oh, leave off, Walsham!" Lila said impatiently. "Maisie needs to come with me."

"It's Lord Beddington at the door, Miss Marleigh," he said with infinite patience.

Lila and Maisie both stopped in shock. Lila stared at Walsham. He didn't exactly look smug at her reaction, but he couldn't resist giving her a very slight bow.

Lila was still staring at him in astonishment. Jonathan, what was Jonathan doing here? Jonathan had never, ever come to her door, not as a guest in one of her salons and certainly not as a friendly morning caller. Not in all the years she had been living independently from the Marleighs. When she went to Sarah Marleigh's funeral two years ago, she and Jonathan had hardly spoken. Barely acknowledged each other with a nod. They came across one another at the odd social occasion and they—by unspoken mutual consent—skirted around each other. But that was rare too. Lila was not invited to the kinds of social occasions to which earls were customarily invited.

Lila glanced at Maisie. Then back at Walsham. "I'll have to see him." She turned to face Maisie who was looking mutinously at her. Lila shook her head. "Not this time, Maisie. Not yet. Let me see what he has to say."

Jonathan knew about the button. He knew that *she* knew about the button. Lila squared her shoulders. Maisie was frowning hard, but she didn't insist on coming with Lila and confronting Jonathan Marleigh.

Lila swept a hand through her hair and made for the parlor. She paused at the threshold, took a deep breath and entered. If revulsion filled her entire body at the sight of her half brother, she didn't let it show. Not too much, at any rate. "Jonathan. This *is* a surprise." Her voice was frigid. Maybe she wasn't entirely hiding the revulsion then.

He smiled his weak smile and gave her a little bow. "I had to return your call, sister. It would have been rude not to. And to tell you the truth, I've always been curious about your home. What would Lila choose? I wondered. All scarlet and gold, or would she keep it understated and make pistachio and champagne her colors of choice? Florals or brocade? Of course, you can afford either. I know you are a successful hostess—I am full of admiration. Though hardly full of surprise. Given your birth and your early upbringing—I mean, Mama and I did what we could, but it is hard to erase a stain of the blood, don't you think? I mean, the Indian touches everywhere, the mirrors, the paisley, the drinks and food I hear you serve, has it been hard to hide it?"

"What do you want?" she snapped.

Jonathan, even though he was dressed neatly enough in

riding clothes, always managed to look as though his clothes didn't fit him properly. Still, he was looking her up and down in his usual blunt way, and she couldn't help remembering that she had been lying on the grass for the last hour. She wondered if she had grass stains at the back and grass in her hair. She couldn't help feeling that he was stripping her naked with his eyes.

"Not so happy to see me today then, Lila. Quite right. Let us get straight to the point." His light eyes and light hair made him look as though he slept underground or in a coffin, as if he hadn't seen sunlight in a long time. "It's not as if we have years to catch up on."

Her face twisted in disgust, but she didn't say anything.

"Quite so, Lila," he said, smiling a little. "I hear that you are housing a certain . . . pregnant girl."

Lila's face froze. She clutched her muslin dress with one hand. How did he know? No one in the house, no one that worked for her, would have gossiped. No one would have intentionally gossiped, though it was always possible to make an unintentional slip. Still, there was a simpler answer. Pritchard. Ezekiel Pritchard. Jonathan's man. He would still be following Maisie. Lila's mind was racing. She was so thrown by this visit and this direct attack that she had no idea what her strategy should be, what she should say. She had no time to plan. What should she do? Deny what he said about Maisie? Would there be any point denying it? What could he do to Maisie anyway? He *knew* they knew. And Sunil was already in prison.

"I have thrown you," Jonathan said, watching her face. "Though I can't conceive why. I simply wish to uphold my promise, nothing more."

Lila looked woodenly at him.

"The girl asked me to help her—financially, I mean. I said yes. I should live up to my promise. That's why I am here."

Lila's mouth curled. "What made *you* agree to help anyone, Jonathan?"

"I would like to see her."

"No."

He raised his eyebrows. "Whyever not?"

She blinked, thinking fast. "She has no need of your help now. She has me."

"But you live month to month, Lila, everyone knows that," Jonathan said gently.

"And you, you little toad, have lost everything you had on drinking and gambling!" She flung the words at him before she could stop herself.

He was watching her, looking amused. "Just so," he said finally. "But you see, I was reared not to pinch pennies."

Neither had bothered to sit down. Jonathan was leaning against a table and he now peeled himself away from it. "Good to know that Maisie is being well looked after. I have no further business, in that case, and will let myself out." He started walking toward the parlor door.

"Funny, isn't it," Lila couldn't help murmuring behind him. "How the people to whom Maisie is close seem to find themselves on the wrong side of the law so often?" She had no idea what made her say it. Maybe something about the nasty little man who was in the room with her. She couldn't even understand the connection her head was trying to make. After all, Jonathan had attacked Tiffany Tristram. Sunil had gotten wrapped up in it. And now Jonathan would simply do all it took to make sure he himself wasn't blamed for what happened to Tiffany. Not that he would ever go to jail for it; it wouldn't come to trial even if he *were* accused. But an accusation like that, attacking a woman at her cousin's party, would not only be a heavy stain on Jonathan Marleigh's name, it would also be an end to his pretensions to the hand of an heiress. Given the state of his debts, he would do anything he could to prevent it, even if it meant sending some other man to the gallows. Still, surely, he was just trying to protect his name? It was nothing personal to do with Maisie. She frowned.

He was watching her, eyebrows raised. "No, m'dear, not funny. Or surprising. Blood always tells in the end." He smiled, bowed, and was again about to exit the room.

"The button," she said desperately. "It was your button. I know you know, Jonathan. *You* know."

He looked slightly bewildered. "You know, I have no idea what you're talking about." Yet he said it in a way that conveyed that he knew *exactly* what she was talking about, and he knew she couldn't do anything about it. As if he *wanted* her to know.

He was at the door again when she flung it at him. "Why did you do it?" She said it almost before she had made up her mind to do it. "Why did you attack her? It doesn't make sense."

He turned and smiled, a half-dead smile. "Again, I have no idea what you are talking about. Because of course, I have not attacked anyone." His pale eyes sparked suddenly. "I'll say this, though, Lila. In the dark, one woman is much the same as another."

And on these words, he left.

She growled, nearly running after him and punching him again. Hopefully this time she would knock him out cold and not just give him a thick lip. What was the man talking about now? This was the thing with Jonathan. You could never tell if he was being cruel—or clever *and* cruel. What did he mean?

He wasn't denying anything. Not convincingly. He knew she knew, and yet, it was as if he didn't care. It was as though he believed that he was above the reach of the law.

She was pacing about in rage, listening to the sounds of Walsham showing Jonathan out—she hoped he had kicked him out, but it was unlikely—and wondering if Maisie would come up from the kitchen herself or if Lila should call for her, when the doorbell rang again.

Dear God, it had to be him now, surely it did.

She pelted to the parlor door. It was Ivor at the front door. Thank God, thank God.

His eyes instantly found her. And her heart froze at the cold, almost blank gaze.

She clutched at her dress, trying desperately to stop herself from rushing to him. Now there was Maisie too, running up from the kitchen. Walsham looked as though he was going to send her on her way, and not too kindly, but Lila intervened and asked Maisie if she could step into the parlor for a moment. Walsham looked as if he had given up trying to have any sort of control on the etiquette in this house.

Both Ivor and Maisie stepped into the parlor, and Lila asked Walsham if tea could be sent up.

Lila took a moment at the parlor door to steady herself. Sunil, it was Sunil that was important. And if Ivor was going to look at her with . . . with hatred, if he was going to blame her for Henry Alston's behavior, well then, so be it. And if he was going to forget about everything they had shared—yet she couldn't help thinking maybe it only meant the world to her. Maybe for him, it was a whim, a passing fancy. Maybe this happened to him all the time. She had just happened to take his fancy this summer. What a fool she was.

She turned from the door and faced the room. Maisie wasn't

sitting down and so Ivor wasn't either. Lila felt stupid indicating chairs, as if this was a normal morning call.

"I would prefer to stand," Ivor said formally.

"And me," Maisie said.

Lila sighed inwardly. She crossed her arms over her chest. "Well?" She gave up pretending.

Ivor filled them in. He had spent all day yesterday trying to find out what was happening to Sunil. He visited him in Clerkenwell Prison. "He's in good spirits. You know how he is, Maisie. He's calm. He . . . has what he needs." He was looking only at Maisie, not at Lila, but at these words, he couldn't help a glance at Lila, and Lila couldn't help thinking that Sunil, poor and alone that he was, must be housed in the worst sorts of conditions, crammed with lots of other prisoners, slops for food, dirt and rats for company, no money with which to bargain for better food or a cell to himself. She shuddered. At that moment, Mrs. Williams came in with a tea tray and everyone was quiet. She asked Lila if there would be anything else and Lila shook her head. Mrs. Williams left. No one made a move to touch the tea.

"They will hold the trial amongst a bunch of others in two days."

Lila was startled. "Isn't that rather quick?"

Ivor nodded grimly. "Yes. I suspect your . . . I suspect Beddington has something to do with that."

"I'll murder that man!" Maisie cried. Lila was already pacing the room, and Maisie was standing right in the middle of it, bristling like a cat. "Just because an earl says so, so an innocent man is in jail! And he'll roast in there for all Mr. Jonathan cares!"

"You think Jonathan is pressing them for a quick trial?" Lila asked Ivor.

"I'm almost certain of it. I expect with someone like Sunil, they would have thrown him in a cell and forgotten about him for a few months if someone *weren't* pressing for a quick conclusion. I've appointed a barrister for him."

Maisie wiped a tear. "Thank you, Mr. Ivor," she said, her voice uncharacteristically small. Normally, someone like Sunil would have no choice but to defend himself in court. The trial would be lumped with many other such trials, and the judge and jury, who would have scores of other cases to see on that same day, would spend five minutes on the case and find him unequivocally guilty. That's how it would normally go. At least, now, Sunil would have a barrister defending him.

"Thank you," Lila said gratefully.

He nodded briefly. "I'll be at the trial. I promise you," he said to Maisie. "I will testify."

He was trying to sound reassuring to Maisie, but Lila could hear what he was trying to hide. He didn't think the case would go Sunil's way. She could hear it in his voice. In everything he wasn't saying. Lila squared her shoulders. "Two days, Maisie. And he has a barrister."

Maisie, whatever her private thoughts, simply nodded. No angry words, no shrieking. Lila watched her apprehensively. All of a sudden Maisie looked very, very young. Not more than a child. And she was heavily pregnant. Horribly thin and very pregnant and the next few days were going to be hard. Lila's eyes flickered to Ivor, but he wasn't looking at her.

"I promise you, Maisie," he said, "I'll do my best."

"I know, sir, Mr. Ivor."

"There's another thing," Lila said. She told the two of them about Jonathan's parting words to her. Since Jonathan had left, she had not had the leisure to examine his words. But now, she realized, they had already unraveled and become clear in her head. "He didn't mean to attack Tiffany Tristram at all."

Maisie was looking puzzled, but Ivor's face cleared up. "That question has been bothering me all along. It didn't make sense for Beddington to attack Tiffany."

Maisie's face finally clarified. "The bounder was trying to attack *me?*"

Lila was at least happy to notice the color and spirit coming back to Maisie's face. She had sagged at Ivor's news. But now she was bristling again. "He thought he was attacking me!"

Lila nodded. "It's the only thing that fits."

"It makes sense," Ivor said. "He went there—to the rose garden—to meet you, Maisie. Perhaps not finding you there, he entered my study, or a noise Tiffany made alerted him to her presence. In the dark, he assumed it was you. Tiffany is quite small, not much bigger than you. And some words that Beddington uttered during the attack—*you wanted me, did you?*—never made sense to me either."

Lila was looking shrewdly at Maisie. "Why would Jonathan try to attack you, Maisie?"

Now Maisie was looking the picture of innocence, which instantly made Lila suspicious. Maisie had always been cagey about her meeting with Jonathan. "How do I know why a blighter takes it into his head to do something, Miss Lila?" she asked.

"If he didn't want to give you money, why make an appointment with you in the first place? And then if he did make the appointment, why try to attack you?"

"I don't know, miss. He was always a funny one."

Lila narrowed her eyes, but instead of responding any further, Maisie excused herself and said she must be off or the other servants would throw her out for dereliction of her new duties.

The exit was so abrupt that Lila had no time to prepare for

being left alone with Ivor. They were both silent and staring at the parlor door.

"I should never have spoken to you the way I did last night. I am unbelievably sorry."

Her eyes flew to his face. Whatever she had expected him to say about last night, it wasn't this. She had been half expecting he wouldn't say anything at all. And she should be glad now that he was talking about it, she should rush into his arms.

But she couldn't. He was apologizing. But his face, it was rigid. He still had that look in his eyes, like he barely knew her.

"Of course, it isn't your fault what happened with Henry Alston." His voice was hard. "Or with Beddington in his house. I know that. I always knew it. It was unforgivable of me to blame you."

She was hardly breathing. He was silent now too. The words were cold and formal. He was hardly looking at her. They still hadn't turned to fully face one another. They were still half facing the parlor door. He turned and walked now, abruptly, to a window, and stood looking out of it, his fists pale and clenched on the window ledge. She was watching him, his profile, barely breathing. She was twisting her hands together. This, this wasn't good. He was apologizing, but it wasn't good. It was worse than if he'd come here in a rage and ranted at her like he did last night.

"My parents had the worst marriage possible."

She started at his words. She certainly wasn't expecting him to say *that*. She walked slowly to another window, some feet away from his. She stood there looking out at the wildflower garden. Now, neither was looking at the other. "I know," she said finally. At least, he hadn't told her about his parents' marriage. But Benjamin Tristram's affairs were hardly a secret. Everyone knew about them.

"My father used to be discreet with his affairs. In the beginning." The voice was expressionless now. Not bitter, or full of rage. Just blank. "But my mother knew about them. In revenge, she . . ." He stopped abruptly. Then carried on. "I would walk into her bedchamber when I was a boy, and there would be a series of men waiting on her while her maid dressed her. Men were at the house all the time. My father would walk into the parlor and find some man . . ." He stopped again. Lila swallowed hard. "It didn't last long. She was only doing it for revenge. Her heart wasn't in it. She barely has the energy for one social evening in a week or a fortnight. A friend or two, no more. But my father lost all sense of discretion and, from then on, paraded his mistresses, one after the other, for all the world to see, but especially where my mother would see them or know about them. It was petty and vengeful. Even though she was only doing it to get back at him. Even though she was doing no worse than he ever did."

"I didn't know. I'm—"

"I'm not asking you for sympathy." The voice was so harsh and abrupt, she stopped. She placed the back of her fingers on her mouth. Then gripped the window ledge again. "I am simply telling you how it is. I apologize for last night. I was completely in the wrong. But this is how things are. I am not—I have never been—cut out for marriage."

"I've never asked you for marriage!" The words flew out of her. Tears sprang to her eyes, and she blinked hard, looking fiercely out the window.

"Yet that was what I was offering."

The words echoed in the silence. And neither could do anything other than stand at their window and stare out into the garden. Her heart was beating so hard now she thought it was going to explode.

"We barely know each other," she said in a small voice. "How can you possibly say you were offering marriage?"

The silence was so long, it had a sound. Then he said, "I suppose sometimes you just know."

She clutched at the lace at her chest. *Sometimes you just know.* But he was speaking again.

"Marriage isn't for me, Miss Marleigh. It never was. I know what it does to people. The cruelties of it—small and big."

"Then let's not get married." Her voice was so small, so low, that she didn't think he would hear what she said. Her throat was burning now. Her chest was hurting.

"I can only apologize."

"Don't." She managed to get the word out, but nothing more. She stood there, staring out into the mild sunshine unblinkingly.

He stood there, at his window for a long time, but then she heard his footsteps as he headed to the parlor door. He was leaving. He had said everything he wanted to say. And he was leaving.

"You're afraid." She said it almost in a whisper. He was afraid. Afraid it would all go to hell. Afraid that that was the *only* way it could go. It was as if the more he had felt in the last few weeks, the more he was convinced it would all go wrong. She wanted to say that her feelings for him filled her with fear too. She was always afraid of losing him, that something would happen to him, a horrible accident; that he would get over what he felt for her, that it had always only been a passing thing for him. She wanted to tell him that loving him felt like fear. But she had no words.

He paused at the threshold. But then he didn't respond to her.

She tossed her head. "We will have to work together—to try to save Sunil."

"I've promised I will do everything I can. And I will."

"With me."

"Of course, with you."

"What next then?" She turned from the window.

He was standing at the door, facing her finally. "I don't think it will go well for Sunil at the trial."

She was pressing her hands together.

"Give me today to see what more I can do. Tomorrow, would you perhaps ride with me at the park?" His face wasn't cold anymore, his voice was neither bitter, nor harsh. It was just formal. He was discussing business now.

She gritted her teeth. Then she made herself smile. Though it hurt her chest. Oh, she was good at business too. "Of course, Mr. Tristram." She gave him a little curtsy, her eyes flashing. "I will be there. I wouldn't miss it for the world."

He looked—she was glad to see—annoyed at her tone. His mouth tightened. Then he nodded and left the room.

31

Lila dressed with care for the park the next day. She wore her best sateen riding habit. Riding habits were dark in color so they wouldn't easily show mud splashes and dirt, and this was dark too. But instead of being in green, navy or brown, it had a rich lilac skirt with a hem of yellow embroidered roses, and the jacket was a darker, richer purple. It fitted her to perfection, framing her broad shoulders beautifully and narrowing to her tiny waist. The skirt, of course, was just full enough to give a mild sense of propriety to her breeches.

She was riding Polly who, after a few days of neglect, was in a frisky and playful mood. Roger, his filigree eye mask in place, was riding just a pace behind her. She let Polly have her head at first and toss off her fidgets, but then when they slowed their pace down again, Lila directed a casual remark at Roger. This made him ride next to her.

After a pause, he said, "People're asking me if I'll be wearing a new mask for the Brighton race, Miss Lila."

Lordy, were people still talking about that? She kept forgetting about it, but then someone or the other would bring it up again. She felt suddenly that she'd love to run it, if nothing else but to annoy the life out of Tristram, who was not in favor of her *making a spectacle of herself*. "We should get you a new mask, race or not. Full gold filigree, I should say. Something more dashing."

He grinned. "Betty will help me find one." He blushed fiercely. "She can't see but she still knows what's best."

She eyed him sideways. Roger and Betty! "Yes, funny how she can see a lot, that one. She's *great* with her hands," she added. Now the man was purple. She couldn't help a grin. "Shall I congratulate you, Roger?"

He sat straighter on his nag. "I'd never do anything without your permission, Miss Lila, and to tell you the truth, Betty would kill me if I did."

She laughed. "Yes. So, lucky for you, you have my blessing. Are you both going to leave me?"

"No, Miss Lila. We never would. Not as long as you wanted us. Would you cast us out if we . . . if we thought about—"

"Marriage? No, stupid man. Of course, I wouldn't. You can't imagine how long I've been hoping Walsham and Mrs. Williams would make a match of it, but I expect Walsham will have an apoplexy if I mention it." She thought about this. "Maybe I *should* mention it," she murmured.

Roger grinned and touched his hat. "I reckon you will, sooner or later."

"Only when he's being especially aggravating."

He was grinning, but then he pulled away and fell back again. Lila looked up to see Tristram—not Ivor, he was no longer Ivor and never could be again—approaching on his horse. She sat straighter. "How lovely to see you, Mr. Tristram. I can't tell you how disappointed I was not to see you last night in my salon."

Ivor Tristram had given Roger a friendly enough nod before

falling in step with Lila, but he didn't look friendly now. He looked annoyed, Lila thought, with a great feeling of well-being. She smiled more brightly than ever. Her smile, she thought, might even be described as dazzling.

"I'm afraid I had other things to do."

"Of course, Mr. Tristram. You're a busy man. Still, my salon felt empty without you."

His mouth tightened. "Were there not enough men there last night to keep you entertained?"

Touché! "Oh, but however many men there were, my interest *for the moment* is fixed on you."

His jaw jerked. Ha. This he wasn't expecting. Marriage wasn't for him, but he had casually assumed that if it *was* for him, then she would fall over backward to accept him. Well, take that, Mr. Tristram.

"I am deeply honored," he said, his mouth a thin line, "and flattered. How long does your interest normally last?"

"Oh, as much as a month sometimes."

The skin around his eyes twitched, just for a fraction of a second, just once. If she wasn't so aggravatingly sensitive to every one of his expressions, she would have missed it. This, she thought, so this hurt, did it, Mr. Tristram? She was pleased to see that she had rattled him. Only for a second or so, but she had done it. He wasn't expecting *her* interest to be fleeting.

But then he turned to look at her. And those eyes. That direct, searching gaze. She had to look away before he saw all she felt in hers.

"Tell me, Mr. Tristram," she said in a cheery voice, "are you backing my friend Kenneth Laudsley for the Brighton race? Or are you backing Lord Herringford's nephew?"

"I haven't had the time to think about it."

"*You* have a matching pair of grays, I'm told. Aren't they tremendous racers?"

He said a few short words about his grays. She had time to study him because he was looking straight in front of him again. He looked as though he hadn't slept in days. His eyes were serious and there was a hint of tiredness about his eyes, more than there had been the day before. She sighed deeply. The stupid, stupid man. She hoped he never slept again.

"I might just give it a go, the race," she murmured.

Oh, now his mouth was tight. A thin line. She sighed as if the sun had just come out.

"You must of course do as you please," he managed to force out.

"Oh, I will," she assured him. "I always do." She eyed him sideways. But then the teasing fell away from her. And her face grew serious. "Are they still holding his trial tomorrow?"

"I'm afraid so. I've tried to change it. But I don't have an earl's standing. Even being solvent doesn't count for as much as a title."

"And your cousin, she still means to marry him?"

"To tell you the truth, I don't know. I'm not even sure she has feelings for him. But she thinks he cares for her, and she's sick of men—me included—who give her nothing but presents. Now she knows I'm opposed to it—her father has always been opposed. I believe it has only strengthened her resolve. But I can't pretend I understand her." They rode in silence. "It's not going to end well for Sunil," he said finally.

She stared straight ahead of her. Yes, he was right. And it was time to accept facts. It was not going to go well for Sunil. Now that he had been arrested, it was going to go badly. The truth was they had known how it would go all along. If he was arrested, it wouldn't go well. They had let themselves get complacent when Jonathan was out of town. "So how are we going to rescue him?"

For a second, his eyes lightened. "I should know you well enough to know you wouldn't give in to despair. Not even for five seconds. I should have known."

She tossed her head. "Yes, you should. Despair is paltry and useless. We simply need a plan. Isn't it possible to . . . swap him with someone else?"

He couldn't help a grin. Her heart nearly cracked in two seeing that smile of his. How was it already so familiar? And why couldn't she loathe the sight of it instead of feeling like she was melting inside?

"We're thinking along the same lines."

She looked quickly at him. "Are we really? I thought you'd tell me to get a grip. I have to say I spent half the night plotting how to swap him for someone else. Someone dressed as a barrister or a curate or something!" She'd spent the other half imagining what would happen if she managed to get Ivor Tristram in a cottage alone, somewhere in the Highlands perhaps, or the Pyrenees, possibly with his hands all tied up with a silk scarf. She had a feeling she knew exactly the kinds of things they could do to each other. She closed her eyes for a second and shivered at the image.

She looked up at him to see him staring at her. She blinked rapidly, wondering how much was visible on her face. Her first impulse was to turn her eyes away but then she stared back at him.

She was completely aware of him. That chest and those shoulders. The deliciously flat, broad chest that she wanted to press herself into and lose herself in. Those brows of his, the way his eyes didn't miss a flicker of expression on her face. He made himself look away.

They rode in silence.

"Of course, if we swapped him with someone—another Indian-looking man," Tristram finally said, "*that* man would be hanged in Sunil's place."

"Yes. That occurred to me. It is a problem. I don't suppose you know someone who *deserves* to be hanged?"

He gave her an abstracted smile. "If we swapped Sunil for someone who is already dead—"

She nearly fell off her horse and stared at him. Polly jerked a little at the sudden movement and, since she was already irritated at Lila for not riding her so regularly in the last few weeks, it took Lila a minute or two to get her under control again. Lila absently stroked her horse, but she was staring at Tristram. "*Can* we do that?"

"Carrying a dead body through the arches and tunnels of Clerkenwell all the way to Sunil's cell. Placing it there while all the other poor souls crowding there watched us and then walking off with Sunil. No, we can't."

"You have another idea."

"It probably wouldn't work."

She looked eagerly at him. "Tell me."

He stopped under an elm. And they faced each other. "There is always a chance the court won't find him guilty."

She flicked her head. "A negligible one."

"I agree with you. I'm simply explaining that I'm working on the contingency that he will be sentenced to death. I am also taking it that Tiffany will not step in to help Sunil. She is convinced of his guilt. These are the facts."

"And we need to accept them. I think that is the only thing

we can do. If we keep hoping there will be a reprieve, and we wait until there is a guilty verdict, we will have lost time. How long will he have?"

"The trial is tomorrow. There is a scheduled hanging three days after that. It would be unusual if Sunil were thrown into that lot. But I'm guessing that that is exactly what will happen because of Beddington's involvement. That means, except for the time in the courthouse, Sunil will be in his cell for the next five days, where it is almost impossible to swap him for a body."

"When then?"

He glanced at her for a second, then carried determinedly on. "I can only think of one thing. It isn't ideal, because it means he will still be incarcerated for the next five days. And if it doesn't work, we will have lost our only chance and we won't get another one. But I cannot think of another way. Just before the hanging, he will be in an empty room for five minutes and that's when he has the opportunity to speak to a priest. It is the only time he will be alone."

She stared unblinkingly at his face.

"The priest would get in to see him, not through the warren of the prison, but from a different door. That is what happens for the prisoners who request a conversation with a priest."

"And?" She sounded a little breathless. It was a mad plan.

He answered the unspoken question. "It's almost impossible that it would work. I have to be honest with you. Even if the priest could get a body in—which is by no means certain— the swap might be discovered. Or the priest may not have the opportunity to make the swap at all."

"How would we get a priest—?"

"It would be Hector, my man, dressed as a priest. His father was a priest. He can pull it off."

She couldn't help a flicker of something, of hope. He had been thinking about this, obsessing about it just as she had. Maybe, she thought with a slight sinking of her heart, that was the only reason he wasn't sleeping. Maybe it had nothing to do with her. But then she shook herself at the selfish thought. "What if Hector didn't have to go in there carrying the body? What if . . . don't they get deliveries of food?"

He smiled at her again, looking a little amused. "They do. I don't know if I can get a body through the door—or what they would do with it once it was inside. But it is a possibility."

"In a sack or a wooden box!"

"It's possible, but full of holes."

They rode in silence again, Lila's mind racing. "What if . . . don't men die in there every day? It is a large and unhealthy place, isn't it? What if—what if—well, wouldn't an undertaker go in there to bring the bodies out to be taken for burial?"

He looked arrested. "That's actually a rather brilliant idea," he said slowly.

She smiled. A genuine smile for the first time that day, an actual feeling of joy. The first real flicker she had felt ever since that meeting with him in her parlor the day before. "Could we do it?"

"It's a good idea. Let me see if anything can come of it." He was looking at her. "Lila—Miss Marleigh—I wouldn't get your hopes up. And I don't think you should tell—"

"Tell Maisie? I won't. In fact, I don't think we should tell her if Sunil is sentenced to die. I think I will tell her there has been an adjournment or something. She's—she's heavily pregnant. I don't know what would happen . . ."

"I agree with you. Will you let me take my leave? If we have to pull this off, I have a lot to do."

"What about after? What if we can get him out?"

"I am already on the lookout for a body. If they think he died from natural causes—if it's just before the hanging—I expect he . . . the poor sod, whoever it is, if I can find someone—will be taken for burial with the others that are hanged that day."

"Yes, but what happens to Sunil then?"

"I'm working on it, Miss Marleigh."

"Thank you," she said with real gratitude. And she watched him ride off.

32

I vor spent the rest of that day trying to work on the details of a plan—if it could be called a plan. At the moment, it was full of holes. It was true, a man entered the prison site in a large carriage run by a team of horses, every day, to take the dead from the prison to be buried. But the dead were taken *out* of the prison, not taken *into* the prison. If an internal swap could be managed, leaving one of the prison's dead in Sunil's place, it would be a possible solution. But though there would undoubtedly be other brown-skinned men in the prison, there was no saying that one would die of natural causes on the exact day they needed him to.

Hector was at the Docks every day, hoping to get news of a dead or dying lascar. There was something ghoulish about it, Ivor thought grimly, as he sat with a glass of brandy after dinner, after another exhausting day. Unless you thought about the alternative, which was that an innocent man would be hanged.

He had called on his cousin Tiffany last night. But she was set against Ivor, since that mischance of a meeting in Vauxhall. She was convinced that Sunil was her attacker. It was clear that—instead of easing off with time—the distress and fear of it had only gotten worse for her since the attack. She was still haunted by it. He urged her to speak about it, to a trusted aunt or older cousin, if not to him, but she looked defiantly at him and told him she would only be better once the man was sentenced to death.

"Jonathan will see to it, if you won't." She flung the words defiantly at him.

He started at that. Somehow, he hadn't expected such an open attack from Beddington. "Did you tell him that I . . . suspect that he is the culprit, and not the lascar?"

Tiffany, dressed as she was for a musical evening, in a gown of gray silk with all-over silver embroidery, her hair in ringlets that framed both sides of her face, had simply carried on pulling her gloves on. "Of course, I didn't. It's spiteful of you, Ivor. I've never thought you and Papa would oppose me like this. But Jonathan will be in my life forever, and I am not the one to set you against one another. He is the one who found that man who attacked me and had him arrested."

He looked steadily at her. "Was he now?"

She flicked her head. "*I'm* not without resource. That night . . ." Her voice faltered for a second, but then she gave him a defiant look. "That night I saw you in Vauxhall, I had my groom follow them to Whitechapel where the lascar was holed up in a . . . in a brothel." Her mouth was a thin line. "I knew where they lived. But I didn't know what to do with the information. I bided my time until Jonathan came back from Yorkshire."

So that was how it had happened. It had been Tiffany whose information had led to Sunil's arrest—with Beddington's help. "Uncle Arthur is still against the match?"

"Oh, so what if he is?" she said impatiently. "It is only stupid prejudice against someone who doesn't have the same wealth as you."

"Do you love him, Tiff?" he couldn't help asking again.

She was pulling on and smoothing each finger of her gray silk glove. "He doesn't treat me as though I'm not there."

It wasn't exactly an answer to the question. Was she so desperate for love that her belief that Jonathan Marleigh loved her was enough for her to want to marry him? Did she feel more than that, or was that it? The image of Beddington's thick lip rose forcefully in Ivor's mind. It was odd because Jonathan Marleigh came across as weak and resentful—and potentially violent. Why couldn't Tiffany see it?

The men in the Tristram family were hardly the best role models, he thought angrily. If she was interested only in weak-willed men, whose fault was it? He found himself wishing he had taken more of an interest in her over the years, been there for her.

But there was no arguing his case with Tiffany now. She was convinced of Sunil's guilt, and she was sure her father and cousin simply wanted to peel her away from Jonathan Marleigh because he was impoverished and in debt—and that they would do it at any cost. Ivor saw that there was no point arguing further. Lila—Miss Marleigh—was right. Facts had to be accepted, and they had to be accepted quickly. At the door, he had stopped one more time though. He couldn't help it. He turned and asked Tiffany one further question. "How is Beddington's horse-riding injury?" It was a shot in the dark.

"Oh, it was only affecting him . . ." She frowned. "I can't remember when. But it wasn't for long. It was on—"

"The day of the party," Ivor said. "Rather like a groin injury, wasn't it?"

He did at least have the satisfaction of seeing her stare.

Hector knocked and entered the parlor now as Ivor sat there

nursing his brandy. Ivor indicated for him to get himself a drink. Hector hesitated, as he always did. Ivor made an impatient gesture. Even when Hector unbent and got himself a drink, he perched on the edge of a chair with it. Ivor felt again that pang of regret, for those days when there wasn't such a gap between him and Hector. Things had been simpler then. Life had been easier. There were fewer formal hierarchies that couldn't be bridged. Fewer demands on his time and attention—in fact, truth was he could do exactly as he pleased at all times. He didn't have the weight of running the estate, of paying his employees, his staff, his farmers, making sure he wasn't bleeding them dry and yet the estate was still surviving. When he was up at Oxford, he could forget the mess his father had made of the estate, and he could escape the ruin of his parents' marriage.

Oh, and another thing, there had been no Lila Marleigh in those days.

In fact, his life had been miraculously free of Lila Marleigh until some weeks ago. He thought nostalgically about his Lila Marleigh–free life—it had stretched on for quite a long time. If only he had had the sense to appreciate it. He gulped down more brandy.

Hector was eyeing him sideways, but he didn't remark on the drinking. Instead he filled him in on the day's findings. The men discussed the chances of pulling off what they meant to try. The plan was for Hector to enter the premises dressed as a priest. In the meantime, for Ivor to find a way to load a dead body into the undertaker's carriage. And then for Hector to find a way to place the body in the confession room and smuggle Sunil out in the guise of another priest. Often more than one priest was in the prison for a visit and Sunil, if his clothes were right, and especially on the day of a mass hanging, might be taken for another priest on his way out of the prison with Hector.

The plan was almost certain to go wrong, Ivor thought darkly. When said out loud, it felt less like a plan and more like a farce. They had a few days to work on the details, he told himself.

He looked at Hector and realized that Hector was watching him.

"Been digging deep, Mr. Ivor?" Hector remarked.

"What of it?" He *had* been drinking steadily for the last hour—or was it two?—but so what? Hector knew better than anyone that he could hold his drink.

"Not going around to Miss Marleigh's tonight, sir?"

Ivor scowled. He wished his staff would leave him be. "Drop it, man, before I start regretting that I offered you a drink."

Hector drank in peace. Ivor thought he was getting off easy—Hector wasn't normally so undemanding, but then Mrs. Manfield came into the room. She frowned at the sight of Hector, sitting there, not looking entirely comfortable, but drinking with Ivor. It didn't happen often, but it was hardly the first time. Why couldn't she mind her own business? Ivor thought belligerently. Really, he was giving his staff too much rope.

"Bad analogy," he muttered. "*Too* apropos."

Hector was looking at him.

"What?" Ivor said querulously.

Mrs. Manfield poured him a coffee.

"I was just saying that I'm sorry we're not going to Miss Marleigh's tonight, sir. They do a fella a nice cup of tea in there if you nip down to the kitchen. They're not high in the instep," Hector elaborated. "Only reason I was asking."

Oh, they were still talking about that. "Do you not get a cup of tea in this house?" Ivor asked irritably.

"Reckon it's sweeter there."

"Don't let Carly hear you say that." Ivor raised his glass.

"Don't tell Carly I said it, will you, sir?" Hector said, actually looking alarmed.

Mrs. Manfield gave Hector a quelling look. He meekly took a tiny sip of his drink. It was good to see that at least Mrs. Manfield could make Hector quake, even if Ivor couldn't.

She placed the coffee next to Ivor. "Will you be going to Miss Marleigh's tomorrow night, sir?"

"Good God, Mrs. Manfield, I suppose you can't get a decent cup of tea in this house either!" He looked crossly at his staff. "Can a fellow not be allowed to enjoy a glass of brandy in his own home without being—without being mauled about?" he said viciously. Then he rubbed his face. "I apologize for the outburst, Mrs. Manfield. Perhaps it is time I went to bed." It was past midnight. He wondered for a second what Lila Marleigh was doing. No doubt trying to find another poor soul to torment, now that her interest in Ivor was sure to wane. She had said as much. That her feelings for him were only for the moment, that they would pass. He downed his glass.

Hector and Mrs. Manfield, usually somewhat jealous of their domain, protective of who got to look after Ivor more and better, actually exchanged glances. Hector and Mrs. Manfield! This put Ivor in a worse rage than he was already in. He thumped his empty glass on the table next to him and came to his feet. He swayed a little. Hector stood too, rather suddenly.

"It's just when I first started walking out with my Carly, I was that terrified too, sir. It can take a man in that way." Hector said the words in such a rush, Ivor could hardly understand him. Ivor stared at Hector. Hector was still standing there, and now he was blushing hotly.

"Terrified?" Ivor said furiously. "*Terrified?* Have you gone mad? Have you both gone mad? Do I give my staff permission to badger me about my private business?" Who said anything about being terrified? The presumption.

Hector looked not mortified or abashed as he should, but more . . . philosophical in defeat. He even had the effrontery to slightly shrug at Mrs. Manfield. Ivor nearly grabbed his glass and flung it across the room. What the devil was the matter with them all?

Hector was about to leave the room, brandy glass in hand, after another significant look at Mrs. Manfield. But Ivor stopped him. "Since when do you let me off the hook this easily, Hector?"

They were both looking at him now.

Hector shrugged. "I reckon I never let you off the hook, Mr. Ivor, but this seems maybe out of my depth," he said, looking apologetically at Mrs. Manfield, "seeing as we've never crossed swords over a woman, and it seems, well . . . bigger than usual. Maybe it's not my purview, so to speak."

"None of your business, more like," said Ivor succinctly.

"As to that, I don't know, sir. Your humor *is* my business. It'll be me you'll be flinging your boots at when you're in a bad mood, not the neighbors."

"Go to the devil," Ivor said. He reached for his empty glass. "Is someone going to fill this up for me?"

Now they were both looking sideways at one another. Hector took it on his shoulders, in the air of a martyr. "I reckon you've had enough, Mr. Ivor, if you don't mind me saying."

"I do bloody well—pardon my language, Mrs. Manfield—I do mind your saying it, damn your impudence—pardon me, Mrs. Manfield. And as a matter of fact, it isn't."

Hector scratched his head. "It isn't what, sir?"

"It isn't big," Ivor said, in the nature of pulling out a rabbit from a hat. "So take that. It isn't big at all. It is a tiny passing thing. It'll pass. And as for being *terrified* . . ." He placed his hands on his hips and stood there, shaking his head. "It's no worse than what Miss Marleigh said. Afraid. She said I was afraid. That was her verdict. Afraid of what exactly?" he demanded, staring from one to the other. "*Of what?*"

He was staring at Hector, but it was Mrs. Manfield who answered. Rather to his surprise, given he wasn't expecting an answer at all. Since the last few sentences he had uttered made hardly any sense, it was a wonder to get a response.

"Most people don't mind when love feels good, Mr. Ivor," she said diffidently but purposefully. "It's when it feels like fear, they don't like it."

Ivor stared at her like she had gone mad. "*Love!*" he expostulated.

Mrs. Manfield stood there, one hand crossed over the other. "It's just, sir, in my experience love doesn't come without fear. Not real love." She looked kindly at him. "It always throws a man more than a woman, I've seen. A woman, in my experience, is not so frightened of it. Not so frightened of fear, I mean."

For some moments, Ivor couldn't trust himself to speak. "*Why* in the name of all that's good are we talking about love at all! I barely know the woman!"

"It's a bit like a thunderbolt, sir." This from Hector. "As if you've been waiting for something . . . that you didn't even know you were waiting for—and then it punches you in the gut, sir. Turns out it's there to stay. And then there you are."

Now Ivor was completely flabbergasted. Of all the . . . my God, the effrontery of it!

He summarily dismissed them, saying that he had a good mind to replace all his staff, but especially the two currently in his parlor for their damned interference, then feeling that he had been rude, he stalked to the door, called out to them to have a good night, and dragged himself off to bed. The sooner he could be done with this entire sorry business and leave for Sussex, the better for everyone, especially for him.

The next morning, after spending the worst night in bed he could remember having in a long time, he went straight to court. The courtroom was more packed than an anthill. The jury was loud, the judge bored, everyone worse for wear in the hot room. And the outcome was exactly as expected. Sunil's hearing was wedged between countless others. It took all of five minutes.

The prosecutor, a man who had the habit of talking under his breath in a rolling monologue, simply reported that Jonathan Marleigh, the Earl of Beddington, and Miss Tiffany Tristram, daughter of Mr. Arthur Tristram, who was a true gentleman, had testified that Sunil Mehta, the lascar standing in court today, had violently attacked Miss Tristram in the home of her own cousin Mr. Ivor Tristram and then absconded by way of the window. The man was deranged and dangerous, had evaded capture by a most enterprising Runner (who gave his testimony as to Sunil Mehta's dangerous and evasive character), and it was for the good of society that this man should be put permanently out of the way. Ivor's brief testimony that no one had seen the man attack Tiffany was paid no heed to. The man was aggressively holding Miss Tristram's arms when the lights came on. There was simply no other explanation but that he was her attacker. And of course, Lord Beddington had himself identified the accused man. He saw the lascar with his own eyes, as he was one of the guests who rushed to the rescue when Miss Tristram screamed.

Ivor briefly closed his eyes at that piece of information. Of course, Jonathan Marleigh had himself identified the man as guilty. Sunil's fate was sealed.

He was sentenced to be hanged in three days' time in a public and mass hanging, as was the custom. It wasn't, however, the custom to send a man so quickly to the gallows after his sentencing, and Sunil looked startled when the date was set. Ivor looked steadily at him, trying to convey that they were going to get him out. But all hope seemed to be gone from Sunil's face. Ivor had never seen the man look like that. Ivor himself could look willful and grim, Lila was headstrong and temperamental, and Maisie could bring the house down when she was in one of her moods. It was Sunil who was always calm, always the voice of reason. Not anymore.

Ivor walked home from the courthouse, trying to work off his frustration. Even though there were no surprises at the courthouse, and the hearing had gone exactly as he predicted, he was still thrown. He felt that admitting to Lila Marleigh that he had had no impact whatsoever on the outcome was impossible. He wanted to sweep in and tell her that he had already managed to save Sunil Mehta. He didn't want to say to her that he felt completely helpless.

He came to an abrupt standstill as he turned into Berkeley Square.

The man he was staring at halted too and swung his cane. "Was hoping to run into you."

"Were you, sir?" Ivor said, his face taking on that same expressionless cast it always did when he was confronted with his father.

Benjamin Tristram looked like his usual self. There was more gray in his hair now, Ivor thought, practically every time he saw him, and he had a feeling that his father was steadily shrinking a little from his robust, muscular stature year by year; but he was still only in his fifties and not a bad-looking man. Ivor had inherited his broad shoulders and muscles from his father. The blue eyes were his father's too, as was the broad, open face, though the darker coloring was from his mother's side. Yet there was a softness to his father now, around the middle and the jowls. He had been a strong, athletic man in his younger days, and was still energetic, but he was losing the robust look. The years of drinking steadily through the night were starting to catch up.

Ivor sighed. He didn't have the energy for this. Over the years his hatred and anger for his father had mellowed into something he called indifference, perhaps tinged with impatience. But today, he was gritting his teeth. How the lord did his father have an unerring way of turning his son into a resentful fourteen-year-old again? "What can I do for you, sir?"

"Had a letter from your mother's doctor. He says she might only have a month or two."

There was a frown on his father's brow, but not much emotion beyond that. This didn't surprise Ivor. Benjamin Tristram was much easier with situations he enjoyed, that were comfortable and put him at his ease. The darker emotions in life, he was not so very good at those. In fact, most of his life he had been excellent at avoiding anything he didn't want to confront. Anger wasn't great. Discomfort was awful. Fear was not to be admitted to or contemplated.

For some inexplicable reason, this thought put Ivor in an even worse mood. "I have some business to finish in the next few days," he said to his father. "I plan to spend the rest of the autumn in Sussex." He hesitated. "Do you plan to come?"

His father looked uncomfortable now. He blotted his brow. "I was never very good at that sort of thing, my son. And Heather, she'll be happier without me."

"What sort of thing, sir? Have you lost a wife before?"

Benjamin Tristram lifted his chest. "No need to take that tone. Always find you very high and mighty. Just because you've saved the family estate from ruin—no need to lord it over the rest of us. I *am* your father."

"I am unfortunately completely aware of it. If there's nothing else . . ."

Now his father looked even more uncomfortable. "I hear you're spending time with Lila Marleigh."

Ivor went cold with rage. His nostrils flared. He didn't feel as though he could trust himself to respond. Somehow, he realized, he couldn't bear to hear her name uttered by his father.

"I've never interfered in who you spend your time with," his father said hastily, perhaps reading his son's face correctly. "Don't intend to start now. No need to look so thunderous. It's just your mother thinks—"

But Benjamin Tristram didn't seem to know how to complete his thought. Ivor did it for him. "That Miss Marleigh is your mistress?"

His father flushed and said, "Yes, she does. Don't know how she got that in her head. Wasn't from me. Someone must have said that I was spending one too many an evening at Miss Marleigh's salon. And I suppose it isn't my kind of den, the stakes are too mellow. But here's the thing. Lila Marleigh, she's as charming as they come, rarely seen a woman who was more so, but she knows how to keep a man in his place. Don't know how she does it. But she does and there it is. Does it in a way that the man leaves with his pride intact, I'll say that for her. A man of sense always knows how far he can take it and no further, if you get my meaning. The thing is," he inserted a finger uncomfortably in his cravat and pulled, "I might not have denied it, when your mother confronted me. But there's nothing in it. So there it is."

His father said it all in a rush. But then his eyelids flickered. So there was more to it. Ivor stared steadily at Benjamin. "You may as well tell me."

Benjamin looked even more belligerent. "Always that tone, Ivor, always the high-and-mighty tone! There's nothing more to tell." He must have seen the look of loathing on his son's face because he flicked his head. "Nothing important. I may have—inadvertently—let people think that Miss Marleigh was in fact my mistress. And rumor got around. And as I said, I didn't deny it when your mother confronted me."

"And why is that?"

Benjamin looked uncomfortable now. Ivor almost gave up then and there. What did it matter now? What could it solve? His relationship with Lila was already in a shambles. He wasn't cut out for it—love, or torture, whatever it was. He was—yes, maybe they were all right—a coward. But then, seeing his father's faltering face, he suddenly knew the answer.

"So there is a mistress, but you can't say who it is."

Benjamin almost looked relieved. "Wouldn't say it to anyone but you. But yes, there is someone. Different from my usual. Respectable."

"Respectable?" Ivor knew he sounded disdainful and disbelieving.

Benjamin bristled. "She is, and I don't care for your attitude! She's married, if you must know. And I can't let her name be smirched. Keep it to yourself, if you please!"

Ivor looked at him with contempt. "It's none of my business."

Benjamin nodded. "Yes, you were always that way. High and

mighty, but your principles are in the right place. And no need to say it, you didn't get that from me—your principles, I mean. But in this case, I want to do right by the woman. She is . . . she's married. She's a friend of Miss Marleigh's. She goes to the salon, it's where I met her. When people started assuming that it was Miss Marleigh I was visiting, I just didn't correct them, see? It would hurt the woman's reputation."

Ivor did see, unfortunately. "And Miss Marleigh?" he said softly. "What of her reputation?"

"She's a salon hostess."

Ivor's mouth curled.

Benjamin hurried on. "Miss Marleigh is a good sport. She wouldn't want Annabel—the lady in question, I mean—to be in any kind of a fix. I expect she didn't correct the assumption people made either."

Ivor felt nothing so much as drained. Yes, Lila—Miss Marleigh—wouldn't care what people thought of her. She'd protect her friend. And she'd laugh in the face of anyone who dared judge her. And what did it even matter now? He rubbed his forehead where there was a pain that would perhaps never go away. "I expect she didn't. Now if there's nothing else . . ."

His father was looking at him with an unusually shrewd look in his eyes. This, thought Ivor, was also the problem with Tristram men. They were good at reading faces and minds—the better to make a quick getaway when there was trouble brewing. His father no doubt found this skill most useful in his life.

"Anything in it?" Benjamin asked. "This rumor that you've been seen in her company, in Miss Marleigh's company, I mean?"

"There isn't." Ivor turned and started walking toward his door.

"Ivor . . ."

He turned. He was exhausted.

His father was still looking at him with that strange expression. "Just because things weren't so good between your mother and me . . ." He stopped abruptly.

Ivor stood there, feeling strangely helpless. For once, he thought raggedly, for once, could Benjamin Tristram just act like his father?

His father surprised him.

"It's not always like that. The way it was with your mother and me. It isn't always so . . . so tortured. Not between people who're suited to one another. Some people just aren't." He raised a hand in goodbye. "I'll be seeing you. When you're in the country—let me know when . . ."

Ivor didn't trust his voice to respond. But he nodded.

33

There was one last conversation he had to have with Lila Marleigh before the date of Sunil Mehta's hanging. As he drove in the park in his curricle, her groom Roger Manson following discreetly behind them, he thought the last meeting couldn't have come fast enough. He wanted never to see her again. After tomorrow, he never would. After this conversation they were having today, they need never speak again.

She wasn't dressed for riding. She had taken a hackney here to the park and he came in his curricle and had taken her up, as they had planned. She was wearing an overdress the color of translucent coral and an embroidered underdress, of a rich burgundy cloth. Her hair, as always, was dressed simply, the waves forming a halo around her face, and she wore light jewels in her hair, like crystal flowers.

Ever since he had told her he couldn't see her anymore, she had taken on her hostess persona with him, smiling, being charming or speaking business, nothing more. He had never before thought that people could use charm and friendliness to keep other people at a distance. Lila Marleigh was very good at it.

Except then he'd catch a dangerous glitter in her eyes when she didn't know he was looking. She was angry with him and, as usual, when she was angry, she was being even friendlier and more animated than usual. It was more maddening than if she would just curse him to hell.

And he knew just what to do to put her in a good mood again. To make her soft and open in his arms. He knew exactly what he could do.

Damnation.

Tomorrow couldn't come quickly enough. The one thing he wanted to do was finish this business with Sunil and go home, where he could get sucked into the endless demands of the estate and forget all about her. Oblivion couldn't come fast enough. And in fact, if he couldn't forget her, then at least he'd take himself out of her orbit. Go where there would be no temptation to see her one more time. He wished Sussex were in the far reaches of Mongolia.

"Miss Marleigh," he said, as she sat with her hands in her lap, looking demure and beautiful and not at all dangerous, "I wouldn't be honest if I told you that this mad plan is going to work. It is unlikely to."

"It is the only one we have," she said, frowning, looking straight ahead of her. "It *has* to work. Maisie is already suspicious." Her voice broke slightly, and she put her fingers up to her mouth. "It's just I keep thinking if we can't save him, then Maisie won't even get to say goodbye. She doesn't know it's tomorrow. Yet, yet I can't make her go through another hanging. And if something happened to her or the baby . . ." She stopped abruptly.

He could hardly sit in his curricle with her, in the view of all the morning riders and walkers in the park, and reach out for her hand. Yet though he could resist—just about—the sight of those glittering eyes, it was harder to deny her when she was feeling helpless. "I will do everything I can," he said. "Afterward, how would it be if Sunil came to Sussex, to my estate, and tried to make a life there? The Runners won't be looking for him anymore if they think he died. He could be just another lascar who worked on a farm."

He could curse himself for those words.

Where had they sprung from? He had had the idea a few days ago—where else would Sunil go, after all? London would be too dangerous. The Runners might stop looking for him, but Ivor was not at all certain that Jonathan Marleigh would. He could work on a farm in Sussex. Yet, then he had dismissed the idea. Wasn't he just trying to hold on to some connection with Lila Marleigh? If Sunil and Maisie worked on his estate . . . but it was too late to take it back. She was already nodding.

"That's kind of you. I've been thinking they couldn't live in London. Maisie, I would have Maisie with me, if Sunil—if he—if our plan didn't work. But if it does work and he lives, they should probably get out of the city for a while."

"This is the bit I'm stuck on. If Beddington somehow sniffs trouble, if he is on Sunil's trail or if he warned the Runners—"

"Then how would Sunil get away from the city? Yes, it is a problem. And when Jonathan came to my house, I have to say, I don't think it was to offer anything to Maisie. I think it was . . . more of a warning."

They discussed this question. How to get Sunil away from the city if he managed to escape.

They sat in silence as he niftily drove his grays around a corner. Yet he was entirely attuned to changes in her expression. She had been looking thoughtfully into the distance, but now her eyes were alert, and she was sitting straighter. He couldn't help but be amused. "Miss Marleigh, I can't help but think that you've had an idea."

She turned bright eyes toward him. "You know, I think I have. I might just have. As Kenneth always says, shout out your secrets, don't hide them in the dark."

She told him her idea.

34

In the end, Lila couldn't keep the truth from Maisie. Simply because Maisie had found out that there was a public hanging the very next day and ferreted the information out of Lila that Sunil was one of the twenty-two people scheduled to be hanged, three at a time, on the following day. She was speechless. Though not for long. "Were you planning to tell me or were you planning to let him hang and for me never to know a thing about it?"

On reflection, Lila felt she had been very stupid. "I was scared it would hurt you—or the baby—if you knew," she said nervously.

"It'll hurt me worse if he dies and I never get to say goodbye!"

"Maisie, I don't want you to say goodbye. I want us to get him out. He—Sunil—feels the same. Mr. Tristram says he's going to do everything he can to get Sunil out. There *is* no reason to say goodbye." All night she had tossed and turned, trying to claw awake, so she could stop seeing the executioner put the noose around Annie's neck. Over and over, all night long, Annie's accusing eyes had stared at her. Not only for letting Annie down, but also Maisie. She had woken up feeling like she couldn't face another day.

Maisie was adamant that she wanted to see Sunil before it was too late. And Lila didn't see how she could refuse the girl, didn't see how she could say with any conviction that there was no need to say goodbye, that they would save him somehow. The night before the hanging, Hector escorted Maisie to see Sunil in Clerkenwell.

When she came back, instead of being downcast, she was more furious than ever and determined that nothing should get in the way of Sunil's escape.

The next day, Tristram's groom escorted Maisie in stages down to Sussex to wait for Sunil. Lila had suggested that she wait in London to see—to see what? Maisie had demanded. To see if Sunil made it out alive or not? She threw the words at Lila like a challenge. Lila meekly agreed that the groom should take Maisie down to Sussex to wait for Sunil.

On the day of the mass execution, Lila arrived early to the Old Bailey in a curricle. If she had imagined that being early would mean that she could escape the throng, she would have been mistaken. As it was, Tristram had warned her how it would be. He had said there would be a mass of people there. For some reason, she hadn't realized how visceral it would be. To be here, at the second hanging she had witnessed in her life. She clawed at her throat. The people, the clamor, the crowd braying for blood. The same, just the same, except much bigger.

Roger was standing behind the curricle, the new elaborate gold filigree mask—which covered much more than his eyes and reached down to frame his mouth—well in place.

"Good God," Lila said for perhaps the sixth time. "Do the people of London have nothing better to do than throng to see a hanging?"

"Twenty-two hangings, Miss Lila. Twenty-one, if we can help it," he added optimistically. "No one wants to miss it."

The gallows were all set up, three nooses dangling in the light breeze. The day was clear, not a cloud or a drop of rain to mar the proceedings. Every one of what looked like about ten thousand people would have a clear view. It was nothing short of bedlam. Lila was worried she would faint.

Not only were there people of all classes and types, wearing all kinds of clothing, but also carriages and phaetons and curricles. Children and their uncles and grandparents. Street vendors doing brisk trade, selling tea and hot pasties. Dogs and cats and no doubt hundreds of mice.

Things had already gone awry with their plan.

Hector had managed to find a body and paid for it too, Tristram had told her grimly this morning, before they made their separate way to the Old Bailey. A similar height and build to Sunil, and dead only a few hours, but the body wouldn't stand up to any closer scrutiny. However, that wasn't the main problem. The main problem was that the plan had fallen apart at its weakest link. The undertaker wouldn't be heading into the prison before the mass execution. He would be waiting for the bodies *after* the execution of the twenty-two prisoners. There was simply no way to get the body into the prison and make the swap with Sunil. Still, Hector visited Sunil to say the last rites (ostensibly) and updated Sunil on the latest plan.

The latest plan, Lila thought. It would be a wonder if it worked. No, not a wonder. It wouldn't be a wonder. It would be a miracle. She looked desperately about her.

The gallows were set up on a raised platform. The accused men and women scheduled to be hanged today would be brought out into the open from a side door in threes, then they would walk all the way up the steps to the platform, where three would be hung at one time. Lila's curricle was parked not far from the gallows, at the street corner. A quick scan showed that not only were people making full use of the street and square to watch the hangings, but were also perched all around in windows, on rooftops, and on the roofs and courtyards of nearby shops and of St. Sepulchre's Church. Many looked as though they had in fact slept the night outdoors just to get a better seat this morning.

Standing there, minding Tristram's matching pair of grays, Lila couldn't help thinking that the plan was hopeless. It couldn't work. There were eyes everywhere. People seemed to have come not only from all parts of the city, but from the countryside, judging by the carts piled with farm implements and all the different accents she could hear around her, jumbled threads of different-colored yarn. There was something ghoulish about it, and she felt perverse for standing there, waiting to watch people being executed. But what choice was there?

And then she saw another curricle. There were a hundred people at least between them, or perhaps two hundred, but it was unmistakably Jonathan, dressed in a puce coat. He saw her just as she saw him. He tipped his hat. She stared at him in loathing. To not intervene as an innocent man was sent to the gallows was one thing, but to come and watch that man hang—she didn't think she could hate him more. Her hand was itching to punch him again.

Then, to her immense surprise, handing his reins to his groom, he descended from his curricle in a leisurely way and pushed his way through the crowd to where she sat waiting. He tipped his hat to her again and then, not waiting for an invitation, climbed up to her curricle and sat himself next to her. She wanted to protest on principle, except there was no way to hear him if he was standing on the ground next to her, the tumult around them was so loud.

"Nice horses and a nice seat," he said, eyeing first the grays and then the curricle. "Not yours, I take it?"

"Ivor Tristram's," she said shortly, keeping her eyes fixed ahead of her and not turning her head to look at him.

"I felicitate you. I didn't know you were so close that he would let you borrow his racers."

"Indeed," she said frigidly.

"You look ready for racing. Don't tell me that you will take part in the Brighton race today, after all the times you have denied that you would?"

"I fully intend to."

He laughed. It actually sounded genuine. "I take my hat off to you, Lila. I knew you were cold-blooded, but this beats everything. You'll stay at Newgate to watch that man being hanged and then meet up with Herringford's nephew Horatio for the Brighton race! Where, the other side of Westminster Bridge, is it? Capital! A stomach made of steel! And if it makes you the talk of the town, even better for your salons."

She didn't dignify this with a response. Her reputation would only plummet if she were known to have let every man between London and Brighton ogle her and size her up. But that's not what this race was about. She was going to run the race, she had to. And if she didn't care about the opinions of all the men between London and Brighton, she certainly wasn't going to worry about Jonathan Marleigh's.

"Well, I *am* known to be eccentric," she said lightly.

"I see your man has a new mask on for the occasion. Is that to celebrate the hanging or your first curricle race?"

She flung the words at him. "And what about you, Jonathan? Come to enjoy the fruits of your labors?"

He didn't answer for some moments. She felt him pick a

bit of lint off his coat. "Letting some innocent man hang wasn't part of the plan, believe it or not, sister. I merely wished to give Maisie a fright. People should know not to threaten their betters."

This truly surprised her. Her eyes flickered, but she didn't display any obvious surprise. What did he mean when he implied that Maisie had threatened *him*? And he was implying that that's why *he* attacked Maisie. But she had to clear up something else first.

"What did you hope to get out of attacking her?" she couldn't help asking.

He looked surprised. "Nothing more than giving her a fright, of course. Everyone chose to think of it as a sexual assault when it was Tiffany Tristram. But you surely don't think that I'd stoop to *that* on someone like Maisie."

Jonathan looked disgusted. Lila almost laughed in his face. But what did he mean that Maisie threatened him?

"She had good reason to threaten you, as well you know." She blagged it out, hoping it would elicit a response. It did.

"Some chit out of the gutters threaten an earl. Come now, my darling, I know you've come from no better yourself, but surely even *you* have some sense of what is right and what wrong."

This made her look at him. Not the slur on her or her mother—that she was used to—but what he said about Maisie. "Who put her there in the gutter in the first place, Jonathan?" The rage that filled her now took even her breath away. It wasn't just the words; it was that Jonathan was so utterly sure of his place in the scheme of things. The relative place of him, the Earl of Beddington, and Maisie—a no one, a prostitute. To him there was no question of the social hierarchy. One of them was simply better than the other. One deserved a better life, a better outcome. She could see it, he felt the same about Sunil. Sunil's death, in Jonathan's eyes, did not matter. It was collateral that he was more than willing to accept. She didn't think she could feel this much hatred. More than hatred for him, she felt loathing for the blood-tie between them. It made her want to scourge herself.

He was looking at her, no expression on his face at all.

"*We* put her in the gutter, Jonathan. You—the Earl of Beddington—you let her run away when she was seven, you let her mother hang. If she was from the gutter, it was because we put her there."

He didn't say anything for a long time, but she was surprised to see that he looked almost relieved, as though she had said something that . . . that what? What was he relieved about? Her eyes narrowed in suspicion. What had he thought she was going to say? My God, the man was confusing and maddening.

"She belonged in the gutter in the first place," he said mildly. "Her mother would have slept with any old dog—"

"Oh, shut up!" she screamed. Admittedly, since they were having to yell at each other just to make themselves heard, this sounded no louder or worse than the rest of their conversation. "Shut up and go away! What do *you* know about Annie Quinn? What can *you* know about Maisie or whoever her father was? How dare you judge?"

He looked curiously at her, and she felt as though the thin sunlight was glinting not on but *through* those strange eyes of his. "Always good to see you, Lila. Always so full of fire. I find that such a desirable quality. Don't think too harshly of me. This hanging will teach Maisie a much-needed lesson about how to treat her social betters. I'm afraid living as she did in our house when she was young must have given her a false sense of her own importance. This will remedy it, perhaps. Oh, and don't be late for your race. If you are late and you lose, you still lose."

She was so furious at everything he had said, at his *face*, that she couldn't take the time to try to decipher what any of it meant. His words hovered in the air. Maisie had threatened him with what, for what? Teach Maisie a lesson? Why? Still his words hung there. But she was too raging mad to decipher any of it.

35

She couldn't see Ivor Tristram anywhere, but then—in this cram of people—she didn't expect to. She knew he was here somewhere. Her shoulders were rigid, her eyes intent, trying to look at each face in the crowd, but she knew at least that Tristram would be there.

"Roger, how much longer?"

Roger perhaps had even keener eyes than she. "Not long, Miss Lila."

"You know what to do?"

"You have it right, miss. I do."

She took a deep breath and waited.

Finally, it was time, and the first three prisoners came out of the door in the wall. Their hands were tied behind their backs. All of a sudden, Lila felt sick. It was one thing to be waiting here, taut as a string, to rescue Sunil. It was another that she had to sit through who knew how many hangings before Sunil came out for his turn. Who knew what these men had really done or were falsely accused of doing? Annie, poor Annie. Annie's face kept swaying in front of her eyes. I'm so sorry, Annie, she kept saying in her head.

"Do we have to watch?" she found herself saying. Yet she needed to stay alert. She had to stay focused. There wouldn't be much time. It took less than half a minute for the prisoners to come out through the door and start climbing the steps up to the platform. That was the time they would have to rescue Sunil when it was his turn. Less than half a minute.

She eyed the Runners and the constables who were patrolling the area. She felt even sicker now. How could it possibly work? What, she wondered, was the sentence if you were caught helping someone escape the gallows?

She closed her eyes as the three nooses were placed. And yet she heard—or fancied she heard—the sickening pulling sound. The bile rose in her throat and she frantically swallowed. She had to hold it together. She had to. And she wasn't sure she had heard the hanging at all. Because the crowd was—unbelievably—cheering, screaming, yelling for more. Her insides turned. This was the wrong place to be, she thought. What was she doing here?

Three men executed. She couldn't bear looking. She wondered if they were dead yet or still hanging there, twitching. It took forever, it seemed. By the time the men were dead, by the time they had been taken off the nooses, it seemed an hour at least had passed. Though it was probably not half that much. The bodies were cleared off the podium. The door opened again. She was looking now. She had to. She wouldn't get long. Half a minute, no more. She had to get it right or they would miss their chance.

Sunil wasn't in this set of three either. And there was a woman there, a girl, who looked no older than twenty. Leila nearly moaned out loud. Or maybe she did moan, she couldn't hear her own sounds. The entire process was repeated. The crowd jeering and cheering, people half hanging out of the windows, some even falling out—and who knows where they ended up? The three prisoners walked up the stairs to the platform, the nooses, the sickening sound that Lila was sure she heard again, the screaming and cheering that followed.

When the third set came out, and Sunil wasn't in this either, she felt as though she was stuck in a nightmare. The horses were getting restive now. They had behaved remarkably well given what they were witnessing. But Tristram had told her they were used to the cheering crowds at prize fights. She had no idea what the crowds were like at a prize fight, but the horses must be shockingly well trained not to bolt in this crowd. She hoped they *were* shockingly well trained for what they were about to do.

If the bloody guards would ever bring Sunil out, that is.

Sunil was in the fourth set of men. Lila was nearly sick there and then, except there was no time to be sick.

No sooner were the three men out of the door than a shot rang out. Then another, from what seemed like a different part of the arena. And then yet another. There was true screaming now. Gone was the cheering, and the horses all around were in a panic. A lone horse seemed to have gotten away from his owner and was pelting straight for the bottom of those steps, where the three men still stood. She was watching it, every nerve in her body tight as a bow ready to release an arrow. The horse caused so much mayhem that people were screaming, running out of the way, guards were blowing whistles, people jumping nearly out of their skins. The horse careened all the way down the narrow path that was open next to the building, between the building and the platform. It careened past and kept going. Every eye in the arena was on the pelting horse. Even Lila couldn't help watching the horse. It was only when she felt a slight sway in the curricle, as if someone had stepped off it and then someone had stepped onto it again, behind her, that she came back to her senses. She dared not look behind her to see who was standing there. But she didn't have to. Because at the head of her horses, in front of her, a man, with burn scars around his eyes and a hat low on his head, tipped his hat to her. Roger. Thank God. It was Roger. That could only mean one thing. Sunil was standing behind her on the curricle.

Her eyes automatically swerved to the bottom of the platform again. And although everyone was watching the horse that was now pelting away in the distance, a dead body had been discovered at the bottom of the platform. Not yet, she told herself. She couldn't move yet. No one was leaving. Everyone was watching first the horse and next what was happening at the bottom of the steps. A murmur was going around now, and eyes were turning from the horse to the next source of drama. Roger had already melted away into the crowd.

A murmur finally reached her. It seemed that one of the prisoners had died of shock or perhaps an injury from the runaway horse. More likely shock, people were saying.

"The man looks nothing like me." She heard the words uttered behind her, close enough that they didn't need to be yelled. The voice was bitter and philosophical at the same time.

A hysterical gurgle rose in her. She desperately wanted to leave. Yet no one else was leaving. Trying to leave now would be premature. It would be conspicuous. If she waited for this round of hangings to be done . . . the thought made her feel faint. She wanted nothing so much as to get out of here.

And then through the crowd, through the melee, she caught sight of Jonathan. She had forgotten him in the drama. He was watching as the two remaining prisoners were hanged and the third, the dead body, was flung with the other dead bodies. His eyes were narrowed. Her heart started pounding.

Just as she was thinking they had to get out of here, that they had already left it too late, Jonathan turned his face in her direction.

He knew.

"Come now, darlings," she said to the horses. Who knew why she bothered, since no one could hear her? "It's time to leave." She deliberately made herself not look at Jonathan again. He knew. He knew about the switch.

After each set of hangings, a handful of people shifted, either to take a break, give up, or simply to try to move to a better spot. She and Tristram had decided she should wait to leave only after the last set. But there was no time. No time to lose. Jonathan knew.

It took what felt like hours to find some way to turn the curricle and make her way out of the throng. It was only made possible because people tended to scramble out of the way if two enormous horses were plowing through their ranks. People did scramble out of the way, though not without a lot of yelling and cursing at her. Some of them were yelling to her to be less craven and stay and watch the rest of it. Others were telling her to be wholeheartedly sick and be done with it. She was called more vile names than she had ever heard in her entire life put together. Mostly for the evil of blocking the view with her horses or making people leave their hard-earned spot.

Finally, she was out of the writhing mass.

The first thing she did when she was clear of the crowd was not to give the restless horses their head and race toward Westminster where the curricle race was to start, but to stop the vehicle, lean over the side and be comprehensively sick.

"I apologize," she said to Sunil afterward, wiping her mouth on the back of her hand. "It has been building for the last hour or so."

She heard the sounds of horrible retching behind her and as almighty a splash on the cobbles as she had just made. "It has been building for nearly a week," Sunil said behind her, wiping his mouth on the back of his hand.

She couldn't help a laugh. She risked a glance behind her. Mask in place, hat low on his head, the man could well be Roger Manson.

She gave the horses their head and, at her urging, they flew.

36

The race began on the other side of Westminster Bridge, and indeed, as soon as she was in sight of it, her opponent, Lord Herringford's nephew Horace Tupphorn, touched his hat to her, gave her an unmistakable leer, and was off at a tearing pace. She sighed and said the word *Novice!* and was off at a much steadier speed. "At least we can safely say that the man is definitely related to Lord Herringford," she said to no one in particular.

The race had begun. She had been saying for weeks that it was just a rumor, that of course she was not running it. And funnily enough, even though she had meant it, no one had really believed her. And here she was.

Oddly, despite the urgency of the situation they were in, Lila couldn't help feeling a tiny bit excited that she was doing this. Running a race to Brighton, something women never did, not because they couldn't, but because it was seen to be fast and would cause a scandal. She kept a neat and steady pace until the first change of horses came up.

When they changed horses in Croydon, her opponent Tupphorn was nowhere in sight. He had clearly taken the opportunity to let his horses go as fast as they could. But Lila, though new to racing, was not new to driving a curricle or a pair of horses—though admittedly, Tristram's were a finer pair than she was used to—and knew to pace herself. Plus, Kenneth had given her clear instructions. No one could have been happier than him to hear that she had decided to run the race after all. "I knew you had it in you," he said when she told him—just yesterday—that she wanted to run the race in his place, after all. She asked him for tips, and he gave them, freely. "But promise me you'll win," he said. "There is only my reputation on the line, you know!" She had guiltily said that she would try her best. Knowing that Sunil's safety would have to be her first priority.

Between Croydon and the next change of horses at Horley, she saw Tupphorn's curricle several times. Toward the end, before the change in Horley came up, he was lagging, as predicted, and she passed him and stayed ahead all the way to the second change. She also noted with some aggravation that he wasn't the only one leering at her. Several men she passed were looking her up and down and a few holding their quizzing glasses at her. "I never knew the London–Brighton road had improved to this degree!" shouted one young buck after her. "Good gad!" yelled another. "Take me up with you, goddess, won't you!"

As always, leering men only made her sit straighter, her posture more perfect, and her bearing almost aristocratic. She couldn't help it. And Kenneth was right. There was something exciting about running the race (even if the real reason was to get Sunil out of the city), but it wasn't just that. It was also exciting to thumb her nose at convention. She couldn't help that either.

After Horley, the same thing happened again. Tupphorn, who had turned out to be a muscular—very top-heavy—and pimply young man with his uncle Lord Herringford's jowls, let the horses go again and was ahead of her for at least half the way to Cuck-field. But then she overtook him again. Really, if the man refused to learn anything, then after the change at Cuckfield, and halfway to Marine Parade in Brighton, the race would be hers.

Except for the minor problem that she couldn't do exactly what she pleased. She had to think of Sunil and not the damned race.

It was at the last change at Cuckfield that Maisie, escorted there by Tristram's groom, should be waiting. Tristram and Hector, after causing the mayhem with the pistol shots and runaway horse and dead body, should also have left the gallows at the Old Bailey before she did, not slowed because of the traffic up to the bridge, and they should have ridden down to Cuckfield. They should also be waiting for her there.

"I suppose you can make the switch with Roger as fast as they can change their horses, can you, Sunil?" she found herself saying. Since Horley, she had managed to cross Tupphorn again, and was now a good while ahead.

"What, so you can get Roger Manson back and finish the race?" Sunil sounded as though he was grinning.

At least the man had the heart to grin. He looked pale and emaciated, the one or two glances she had given him.

"It would be poor sport not to at least *try* to win."

He chuckled. She chuckled too. In fact, soon they were laughing so hard, she was in danger of overturning. Tears were streaming down her face, and it was all she could do to keep her eyes open. At the inn in Cuckfield, a lightning change of horses wouldn't cut the mustard. She needed a reason to dally, to give Sunil enough time to switch with Roger Manson. He would then find Maisie, and Tristram's groom would escort them to Tristram's estate near Rye.

And Lila would be damned if she didn't attempt to make

up for lost time and try and win this blasted race. She wouldn't have it be said that a woman couldn't do it. That a woman had had the temerity to enter this male domain and then hopelessly fail. And Kenneth would kill her if she didn't at least try. Plus, she couldn't help it. Even though Tristram had agreed that the mad plan might have a chance of working, he still didn't like the idea of her running the race. He hadn't been able to give a very clear reason why, simply asserting that it would make her a spectacle for every man on the road and the speed of the race was hardly safe. She reminded him that neither of those factors was his concern. He did not know what to say to that.

Still, race or no race, she had to slow down the change of horses in Cuckfield. She could do some minor damage to the curricle and then wait for it to be fixed, but she neither wanted to damage Tristram's curricle, nor delay more than needed.

She reached the coaching inn at Cuckfield where the last change of horses was to take place. The ostlers hurried over. "Lemonade, please," she said, as if she were a poor female about to faint. She realized she was actually parched. The men, of course, were ogling at her temerity, to sit there like that on a curricle on the high road, with just a groom for company. It was unheard of. "What are you staring at?" she snapped at the man changing the horses. "Have you not seen a female before, or is there soot on my nose?"

His eyes nearly fell out of his face; he bowed about five hundred times before running off, probably to tell everyone he met what shocking thing he'd seen outside the inn. She descended from the curricle with a great deal of dignity. Another thing Kenneth had taught her. When doing something shocking, do it as if she didn't give a farthing what anyone thought about it; don't show doubt, don't hesitate.

Sunil made a show of looking after the change of horses as

he had done previously at Croydon and Horley. She made her way to the back of the inn, where Tristram had said he would be waiting. From the little garden at the back, she could look into the back parlor.

Her blood froze when she looked inside.

Tristram was not there. Neither was Hector. There were only two people in the room. Time slowed down and almost stopped.

Lila opened the back door and stepped into the room. The room with its white mottled walls and black beams looked comfortable enough. With thick wood furniture and some red upholstery. But Lila was only dimly aware of the décor. Quietly, but not so quietly that she startled the life out of the two people in the room, she entered and stood there, just inside the door. It was Jonathan Marleigh backed up against a wall and Maisie—a very pregnant Maisie—holding a cast-iron poker to his throat.

"Don't tell me to let him go, Miss Lila," Maisie said, without even turning around to see who had entered the room. "For one thing, it ain't none of your business, so far as I can see. And for another, I just won't do it."

Lila couldn't help thinking every hair on Maisie's body was standing on end. The chit was bristling with fury. She couldn't see Maisie's eyes, but it wouldn't surprise her to see embers simmering just below the surface.

"I don't know why you're here, Jonathan," Lila said calmly, taking her gloves off and placing them on the table. The room was clearly a back parlor that could be reserved by some of the inn's wealthier guests, and was furnished comfortably with chunky hardwood tables, made of something sturdy like oak. It even had a little sofa in front of the fire, now that she could see it properly, though no fire was lit at the moment, since it was still a mild autumnal day.

"Don't you?" he said in a commendably calm voice, given that he was very near being impaled on an iron poker. Seeing Maisie's utter focus on Jonathan's jugular and the murderous gleam in her eye, there was no doubting it. If he moved, he would die. "I must say, nice trick. They actually think the lascar died of shock from a wee runaway horsey. No one even questioned that it was the right man. Though, I admit, I cannot for the life of me tell the difference between one native man and another. They all look the same to me."

Lila swallowed, really hoping she wouldn't be sick again. "Why don't you let him go, Jonathan, now that the law will assume he is dead? You have what you want. Why are you here?"

The door opening behind her startled the life out of Lila. Maisie's attention didn't waver. Jonathan's eyes veered for a fraction of a second but then went back to Maisie. Lila didn't dare turn her head to look at the noise.

"Ma'am," a voice that was vaguely familiar. "The race, ma'am."

Lila realized it was the ostler who had been ogling her five minutes ago, who was responsible for the change of horses. Her mouth had never felt tighter as she spoke. "As you can see, I'm a little occupied at the moment."

The man seemed to hesitate, but then the door opened and shut behind her. She wondered if he would raise a hue and cry. She hoped not. It was taking all she had to keep Maisie calm.

Jonathan's attention was firmly on the eye of the poker, but he was speaking directly to Lila. "You know, I am starting to think you might be right. I wasn't thinking, careening down here on my horse. I hated the feeling of being worsted without a fight. But now I think on it, it might have been sensible to save my breath. Now, if you'll just pull this young witch off me . . ."

The poker was now prodding Jonathan's flesh. He made an

involuntary gurgling sound in his throat, but then tried with a great effort to be calm again. The poker cut into his flesh—a mere flesh wound, but there was a trickle of blood now making its way down Jonathan's throat and seeping into his cravat. He blanched some more. "I was never one to be easy at the sight of blood."

"Yet hangings don't seem to bother you at all," Lila said, as if simply making an observation. "Now, Maisie, I'm sure you'll want to see—I'm sure you'll want to let this little worm go."

"That's where you're wrong, Miss Lila," Maisie said. "I reckon one less earl in the world will be a very good thing. It's *exactly* what I want. More I think about it, the more I want it." She actually gave him a sharp poke. Dear God, she was going to sever the man's jugular any second.

"Maisie, saving one man from the gallows was hard enough work. I don't think I have the stomach to try to save you. Don't do it." She heard a crunch of a footstep behind her, outside in the yard. It was hardly there, and since Maisie made a light lunge at that very second, it didn't seem that Jonathan or Maisie heard it. If it was Sunil, he might want to rush to the rescue. If he did, Maisie might just take the moment to drive the poker home. Maisie would swing for it, for the murder of an earl. No one would even bother with a cursory trial. Lila was so tense she could hardly breathe.

"I reckon it'll be worth it," Maisie said. She was practically spitting in the man's face.

"You wouldn't kill your own father, Maisie."

Lila nearly toppled over in shock at Jonathan's words. She glanced at Maisie's face. But that hadn't altered, not even by a flicker. "You reckon I wouldn't?" she was saying.

Lila realized—with a sense of everything shifting around

her and yet things finally falling into place—that Maisie knew. Maisie knew the impossible. The thing that hardly made sense to Lila and yet it made all the sense in the world. "Have you always known?" she found herself asking Maisie in almost a whisper.

Maisie's eyes didn't waver from Jonathan's face. Her hands didn't tremble either. "No, miss. Not always. But Ma told me before she died. And this man here said come back if you need anything. Not that I ever believed him." She did spit this time, over her right shoulder. "But then, fool that I am, I figured the babe's grandfather might be interested in its welfare."

It was ludicrous imagining Jonathan as a grandfather. He was not even forty. But then Maisie herself was only seventeen. And Annie hadn't been any older when she came to the Marleigh home, pregnant with Maisie.

Jonathan's lip curled. "You know, I might have been fool enough to give her some money if she had just asked for it, for her child. But she threatened me," he said to Lila. "Said she'd tell everyone that I was her father. Me, an earl, the father of some bastard child. And who knows if I am or not? We only have Annie Quinn's word for it. What was I supposed to do about that?"

He meant it too. He truly believed he was within his rights to attack Maisie because she threatened to reveal that he was her father. "So you attacked your own daughter," Lila said, her voice dripping with disgust.

"She deserved a fright. I only meant to frighten her. It wouldn't have gone any further if—"

Lila could almost laugh, if the situation weren't so serious. "If you hadn't—like the idiot you are—attacked the wrong woman in the dark."

He didn't respond.

Then Lila thought of another question. An important one. "Is that why Sarah hired Annie in the first place? Because she knew *you* made her pregnant?" Lila said to Jonathan with all the disbelief and loathing she felt.

"That's Lady Marleigh to *you*," Jonathan couldn't help saying, his lip curling. There was hardly less loathing in his face and voice. "Of course, Mother didn't know. What do you take me for? I convinced her we needed Annie to look after the three of you brats. She saw reason. And Annie stayed out of my way, and she kept . . . Maisie out of my way too. I thought it was the right thing to do, to offer the brat a roof. But I regretted my generous impulse when Annie started asking me to pay for Maisie's education."

Lila clutched her throat. The ground had shifted at the revelation that Jonathan was Maisie's father. Yet, here it was, shifting yet again. "You—you bastard. *You* put that jewelry box in Annie's room!"

For the first time, Maisie was rattled. A little squeak came from her, a sound of pain and surprise. So much so that she wavered, and even though the poker pushed deeper, she was just unsteady enough that Jonathan seized his advantage. Before Lila could react, or Maisie could find her steady hands again, the poker clattered to the floor, and Jonathan Marleigh was still in the same place as he was, his back to the wall, and so was Maisie, but now there was a pistol in his hand, and it was pointing straight at Maisie's belly. Lila's hand instinctively came up to ward something off. She was barely breathing.

Maisie looked unabashed; looked, in fact, ready to charge at him and consequences be damned.

"Maisie, don't move a muscle," Lila said quietly. "Don't move a muscle." No desperation. She could not afford to sound desperate.

There were noises behind her. Jonathan's eyes flickered this time. Some more people entered the room, but Lila didn't dare turn to look behind her to see who it was.

"Drop the pistol, Beddington."

Lila could almost have sagged in relief. It was Ivor Tristram.

He came to stand beside her. She caught his eye. There was something there. Some warning, or some message. She looked uncertainly at him. She wasn't sure what he wanted her to do. But other than that glance, he was not looking at her. His eyes were on Jonathan.

"Good to see you, Tristram," Jonathan said, his mouth curling. "You're right. I have no wish for bloodshed. It would be most inconvenient. I just want to leave. But I want a gentleman's word that you will never come after me for this."

"I'll come after you," Maisie growled.

Lila squeezed her eyes shut for a second. Really, Maisie, was this the time? A pistol was pointing straight at Maisie's belly. If Jonathan let it off, both Maisie and the babe would die, and Lila knew it; she would never get the sight out of her mind, ever. How would she ever live with herself? A sense of unreality, of desperation was stealing over her. A sense of time slowing down, but unstoppable. Of inevitability.

"Maisie." It was Sunil's voice. He had stepped into the parlor too, with Tristram.

For the first time, Maisie backed off a little. Lila saw her chin tremble, though she didn't take her eyes off Jonathan. Jonathan was looking at Maisie too, his pistol unwavering. "Come now, marry this man and have lots of half-caste brats," he said.

Maisie growled. Lila's fists clenched again. Really, did the man not have any sense of self-preservation?

"We won't come after you," Lila found herself saying in a strangely hollow voice. Could anyone else not see sense? Why weren't they promising this—this *worm*—anything he asked for? If he pulled the trigger . . .

"Except of course you will not be allowed to marry my cousin." Tristram's voice again.

Lila gritted her teeth. Was *this* the time? This was the time to get Jonathan Marleigh and his pistol off Maisie's belly and out of this room. Not to be bargaining for Tiffany Tristram's marriage. What was wrong with Tristram and what was wrong with Maisie? Now was the time to pacify, not enrage or worry Jonathan Marleigh.

Jonathan grimaced. "Well, you see, that is a bit too much to ask me, Tristram. Why did I go to all this bother if I have to give up the prize in the end?"

The prize. Yes, thought Lila. That was exactly what Tiffany Tristram would be to someone like Jonathan. Not a woman with a heart and soul, not a person, but a prize.

"You can't expect anyone to countenance the match, Jonathan. And anyway, what bother did you go to? What did you do that was so onerous?" Tristram's voice was calm.

What did you do that was so onerous! What a question.

But then Lila stopped hyperventilating at everything that was coming out of Tristram's mouth and focused on that glance he had given her. He was trying to do something. She had no idea what. If he was trying to get Jonathan to confess, well what would that do? It was only their word against his. But it was perhaps better to play along.

"What *did* you do, Jonathan?" she said scathingly, watching the eye of the pistol with her heart galloping in her chest, but her voice calm. "What trouble did you go to? Hired a few scoundrels to scare a few people away?"

His lip curled. "It was a mistake. And well you know it. From the start. I never meant to attack Tiffany. I . . . care about her."

Lila couldn't stifle a bark of laughter. "Care about a woman, Jonathan? Care implies love and respect, doesn't it?"

Jonathan looked at her with loathing. "Just because I have no respect for a woman of *your* stamp doesn't mean I look down on all women. *You're* a slut, like your mother before you—"

Before she could think about it, Lila charged in his direction, claws out, rage on her face. But her wrist was caught by Tristram.

"Let me go!"

Tristram's hand was firm. Jonathan's pistol was now pointing at her head.

"Why did you attack my cousin, Beddington, if you care about her?" It was Tristram's voice, calm as ever. Both Maisie and Lila were seething now. And Sunil was still behind them, not daring to move a muscle or utter a word. Jonathan's finger was flush on the hairbreadth trigger. Either Lila or Maisie was as good as dead if he moved it a fraction.

"I meant to scare Maisie. I had no idea Tiffany was in the room. I didn't know it was Tiffany I was struggling with, in the dark. When I ran out of the room, the lascar must have come into it. When I rushed back into the room with the others, they all took it that the damned lascar had attacked your cousin. It was mighty convenient."

"So, you joined in the fun and accused him? And then made sure the Runners got him and sent him to the gallows? You little worm!" Lila cried.

"It wasn't meant to go that far," Jonathan said. "If the two of you hadn't interfered," his glance swept over Lila and Tristram, "I'd have scared Maisie and her lascar off. But you took it up and I realized I had to take it further." He motioned with his pistol. "Now that's all clear, perhaps we can go back to negotiating."

"There is no negotiation," Tristram said. "There is no way that you will ever see Tiffany again."

Jonathan's lip curled, in a familiar expression. "You know, she was starting to wear on me, I have to say. She can be a little clingy."

Lila couldn't help letting out a little growl. "You vile little toad!" she said.

Jonathan merely looked contemptuous. "I have no wish to use this," he said, waving his pistol. Then he pointed it straight at Lila's head. "But I need your word, Tristram. I let you go now, and this never comes up again."

"I think not, sir."

Everyone froze in shock at the sound of the new voice. Everyone that is, except Tristram, who was apparently expecting it. Jonathan was staring at whoever had entered the room. Lila didn't think she could turn to look. Maisie's eyes were fixed on the pistol too.

"Who the devil are *you*?" Jonathan asked.

"A Justice of the Peace I happened to find traveling from Brighton to London," Tristram said calmly.

Nothing much changed, except Jonathan's mouth curled and the pistol moved back to Maisie's belly.

"It's over, Beddington. This man has heard everything you had to say."

Jonathan's face contorted with rage. He straightened his arm and aimed the pistol more assuredly at Maisie's belly. And then it was hard to know what happened next. Except that Lila launched herself at Jonathan, there was a retort, a sharp jolt, and darkness.

37

Time stopped as Ivor watched Lila fall.

He felt that he had been standing there, in that back parlor of the coaching inn, his entire life, watching her fall. And yet he caught her, caught her before she fell to the floor. Caught her to him and held her, held her with everything he had.

For the next few minutes, he wasn't aware of what was going on around him. For the first few seconds, he needed to know where she was hit. Her head, her chest, her belly, no, all clear. It was her shoulder. It was bleeding profusely. Linen, he needed linen. He had to stop the bleeding, or she'd bleed to death and then it wouldn't matter that she hadn't been shot in the head.

She was pale, very pale. Her eyelids weren't even flickering. And his heart nearly stopped when he couldn't find a pulse. Except it was there. It was faint and slow, too slow, but it was there. He carried her over to the settee. There was noise and bustle around him. But he didn't know what was happening. He was automatically putting pressure on the wound and his hands were filling with blood. Lila's blood, gushing out of her with each one of his heartbeats.

Maisie was on her knees next to him. "Miss Lila," she was

saying. She was holding one of Lila's hands. "Miss Lila, why . . . why does she always have to think she knows best!" she cried, her voice cracking. "Always!"

Ivor felt that he would have quite a lot to say on this subject at another time, but right now, all he could see were Lila's unmoving eyes.

Sunil must have been out of the room for a few minutes, because he came rushing back in. "I've asked for a doctor, Mr. Ivor. The innkeeper has given us a direction, and Hector has gone to fetch the man." He had a woman with him, who brought in boiling water and large strips of clean linen. The first thing to do—Ivor had to focus. For the next several minutes, he and the woman bound Lila's wound. The bullet was wedged in there, but that would have to be taken out later. For now, he had to stem the bleeding. He had to clean the wound. He did so, with the woman's help. Cloth after cloth was bound to stop the bleeding. It was endless minutes of his life. He was fighting for it. Fighting, he thought, for his own life.

When the woman left with a bloody basin of water, he bent over Lila. "Wake up, Lila. Darling, open your eyes. It's all over now. Wake up, Lila." His voice, he wanted it to be commanding and firm. He wanted her to know he wouldn't take no for an answer, wanted her to know there was no real worry, that she would recover. The bullet would be taken out, it would heal, it wouldn't get infected. He wanted her to know. But he felt his voice was coming from the end of a long and empty hallway. "Lila, my love. Wake up now." She was pale, so pale, as though she had been drained. And he couldn't be sure, couldn't be sure that everything he had done had stopped the bleeding. What if it hadn't? The urge to touch the bandages to check was so strong he had to clench his fists.

"Come, Miss Lila," Maisie said, "open your eyes now. If you think you're going to make me feel bad . . ." She was earnestly crying now. Sunil was kneeling beside her and rubbing her back. Ivor couldn't help thinking this was hardly a happy reunion for the two of them. They'd barely had a second to acknowledge each other. Maisie was sobbing. She'd stood firm in the face of a pistol pointing at her belly, at scraping a man's throat with a heavy iron poker. But now she had crumbled. She was crying on Sunil's shoulder.

Time ticked on. Surely, Lila should have woken up by now. Surely it was taking too long. And where was the damned doctor? How long did it take to get the doctor? If it always took this long, how did anyone survive?

What if the man didn't make it in time? What if she was still bleeding and Ivor couldn't see it, would only see it when it was too late, and she was moved, and the sofa was soaked underneath her? What if the doctor came and extracted the bullet and she died of inflammation? What if she was in terrible pain right this second? Where was the damned doctor? He would crawl out of his skin if he had to take this much longer. He wanted to pace up and down the room, or punch something to a pulp and hopefully hurt himself really badly in the process, but that would mean taking his eyes off her face. Her pale, pale face. What if he never heard her voice again?

"What did you call me?"

The words were murmured, so low that he wasn't sure he had heard them. Had her lips even moved?

"Miss Lila!" Maisie cried.

He gripped Lila's good shoulder.

Sunil spoke softly. "Come now, let's leave them be," he said to Maisie.

"I'm not leaving the room!" Maisie shrieked.

A smile hovered on Lila's mouth. "I have no idea why anyone—anyone needs to leave the room," she said.

"I have some idea," Ivor said, and kissed her somewhat fiercely on her mouth.

"Are you trying to kill me?" she said faintly.

"Oh," Maisie said. "You're right," she said, clearing her throat. "A bit of fresh air would be maybe good for the babe."

The two of them got to their feet and with more words about how fresh air would be good for the health of the baby and for Maisie, they made to leave the room.

Ivor had to ask them before they left. "Beddington?"

"Mr. Peterson has him, sir."

"Who the devil is Peterson?" Lila asked. Her voice was weak, too weak for his liking, but he was happy to hear her cursing.

"I love it when you swear," he said soulfully. He meant it. "I wish you'd do it more often."

She laughed and then broke it off abruptly. "Damnation. What have you done to my shoulder?"

"Well, that's the maddest thing I ever heard!" That was Maisie. She was no longer weeping. "Who jumped straight in front of a gun! Not me! Not Mr. Ivor! Not Sunil! Not—"

Sunil clamped a hand around her shoulder, perhaps sensing that the list of persons who had not jumped in front of Beddington's gun could be rather long, and it wasn't clear if it would only include persons who happened to be in the room at the time, or also others who'd been nowhere near it.

"At least I wasn't trying to get myself hanged for impaling a man on a poker," Lila said with asperity.

Maisie had more to say on this subject, but Sunil steered her firmly to the door, saying over his shoulder that the Justice of the Peace, Mr. Peterson, had the Earl. Ivor couldn't help it. He felt compelled to say it out loud. "He's still an earl. Nothing might come of it. We must all be prepared for that."

"He might leave us alone, sir, if nothing else," Sunil said. Then he ushered Maisie out. Ivor turned his head and watched them step outside. He watched them cross the yard and sit down, side by side on a bench, holding hands. Maisie seemed to be weeping again.

He turned back to Lila. "If you ever do something so foolish, so idiotic again, if you *ever* do something like that again, I will murder you with my bare hands."

He kissed her again. For a few seconds, she did nothing, she didn't move, and he wondered if he was hurting her. Or maybe she didn't want him, maybe she had lost all interest in him after all, just like she said she would. Then her good arm crept around his neck, and she kissed him back. And he wondered how he had ever contemplated living, if he were never to feel those lips of hers again.

He pulled back and stared at her face. "Lila . . ." His voice cracked.

"Don't you Lila me," she said crossly. "Are you going to turn tail and run away again next time you're afraid, next time you don't behave perfectly?"

"You did say I'm a coward." He drew her hand closer and kissed it. "I *am* a coward, Lila, but I don't see how I can save you from your own *mad* impulses if I'm not next to you all the time."

"I'll drive *you* mad."

"You've already done that." He placed his forehead on her hand for a second, his eyes closed. Thank everything that was good that she was all right. "The doctor is on his way, Lila. It'll—hurt, darling."

"I'll never get tired of you calling me that."

But then she winced, and he had to control himself, stop himself from holding on even tighter to her, as if he could physically stop her from slipping away from him.

They stayed in that position until finally there was a knock on the door. Sunil and Maisie followed the doctor in.

Ivor explained quickly what had happened and what had been done to tend the wound. The doctor, his eyebrows gray and bushy, his face humorous and slightly vague, looked dispassionately at the situation. "If Miss Quinn will stay with me, the men can perhaps . . ." He looked vaguely toward the door.

"I am staying here," Ivor said firmly.

The doctor, Dr. Mannerly, glanced at Lila.

"I'd like Ivor to stay," she said.

Which was just as well, because Ivor had no intention of leaving.

The next half hour was possibly the worst of his life. Ivor reflected that he would take any pain, make any sacrifice not to have to sit through something like that again. For one thing, his hand was about to fall off, Lila was clutching it so hard. But it was her moaning, the sounds of an animal in pain, the tears that were pouring down the sides of her face, unheedingly. It was the knowledge that he had, clear and blinding, that no matter how frightening it was to give himself up to being with Lila Marleigh, how frightening to imagine that her love could fail, that his could, that they could hurt each other, it was much, much worse to imagine a world without her. *That* couldn't be borne. And although it might still be better to steer clear of her, he realized there was a better chance of her surviving if he was with her to take care of her—she clearly had no care for her own safety. But he suspected that he certainly had a much better chance of living to a grand old age if *she* was with *him*.

She was pale and shaking by the time the doctor was done. She had lost consciousness once or twice and made Ivor's heart nearly stop beating, but the doctor said each time that it was for the best. She was shaking now and looked almost green. Ivor imagined he himself was no better-looking at the moment than a corpse. All the color had likely drained from his own face too.

He practically poured brandy down her throat after the doctor was done and Maisie and Sunil had left the room again, and told her she'd have him to deal with if she dared get a fever or an infection.

"You're horribly autocratic. I knew it," she said. "I'll fight you every step of the way, you know that, don't you?" Her voice was faint, and she could hardly hold her head up to drink the brandy.

"I'm counting on it, darling."

Then her eyes opened wide, so wide he was startled. She nearly sat up, trying desperately to prop herself on one elbow, and went even paler. Her eyes were frantic.

"What is it, Lila? The pain?" he asked urgently.

"No, get your hands off me! Tell me—"

"Beddington? They have him, Lila, don't worry. Now lie back and—"

"Damnation! No, the—the—the—"

"Sunil and Maisie? They're perfectly well, Lila! Why don't you . . . ?"

She growled and shook his hand off. Her chin trembled. He stared at her. She said, "The race! I lost the race."

He sagged in relief. Dear God, the woman was going to be the death of him. Tears were pouring down her pale face.

"As it happens, you didn't. Herrington's nephew Tupphorn

crashed his curricle even before he reached Cuckfield, he was driving so recklessly. You either both forfeit the race or you win—he certainly didn't."

She burst into even louder tears. "Oh, thank goodness. Thank *goodness!*"

EPILOGUE

Lila eyed her two sisters. There was something about the hint of honey in the cream of their skin that set the sisters apart from others and yet made it clear that they were related to one another.

Still, many other things were different.

Lila was short, broad in the shoulder, tiny in the waist, and she looked as though she was on a mission to animate the world or fight it, one or the other, often both. There was a frenetic energy about her, a quickness to jump into the ring and aim for the kill, that was less evident in the other two. Her clothes had more color and style too.

Anya was taller. She was willowy, and instead of Lila's loose curls, which skimmed beneath her shoulders, her hair fell in tight ringlets and was fashionably cut at her shoulders. Lila's eyes were a very dark brown, but Anya's were coal black. Her eyes were also more wistful. There was something inward about her face, as though no one was allowed to see what Anya Marleigh really thought about the world and the people around her. She watched you; she didn't like being watched. She was a musician, a sitar player in the Queen's court.

And then there was Mira. Her hair was bushy and dark, but then it turned lighter as it grew, and it was caramel at the ends, almost a spun gold, and she wore it in a severe bun pulled back from her face. If the bun was ever let down, the hair skimmed the small of her back, but no one ever got to see that. She kept her hair and her generous curves under a tight rein.

"So you've asked us to tea—to invite us to your wedding?" Mira said. Her voice was ironic. Even though there was nothing particularly ironic about Lila asking her two sisters to her wedding, even then Mira managed to make it sound as though there was. As usual, Lila bristled, but she was determined to hold on to her temper. She had promised Ivor she would try to.

"I hope you will come," she said coolly. "It won't be immediately. We will wait for some more months because of Ivor's mother's passing." She tried not to sound anxious. She tried not to freeze just so she wouldn't sound anxious. She was gripping her hands tightly in her lap. This was harder than she had anticipated.

"Is that why we're here?" Anya asked. There was nothing of Mira's irony in her voice, but there was passion under her words. Passion that was stronger for being unstated. With Anya, there were deep waters, yet there was a sense that under the deep waters there was an even deeper furnace.

Lila pursed her lips. Ivor had encouraged her to try to keep her temper, damn the man. "That's not the only thing," Lila said. "It's not just the wedding. Of course I would like you to come to that. But it is something else too." She gripped her hands tighter. Her stomach was painfully clenched too. "I also want us to try to—to find our sisters." She lifted her chin as she said it. She hated feeling this vulnerable. She hated to find herself in this position, of asking something of someone that they were likely to refuse. She expected opposition. Derision. Open conflict. There was silence for such a long time in her parlor that she had almost given up on a response when Mira spoke.

"They are here. In this country." The words were abrupt.

Lila looked at her sister in shock. Anya's face was pale as she turned her graceful head to look at her sister. "How do you know?" she asked.

"They followed, not long after us. A few years perhaps. I didn't know at the time, not until I made inquiries recently."

Lila sat there shocked. She had expected outrage or resistance from her sisters at her idea to search for the triplets, but she hadn't expected this. "Do you know where they are?"

"I know they were brought here and given to families who adopted them. I didn't make any further inquiries. I thought if they wanted to be found they would have been in touch."

"*Families?*" Anya asked. She looked as shocked as Lila felt. The word seemed to wedge itself in Lila's chest.

Mira's face was grim. "They were separated."

Tears filled Lila's eyes and a hand went to her cheek. "Separated." The word came out in a whisper.

The triplets. When Sarah Marleigh discovered that the Earl had six children with Naira Devi, she asked for the boys to be sent to London and for the girls to remain in Delhi. But it turned out that all six were daughters. She then asked for the lighter-skinned girls to be sent to London to live with her and for the darker-toned ones to be left behind.

But this was not the cruelest trick she played.

The choice to stay or leave was left to each of the three older girls, to Lila, Anya, and Mira. Each was separately given the choice—to move to London and live with Sarah or give up their place to one of the triplets.

Each of the older sisters made the choice to leave. None of them knew what the others would choose. But that is the choice they made. Lila was seven when they moved. Anya six. Mira five. The triplets only three. They left the triplets behind. They each of them chose to give up the triplets instead of fighting to stay together. And it seemed then that the triplets weren't allowed to stay together either. They were separated from each other too. Lila didn't think she could hate Sarah Marleigh more, but it seemed there were further depths of loathing to plumb. There were greater pools of guilt.

"Why did Sarah bring us here in the first place?" She couldn't help asking it, that old question that niggled at her.

Anya looked just as confused as she felt. Mira wasn't looking at her. Lila stared at her sister. "Mira?"

Mira shrugged. "Perhaps there was a reason. Perhaps we'll never know."

Lila couldn't help thinking that Mira knew more. But she also knew that Mira wouldn't tell, not until she was good and ready. And perhaps she would never be good and ready.

"We have to find them." The words came out of Lila's mouth. The triplets were here, in this country, had been for a long time. They had never searched for their older sisters. But then they were only three when the older girls abandoned them. Did they even *know* they had older sisters? And if they did, why would they care to find them? The older sisters had betrayed the younger ones. Lila would never—had never been able to— forgive herself.

Mira's mouth tightened. "If they wanted us, they would have come looking for us. We cannot impose—"

"Why would they want us?" Anya asked. Her face gave hardly anything away, her posture perfect, her neck long and swanlike, yet those black-beetle eyes, there was fire burning inside them.

No one had an answer. Each sister was lost in her thoughts, her own pool of guilt that could not be shared in case the burden became less acute.

Lila sat there in silence for a long time. She finally said, "I want you in my life. I'm going to look for them. I want you to do it with me. But I'll do it with or without your help." As usual, a conciliatory tone might have been better, she reflected. As usual, she only sounded like she wanted to cut them out.

Mira instantly stood up. "If that's all, I will be on my way."

Lila desperately wanted to say more; her lips quivered with unuttered words, but she couldn't find them.

Anya was the one who dithered. Her hands were clenched in her lap too, not unlike Lila's. A tiny turquoise stone set in a slim ring on her right hand—something of their mother's. She stood up too. "Can't we . . . ?" She was gripping her hands together.

Mira turned her face away. She made no response.

And as usual, instead of reaching out to her sister, to Mira, instead of trying to soothe her hurt, Lila jumped into the fray. "How predictable, Mira," she said. "That *you* should have no feelings. Why should that surprise me?"

SHE TOLD KENNETH about the meeting afterward, when he came to pay her a surprise call, not long after Anya and Mira had left. She didn't tell him about the triplets. He didn't know about the younger sisters. But of course he knew Anya and Mira. He was looking as dapper as ever in a teal velvet jacket and perfectly fitting breeches. There had been no one as excited as he when she won that race to Brighton. Now he looked at her just as lazily as always, sitting there on his favorite chaise, yet there was something in his eyes. "You know, darling, you will never rest easy until you make peace with Anya and Mira. You *think* you will, but you will always chafe at the bit. I know you, Lila."

"I can't make peace with them. *They* don't want to."

He glanced at her face. "Don't they? Or do they in fact want to make peace—and do you too—and yet you are altogether too helpless, all of you, to do anything about it?"

She was standing at the window, frowning out at the garden. "I tried, didn't I?"

He got up from the chaise. "You know I must be off. I am meeting Jeremy Ashton in the park, but I wanted to say hello. But I will say this, Lila. It never ceases to surprise me how many people think they are trying, really trying, to make peace with someone or the other who is important to them. But how, just as often, they are almost always standing in their own way. A never-ceasing wonder."

She turned around to look at him. It was a funny thing how shrewd those lazy eyes could be. And there were few people in the world who knew her as well as Kenneth did. "Neither one accepted my invitation to my wedding." Her voice was tight. How could they have turned her invitation down? To her *wedding*!

"Oh, the time will come when the three of you will be forced to confront each other." Lila looked mulish at the words and he backed off, holding his hands up. "Don't shoot the messenger. All I am saying is that something will force you together sooner or later. I never said it would be me, did I now?"

She eyed him. "You know, Kenneth, one might almost say that you cared," she murmured.

He held up his hands again. "Take it back! Do not say something so vile."

She couldn't help a chuckle. "I don't think I thanked you properly for my winning the Brighton race."

He flicked an imaginary bit of lint from his shoulder. "I would say you were rather magnificent, darling," he said, somewhat to her surprise, "but only a puffed-up arse would compliment his own work."

She grinned. "Which you are."

"I never denied it, Lila, I never denied it."

That said, he left for his tryst with Jeremy Ashton.

"I TRIED TO keep my temper, I really did, Ivor," she said not long after she'd said goodbye to Kenneth, as she and Ivor strolled near the duck pond in Kensington. It was late winter and there was hardly anyone around. The peace and solitude, the hiding away inside their own world together, suited Lila perfectly. It was as though she had been looking for it all her life. It was as if they had reached out, groping in the dark, and found each other. She snuggled deeper into her fur-lined winter coat, the color of mulberries, and pressed closer to him.

He looked amused. "And how did that go?"

She looked ruefully at him. "I said I'd look for the triplets with or without their help. And when Mira said she'd have no hand in it, and Anya didn't give a definite answer, I said I never wanted to see them again. I said it was a mistake to have reached out to them, and why was I so stupid?" She grimaced. "I'll have to ask them around to tea again and apologize, I suppose?"

His lips twitched. But he didn't respond. She appreciated that he didn't feel he had to jump in with an opinion or a solution.

"I've spoken to Tiffany again," he said as they passed under some beeches that were shivering in the breeze. "She is less angry with me than she was. Less wont to believe that I've concocted the whole case against Beddington. I was afraid she would have a broken heart, but she seems able to take it with more equanimity than I believed she might."

"Do you think he will be prosecuted?"

"I doubt it, Lila. I'd like him to be. But despite the gross amount of debt he's under, he is an earl. And to tell you the truth, what would they prosecute him for? For attacking a young lady in the dark—who he thought was a stranger who had entered the premises illegally? For planting a jewelry box ten years ago in another maid's room? For sending an innocent man to the gallows—an innocent man who apparently died before he could be hanged? The best thing is for him to make himself scarce. And at least he has given up on Tiffany."

She thought about it for a moment. "She will get over it. Her pride is likely more hurt than her heart." She thought about Robert Wellesley. "In fact, she's more hurt that she believed in him. That's what we hate the most. That we mistrusted our own instincts."

He pressed her hand. "You had sound instincts about Sunil."

She couldn't help a grin. Two months ago, Maisie had given birth to an amber-eyed, curly-haired little baby girl, and Maisie had instantly handed her—Annie—over to Sunil, saying that the bulk of her job was done. Sunil had been inseparable from the baby ever since. The trio was settled in Sussex. Maisie, Annie at her breast, had taken over the supervision of cleaning out an outbuilding that Lila wanted to put to use as soon as possible. And Sunil was already working on one of Ivor's farm holdings. To speak to them, it would seem as if no shadow of death or betrayal had ever crossed their paths.

Lila would be moving to the estate in Sussex in just a few months. They would sell her house in Brook Street, and Ivor's place in Berkeley Square would be their town residence. He had hesitatingly asked her what she wanted to do with her business once they were married. She said without a qualm that she wanted to give it up. "Are you sure?" he asked. She appreciated the question and the concern that went with it.

She bit her lip and told him that instead she wanted to house and educate women in Maisie's condition. Pregnant young women—pregnant young prostitutes—who had no one to look after them. Or even women like Hannah and Betty whom no one else would hire. She wanted to house them, train them, and make them ready to be employed.

She said it defiantly, waiting for him to say that such a venture would hardly be suitable for his wife, that he'd be damned if he would open up any part of his house as some sort of refuge. He was already taking on the people who worked in her house and offering them employment in Berkeley Square or Sussex—whichever they preferred.

But he only nodded and said that he was getting off much easier than he expected. When she punched him in the arm, he added that he would support her all the way, whatever she chose to do. And no one would say it of him that marriage to him had stopped her from following her heart or her mind. "And," he added, "you'll drive yourself and then me mad if you don't get what you want. I'm a realist."

"What if we start a rescue mission?" she said now, as they strolled in the park.

He glanced at her. He tucked her hand closer into the crook of his arm. "I thought that's what we were doing already."

"I want more."

"Let me know the worst," he said, sounding somewhat resigned.

"That's not very lover-like!" she protested. "Don't you have anything to say about the moon and stars? About how you'd get them for me if I asked for them?"

"No, darling, I don't," he said simply. He took her hand from his arm and kissed it. "But if you come back to my place, I can have a roaring fire built up in my bedchamber. I think I might have something better to give you than the moon and stars."

"A rather high opinion of yourself, Mr. Tristram."

"There are only a few things I am good at. Making you happy—in any way you want, for as long as you want, for as many *times* as you want—is one of them."

"I will hold you to that."

"You can hold me to anything." But then he looked at her with misgiving. "What kind of rescue mission, can I ask—or is it better if I don't know?"

She glanced sideways at him but didn't spare him or his feelings. She had vowed to herself—and to him—that she never would. "Why, to save innocent people from the gallows of course. I wonder how many times we could get away with the runaway horse trick. Though I have a few other ideas too."

"Dear God," Ivor said. "I clearly was delusional when I thought I was getting away easy." He put an arm firmly around her and steered her—to her delight—in the direction of home.

ACKNOWLEDGMENTS

I can't tell if the Marleigh Sisters series has come out of nowhere or if it's been lurking inside me forever, waiting for me to find it. I owe a debt of gratitude to Georgette Heyer, whose wit and sparkle have seen me through many a rainy day and many low times in my teenage years when things looked blue. You make me laugh out loud and weep with longing, Ms. Heyer.

Thanks must go to many wonderful people.

I have a dream team in Lucia Macro and Kate Bradley, two women who cut the bullshit and come up with magic. Love your kickass attitude, intuition, serious publishing acumen, and the way we work as a team. You're the cat's pajamas. Waiting for a time when we can all share a Lila cocktail.

Priya Doraswamy, the day I met you (like a blind-date setup, really), your warmth made me weak at the knees. It's not just how sociable you are and how good at business, but your friendship and the fact that I can call you when I'm doing a pee—these things are everything to me. I cherish how you always take me seriously. And when I say, hey, Priya, crazy idea . . . you say, sure, let's try it. You're a dream.

Teams at HarperCollins UK and Avon (Harper USA),

I'm in awe of your eagle-eyed ways, your insight and creativity. Thanks to copy editors, coordinators, and marketing, especially Penny Isaac, Kati Nicholl, Rachel Berquist, and Camille Collins. To cover designers Ellie Game, Kerry Rubenstein, and Dawn Cooper. Special thanks to Asanté Simons, Chere Tricot, and Meg Le Huquet. Huge and everlasting thanks to Lynne Drew and Erika Tsang for making it all happen.

Chantelle Aimée Osman, to you I owe the blind-date setup. Your generosity and all-round loveliness and creativity help me see another, happier side of publishing.

Michelle Danaczko, your friendship and the shoulder you often offer for me to lean on, your generosity with your time and advice, mean a lot to me.

Carole V. Bell, I know you know this, but I'm in awe of your passion and your championing of diversity. Thanks for reading my work, and I can't wait to share more of it with you. Gigi Pandian and Kellye Garrett, you are two superstar crime writers who continue to inspire, encourage, and rebuild a whole industry. Stella Oni, Winnie M. Li, and Elizabeth Chakrabarty, my creative and driven friends, I can't do without your enthusiasm for all things writing. Writers and creatives I love talking to when I get the chance—Arun Sood, Biba Pearce, Helen Fitzgerald, James Thurgill, Sophie Page, Jheni Arboine—let's talk more. Theo Jones, Bryony Hall, and the Society of Authors, for reading through contracts and seeing things I'd never be able to see.

At Renegade, Florence Izen-Taylor, for your gorgeous enthusiasm and the chats, and Alex Cooke, for your support and professional attitude. Can't wait to work more with you.

Agora/Polis Books, I love doing the Arya Winters series with you. Thanks to *Ellery Queen Mystery Magazine* for thinking a tad outside the box to publish my short story "A Heist in Three Acts." To *Publishers Weekly* and Oprah Daily for being generous in your praise. To Cathie Hartigan and Kate Nash—I can't thank you enough for choosing me for the Exeter Novel Prize, for my mystery novel *Thirteenth Night*. You gave me validation when I really needed it. To Ruth Harrison and the team at Spread the Word, Nazneen Ahmed Pathak and the British Council, Michelle Phillips in your new adventures, the hilarious team at ChickLit4Life, Sara DiVello at Mystery and Thriller Mavens, Sarah Harden at Hello Sunshine, Tayla Burney, and Monica Germana, can't wait to work more with you.

Liz Bunting, Jamillah Ahmad, Ciara Flood, Grainne Butler, and Vikki Hill, thanks for letting me have a moan and reveal my chaotic side. Charlotte Hennessy, for our unforgettable catch-ups and the deep, deep chats. Hannah Marriot and Ruth Mc-Donald, wish you were in town more, dude. Hannah, thanks for the middle-of-the-night title chats. You were right, *that* title felt a little "buttoned-up." Adam Ramejkis, for your approach to creativity and for reaching out. Mei Kan, for all the corner chats—hey, we've got a whole world to save. Andreas Otto and Doro Shoene, for always taking up where we left off as if time hasn't passed.

Siobhan Clay, Danielle Tran, and the wonderful teams at the University of the Arts London. Elena Koivunen, for teaching me a glorious creative hobby, and Margot Bannerman, for teaching me things I didn't know and for scaring the shit out of me. Stewart Williams, for the photos and for making it all comfortable.

For authors Julia Cameron, Elaine Aron, Imi Lo, Elizabeth Gilbert, Brené Brown, and Heather Havrilesky, your writing has reassured me that it's okay to be weird. To Julia Quinn, queen of modern Regency, for your support and for bringing this beloved genre to so many readers. Thanks also to Harini Nagendra, Ovidia Yu, and Sumi Hahn.

My partner and kids for letting me be grumpy and creative and dance-y and crazy, and for always supporting my need for writing, for your adoring ways—you've taught me how to love. Family and friends for challenging me. Anisha, without your support and clear-eyed instinct for books, there wouldn't be a Lila, there wouldn't be an Arya. Thanks for letting me be neurotic and for always saying, "It's okay, that's not too crazy." For always being my first reader, and for knowing beyond reasonable doubt what will work and what won't.

And because we never thank ourselves, I want to thank myself for following my instincts, and for occasionally letting out the crazy with people I trust.